The Trouble with Mages

IMMORTAL QUEST

BY

ALEXANDRA MACKENZIE

EDGE SCIENCE FICTION AND FANTASY PUBLISHING
AN IMPRINT OF HADES PUBLICATIONS, INC.

CALGARY

EDGE

Edge Science Fiction and Fantasy Publishing
An Imprint of Hades Publications Inc.
P.O. Box 1714, Calgary, Alberta, T2P 2L7, Canada

In house editing by Laura Pellerine
Interior design by Brian Hades
Cover Illustration by Tomislav Tikulin
ISBN: 978-1-894063-46-3

EDGE Science Fiction and Fantasy Publishing and Hades Publications, Inc. ac-
knowledges the ongoing support of the Alberta Foundation for the Arts and the
Australian Council for the Arts for our publishing programme.

Alberta Foundation for the Arts

Canada Council for the Arts

Conseil des Arts du Canada

Library and Archives Canada Cataloguing in Publication

MacKenzie, Alexandra, 1954-
Immortal quest : the trouble with Mages / Alexandra MacKenzie.

ISBN 978-1-894063-46-3

I. Title.

PS3613.A3533I46 2010   813'.6   C2010-904489-4

FIRST EDITION
(d-201000714)
Printed in Canada
www.edgewebsite.com

DEDICATION

Dedicated to Caroline Stevermer, my writing mentor, and to Sandy Hereld, my fannish mentor—with love and gratitude forever.

THE TROUBLE WITH MAGES

IMMORTAL QUEST

CHAPTER ONE

Marlen stood before the old brick museum, breathing rapidly in the chilled night air. He needed to find a way to break in.

He looked up and down the narrow side street in Brompton. Not a soul in sight. His choices were simple: he could cross over to the alley next to the museum, use his tools on the low-set window, and be in and out before you could say "breaking and entering."

or he could walk away now.

Marlen closed his eyes and tried counting to ten to calm himself. *I'm not a thief*, he thought, *but I can't run away now. I'm in too deep. All my own fault.*

"Get on with it, then," he told himself. He liked talking to himself. Though it might be wiser, under the circumstances, to try whispering to himself instead.

He looked down the deserted street one more time. *It was now or never.*

"Right. Gem and Mineral Museum, here I come." He darted across to the alley.

The museum surely had an alarm system; the basement window would be no exception. Marlen drew a small leather pouch from his jacket. He pulled out a smooth blue stone, spoke a quick, nervous incantation, then ran the stone round the window perimeter.

He'd had rare use for such a spell before, and not had much time to practice. If it didn't work, at best he would come away empty-handed and at worst he'd wind up in jail. He had no time to waste in jail. Not if he had done what he believed he had done. Not if he had unleashed a great danger on the world.

Steady on. The was no reason to panic just yet. He just had to get inside, grab the stone, and everything would go back to normal.

Marlen put away the blue stone. He shivered, but not from the cold. He rubbed his hands together and gently pushed at the window latch. *It opened easily.* No alarm sounded. He released a pent-up breath and quickly crawled through a curtain of cobwebs into the musty room below. He stopped to listen. Nothing. There was a night watchman upstairs, but apparently the bloke did not possess stellar hearing.

Something large scurried past Marlen's feet. He hopped backwards, knocking over an open crate. "Oh, great," he muttered as rocks thumped across the floor. He froze again. Nothing. Apparently the watchman didn't even have average hearing. That seemed odd, but he wasn't going to question his luck. Time for a torch. He played the thin stream of light over shelves crammed with rocks of all shapes and sizes. There were gaping holes in the cobwebs where the shelves had been disturbed. More crates littered the floor, their lids pried off. *Damn.* Surely they hadn't got here first. It wasn't possible. There was no way *they* could have beaten him to it.

"Bloody freezing," he whispered, rubbing his arms. No one seemed to care about heating the museum basement. As he began poking about among the metal shelves, Marlen's increasingly rapid breaths made a series of white puffs, mingling with the dust he stirred up. Lumpy gray stones lay piled on every shelf. Why anyone would keep so many dreary objects, even in a gem and rock museum, was beyond him. No doubt all the good stuff was displayed upstairs. But the good stuff didn't interest him. He wanted a lumpy gray stone. A very particular one. And he didn't fancy sorting through a few hundred unparticular gray stones to find it.

But he had to find it; he had no choice. Too many rather powerful and decidedly unpleasant people who would be upset with him if he didn't.

He gave up on the shelves and flashed the light across the crates. A rat the size of a Corgi jumped off the nearest one and darted towards him. Marlen yelled, leaped back, and banged into a shelf. Rocks crashed to the floor. He steadied the shelf and himself, shivers running up his back. He paused to listen. The only sound was the rat pattering off. The night watchman needed a hearing aid. Or CPR.

"Fine," Marlen said a bit too loudly. Nerves made him bolder. "I'll make all the noise I like, then." He attacked the crates, dumped their contents out, and tossed rocks with abandon. Adrenalin and the cold air gave him energy he rarely had at two in the morning. Dust got up his nose, his eyes watered, and an annoying itch took up residence in the back of his throat. His jeans acquired half a dozen snags, his shirt changed from white to gray, and his brown leather jacket was soon smeared with rat droppings. He found lots of lumpy rocks, three enormous spiders, and a tin of petrified biscuits. The search proved fruitless, but at least it warmed him up.

He returned to the shelves. It wasn't until after he scoured the last one and decided to call it quits, that he heard the heavy tread of footsteps above his head. "*Now* the bastard decides to wake up," he murmured. Marlen dashed for the window and scrambled onto a rickety pile of crates. He grasped the ledge, got a good grip and heaved himself out.

Breathing a little easier, he clapped his hands together, turned around, and walked straight into the arms of a waiting constable.

The desk man shoved his copy of *Playboy* under the duty roster as Detective Sergeant Nicholas Watson entered the station house. "Evening, sir. Or morning now, isn't it?" He pushed the button to open the thick wood gate beside his desk.

Nick slowly walked through, clicking the gate shut behind him. "Morning, Perkins," he sighed as he dragged his weary body to the back counter where the tea kettle burbled. "Got the word on my application yesterday." He poured a mug of tea then slumped onto a chair.

"For DI6?"

"Yeah." Nick slurped noisily at his tea. "Bloody Domestic Intelligence Bastards."

"Sorry, sir." Perkins idly fingered the duty roster. "Thought for sure you'd make that lot."

Nick slammed the mug on the counter, spilling brown liquid everywhere. "I did."

"Oh. I see." Perkins gulped as a rivulet of tea made its way beneath the roster, straight towards his *Playboy*.

"No, you don't. You know what they've gone and done? Assigned me to my uncle's special, crackpot outfit. Couldn't just put me in with the regular lot, could they? I told Brian not to pull any strings. The bastard."

"He's part of DI6, then?"

Nick swiveled the chair round to glare at him. "Brian Watson heads a special section called PIS. And if you say, 'piss,' I'll knock you across this ruddy room."

"Wouldn't dream of it, sir." Perkins took out his handkerchief and dabbed at the tea. "What's it stand for, then?"

"Paranormal Investigation Service," Nick snorted. "How he connived them into funding it, I'll never know. Dammit, Perkins, I wanted to be out fighting terrorists, not people who've been kidnapped by aliens or are busy communing with the dead. You know what the other DI6 guys call it? The Barmy Brigade. Running around the country checking out housewives who talk to Elvis, mansions possessed by pairs of flying Wellingtons, teenagers in Lyme Regis who can levitate snooker tables. It's not fair."

Perkins nodded. "So you're turning it down, then."

Nick's eyes widened. "I'm doing no such thing. I'm taking the damn job." He jabbed a finger at Perkins' chest. "And I'm damn well going to *show* them they made a mistake. That I'm too good for that barmy outfit. I'll be the best damn agent they've ever seen. I'm not throwing in the towel yet. Bastards." He picked up his mug and downed the rest of his tea. Then, his tirade completed, he tapped his fingers on the desk top. "Anything happening tonight?"

"Just a bit of B and E over at that rock museum. Fellow claims he don't need a solicitor. Wants to talk. Been right voluble, he has."

"Good," Nick leaped to his feet, rubbing his hands together. "Have him brought to the interrogation room. If he wants to talk, I'll talk to him. But he'd better not want to talk all bloody night." He strolled off down the short hallway.

Perkins buzzed the cells, gave his instructions, and pulled out his slightly damp copy of *Playboy*.

"Marlen Smith?" Nicholas Watson turned the cheap plastic driver's license over. "What's your real last name?"

The B and E suspect slouched as far as possible in the hard-backed chair. The tiny, windowless room contained only two chairs and a wooden table. Nick had always found the police station less than inspirational for inter-rogations, as he preferred the kindly, brotherly approach for gaining information. Be pleasant, be polite, take an interest in the person—that was his style. He'd argued for years for upholstered chairs, without success. It seemed logical to him that a comfortable, relaxed suspect made a cooperative suspect. To that end, he'd at least been able to remove this fellow's handcuffs. Nick wasn't worried. He had a good four inches and thirty pounds on the suspect, not to mention his years of police combat training.

"Come on, now," he repeated amiably. "You can tell me. What's your name?"

"Marlen Smith," the man said as he fingered the cigarette burns in the table top.

"Now, now," Nick tsk-tsked. "I mean your *real* name."

"Marlen. I don't have a last name."

"Everyone has a last name." Nick Watson looked at the ID, then across at his charge. Something tugged at the back of his mind, something vaguely familiar about the man.

He studied the photo on the fake license, flicking from it to the suspect. Wavy, shoulder-length auburn hair, green eyes, scruffy-looking overall but with an oddly attractive face. He could have walked out of a Renaissance painting —Botticelli, maybe DaVinci—unusual enough that Nick would have remembered if they'd met before. He tossed the ID aside and picked up his notepad and pen. "I'm sure you'd like to get some sleep tonight, and so would I. So let's wrap this up quickly, all right? Now, then, what did you do with it?"

Marlen's eyebrows shot up. "What did I do with what?"

Nick picked up a thin file folder and flipped through it. "According to the curator," he said matter-of-factly, "who claims to know every rock in the building, a medium-sized lump of granite is missing. This stone is of unknown origin, with distinctive and peculiar markings etched on its surface. These markings are thought to be alchemical, possibly from medieval times. What did you do with it?"

Marlen frowned. "Hell," he muttered.

"Oh, so you do know where it is?"

"No!" Marlen shook his head violently. "I didn't take it. I haven't got it on me, have I?"

"No," Nick tried to sound calm and reassuring, though his patience was starting to fray a bit. "So where have you hidden it?"

"Look, *I* didn't take it. Someone else did. Tell me, what happened to the night watchman?"

"You know very well. You bashed him on the back of the head and tied him up. I thought you were ready to talk to us. Changed your mind, have you?"

"I am talking." Marlen looked crossly at his watch. "Am I going to be kept here all night?"

"Probably."

"Listen, I never went upstairs. And it was quiet up there, anyway. I knocked a lot of stuff about and no one came to check. Someone else had already tied up the watchman. And someone else went through that basement thoroughly before I got there. They must have tripped the alarm on their way out, which is why you lot turned up to grab me."

"Two burglars on the same night? That's not likely."

"I never said it was likely. But it's the truth."

Nick glowered at him. It was past two in the morning, and his kindly, brotherly approach was wearing very thin indeed. "You're confusing the issue. Won't help get you out of here in any case. You still broke and entered."

Marlen shook his head. "You don't understand. I can't sit around here all night. I've got work to do."

"Most amusing," Nick tapped the folder with his pen. "Why should we let you go? You were caught in the act."

"Too true." Marlen gazed at the ceiling for a few moments. "Look, if I tell you the truth, the *real* truth, will you let me go?"

"Depends, doesn't it?" Nick replied patiently. "Try me."

"Okay, but it means mentioning a few things you'd probably rather not hear. Can't be helped, though. I haven't got time to waste."

Nick wondered if he hadn't got hold of a nutter here. He shrugged. "Go on, I'm waiting. Do your worst."

Marlen straightened his posture and gave Nick a steady look. "You," he said carefully, "have got a small white scar on the back of your left knee."

Nick dropped his pen. How the hell could the fool know something like that? Maybe it was just a wild guess. He picked up the pen and pointed it at Marlen. "What makes you think that?"

"And you've got a large red birthmark in the shape of a toad on your bum."

A flush crept up Nick's face. That was no lucky guess. And it was far too personal for comfort. "Who the hell are you?"

"I'm your best friend," Marlen grinned.

"Right. That does it." Nick dropped all pretense of being kindly. "You're on your way to a shrink, sunshine." He rose, but stopped when he felt another one of those damned annoying tugs in the back of his mind. He glared at Marlen. "All right, you little sod, I'll bite. How'd you know about my... birthmark? You know one of my old girlfriends?" *Or boyfriends*, he mentally added; he wasn't going to say it out loud.

"Told you," Marlen replied confidently. "I'm your best friend. Know all about you."

Nick sat down. This was ridiculous. He drummed his fingers on the table. "I think I might remember who my friends are."

"Agreed. Except we first met five hundred years ago, and you've been through a few changes since then."

"Five hundred years," Nick repeated. Maybe it hadn't been such a good idea to take the handcuffs off.

"Mind you, there aren't any major changes," Marlen went on blithely. "Same basic height and build, same dark brown hair, though you do tend to vary the length. I like the short cropped look, it suits you. Same blue eyes — always were able to charm the pants off anyone with those eyes," he smiled. "And you've always been a handsome bloke. No, nothing major. I always manage to recognize you in your various incarnations. Pity the reverse isn't always true."

Nick crossed his arms, opting for the extremely stern approach. Not a word of it made sense to him. "Give me one good reason why I should believe you. And what do you mean by 'incarnations'? People don't really believe in that stuff, do they?" *Certainly not rational people*, he thought.

Marlen steepled his fingers together and rested his chin on them. After a minute or so had passed, he let out a long-suffering sigh.

"*Well?*"

Marlen started, "Sorry. Just collecting my thoughts."

"You must have a lot of them."

"Ah, the good old sarcasm streak. I've always found that trait of yours a bit exasperating. That and your relentless teasing; except, of course, when I can think of a good comeback. You're annoyed, aren't you?"

"Got it in one, friend." *Should have called the mental health people ages ago*, Nick thought. So why was he still sitting here listening to this rubbish? There was something about the idiot... he wished he knew what it was.

"All right," Marlen said. "I'll start at the beginning. Pay close attention, because this is the most important information you're going to hear in your entire life."

"I'm listening."

Marlen took a deep breath. "You were born in 1478 A.D. Your name was Nicholas, it always is, though your surname changes over time. You're mortal. You've died and been, what you might call reincarnated, any number of times. Our official term for it is transmutation of the soul. For reasons which neither I nor my peers have ever determined, only a few mortals enjoy this form of continued existence. The only problem is that sometimes you remember your previous life, or lives, and other times you suffer from amnesia. This particular lifetime, you've got a bit of a memory lapse."

Nick smiled. "Good joke." It finally dawned on him that someone at the station must have found out about his new job before he'd come in. How could they resist taunting him over the Paranormal Investigation Service? Bastards. "Okay, game's over. Who put you up to this? I am not amused."

Marlen shifted uneasily in his chair, "You going to write any of this down?"

"No, I am not. And the joke's backfired, 'cause you've got exactly one minute to start talking sense before I find you a padded cell."

Marlen sighed. "You asked for the truth, and I'm telling it. I was born in 1480, and was made immortal in 1505. In addition to being immortal, I occasionally practice magic."

Nick chortled. "Not as in pulling rabbits out of hats, I suppose?"

"Not exactly," Marlen said. "You recall a bloke named Merlin? He was my tutor."

"Bit of a name-dropper, aren't you?"

"You're not taking me seriously."

"Got it in one again." Nick rubbed his eyes. He'd had enough. He wanted to go back to his flat and fall onto his warm, comfortable bed.

On the other hand, it might not be a joke. There was still the question of how this total stranger—and Nick was no longer sure he *was* a total stranger—knew what he did. A twinge of fear pricked his spine as he thought of the clubs he'd gone to on occasion, before he'd joined the police and

gotten more circumspect. Clubs where it didn't matter who
your partner was, where he felt comfortable being bisexual.
Surely he would have remembered that remarkable red hair
and those large green eyes... and besides, what could he
want even if it *were* that? Not a blackmail scheme, not after
all this time. That had been six or seven years ago, and it
was over with. He had only dated women since joining
the force. What the hell was this fool really playing at?

He stretched his arms. "Look, I told you, the joke's over.
It was quite inventive, I'll grant you that. But you're not
getting out of a night in jail." Nick put his notepad away
and closed the file folder. "Maybe your magician chums
can spring you. But right now I'm tired, and I want to
go home. So you just pop off to the cells, and you have a
good, long think about where you stashed that rock you
stole." He rose and called to the officer from the cells, who
stood just outside the door.

"No, wait!" Marlen jumped up.

"Don't you try anything—"

The door pulled open. As the uniformed man stepped
in, Marlen grabbed the chair and flung it at him. The officer
stumbled and fell backward. Marlen leapt over both him
and the chair and bolted down the hall. Nick scrambled
after him, chasing him into the front room of the station,
where Perkins was still engrossed in his copy of *Playboy*.
Marlen clambered over the gate and dashed through
the station door into the street. He pounded down the
pavement.

Nick was right behind him, closing in. *Christ, I screwed
that one up royally*, he thought as he spotted his quarry
turning down an alley. Well, the bastard wasn't going to
get away from him, and *this* time, the damn cuffs stayed
on.

He bolted into the dark alley, and tripped over a box.
"Hell," he muttered, quite sure that Marlen had deliberately
knocked it into his path. Nick paused for a few moments to
adjust to the poor light. The alley was strewn with garbage
and crates. Clever. But not clever enough.

He made his way rapidly through the mess, emerging
at the other end without further mishap. As he scanned

the street, he caught the flash of white from Marlen's trainers disappearing down another alleyway. He dashed for it.

Nick entered the alley at a fast clip, completely unprepared for the blow that landed squarely in his gut. He let out a moan of pain and doubled over. The little prick had been waiting for him. He'd underestimated the man. Even as he tried to rise for a retaliatory punch, he felt Marlen's fists hit hard between his shoulder blades, and he collapsed to his hands and knees.

"Sorry, mate," Marlen said, and Nick almost believed he meant it.

Then his quarry made the mistake of standing there one second too long. Nick lunged forward, tackling Marlen at the knees, sending him sprawling. He expertly took hold of Marlen's right arm and twisted it round his back, pushing on it as hard as he could.

"All right!" Marlen shouted. "Enough!"

Nick staggered to his feet, pulling Marlen up with him. He slammed him hard against the brick wall. "Right." He took out a pair of handcuffs. "Should've left these on you, you little sod."

"No! You have to listen to me!" Marlen tried to swipe the cuffs aside.

Nick slammed him against the wall again, and punched him in the gut for good measure. No more Mr. Nice Guy.

Marlen slid down the wall.

Nick roughly hauled him up. "I've had it with you. You're on your way to the butterfly ward."

"You," Marlen managed to gasp, "have recurring dreams—"

"Shut up!" He grabbed the collar of Marlen's shirt and twisted it.

"You're riding a horse," Marlen sputtered, speaking rapidly. "The horse throws you while you're crossing a river. You hit your head going down, the water sweeps over you, you're choking but losing consciousness—"

"Stop!" Nick felt his face drain of blood. *Good God, how could he know that?*, he thought, then relaxed his grip. "You *can't* know that."

"The horse is brown with a white streak down its nose. You're wearing a dark blue cloak with a gold clasp."

Nick stepped back, keeping one hand on Marlen's chest. His head was spinning. It wasn't a practical joke... it couldn't be. No one knew about that dream, *no one*. His mind, however, refused to process nonsense. "There's a logical explanation for this."

"Maybe." Marlen stood there quietly catching his breath. "Look, I need to talk to you."

"I've never told anyone in my whole life about that dream," Nick replied. He realized he was trembling, and his voice sounded far away.

"You told *me*. About four hundred years ago."

"That's impossible."

"Say whatever the bloody hell you want. It's true. I know all the details of that dream, and you're the only one who could have told me about it." Marlen paused. "You always wake up screaming, right as you go under for the last time."

Nick lowered his hand. He fiddled with the cuffs. This was insane, and he was a very sane person. But that dream—no, it was a nightmare. "It terrifies me." He didn't know why he was speaking aloud, didn't know why he suddenly felt like really *talking* to this madman. He didn't know what to do, had no idea how to handle this bizarre situation. "I've never even been on a horse. I don't know why I have that wretched dream."

Marlen stared at him for a long moment. "That's how you died," he said softly. "The first time."

Nick stared back. "Died?" he repeated, feeling like an utter idiot. Incarnations... that's what the fellow had been rattling on about earlier. But that was impossible. Except for the undeniable fact that no one in the world knew the precise details of that nightmare.

"I think you need a drink, mate," Marlen said.

Nick slowly put the handcuffs away. "Probably." They definitely needed to talk more. Though he was still quite prepared to find a reasonable explanation, if only he had more time to think it through. He jabbed a finger at Marlen's chest. "I'm not saying I believe anything you've said, but—" He took a deep breath. "You're going to tell me more."

"Good. Anything open this hour?"

Nick nodded. "I did a year's worth of undercover work on the vice squad. I know a place."

The illegal all-hours pub and gambling den Nick led Marlen into looked like a nondescript brick building on the outside, and might possibly have been more descript on the inside, but it was impossible to tell with the gloomy light and heavy pall of cigarette smoke.

Nick got two large whiskeys at the bar then led his charge to a small table in the back. He gulped nearly half his drink in one go, and stared at the glass. He prided himself on being an analytical man, able to work any problem from step A through steps B, C, and D to a rational solution without letting extraneous nonsense clutter his mind. He liked it when the various aspects of his life were laid out in simple black and white patterns—good and bad, truth and falsehood, sane and crazy. This was crazy. It felt as if a huge, fuzzy gray area were trying to take up residence in his mind, and he didn't like it one bit. He had to try to make sense of it.

Except that it didn't make any sense. Nick fingered his glass. "This dream of mine—maybe you're just a good guesser. Sherlock Holmes could do stuff like that."

"Sherlock Holmes was fiction," Marlen replied, sipping at his whiskey. "This is reality."

"What's real is whatever I see with my own two eyes." Nick took another long pull on his drink. "And hear with my own ears." Of course, he had heard it—his dream—in detail. No one had ever told him he talked in his sleep, and he'd had plenty of bed partners. Something odd was going on here, and he had to figure it out. What did this nutter *want* from him? "All right," he said. "Suppose, just for the sake of argument, mind you, that I was born four hundred years ago."

"More like five hundred."

"Five hundred years ago. And let's suppose this—reincarnation—what did you call it?"

"Transmutation of the soul."

"Right. Let's say it really happens. You said it only affects a few people. So why me?"

"Don't know, mate. You're just lucky, I guess."

"That's not what I'd call it."

"Keep drinking." Marlen smiled. "Alcohol always makes this stuff easier to understand."

Nick sighed. Time to try another angle. "Okay, let's say you're a magician—"

"We prefer the word mage."

"Whatever," he flipped his hand dismissively. "If you're a mage, how come you couldn't use your magic to keep yourself from getting nicked?"

Marlen pulled a small plastic card from his jeans pocket and handed it over. "Read this."

Nick squinted at the tiny print. *Handy Wallet Guide to Magic Spells.* "You must be joking."

"Nah." Marlen slouched in his chair. "I made it up for Merlin's birthday one year, but he didn't give it proper appreciation."

Nick read aloud from the card. "*Send messages across hundreds of miles in less than a day.* My, that's impressive. You ever heard of telephones and fax machines?"

" 'Course I bloody well have. But let me tell you, in 1600 A.D., that was pretty impressive stuff."

"I'll bet. *Ease your lord's stressful nights with a sleeping elixir,*" Nick raised an eyebrow.

"Been taken over by the chemists."

"*Make images appear at a distance.* Ah. Television. Videos. What is all this?"

Marlen snatched the card back. "We're outdated, that's what it is. Most of us haven't used any of our magic skills since the Industrial bloody Revolution. No call for 'em." He waved his arms. "Who needs magic when you've got computers, modems, camcorders, airliners." He stopped sipping and downed the contents of his glass.

"Terrific. So what do you lot do all day?"

Marlen took a breath and let it out slowly. "Most of my fellow mages have become stockbrokers."

Nick choked on his drink. "You're not serious," he got out between coughs.

"Why would I make up something that ridiculous?"

"God only knows." Nick cleared his throat. "Magical stockbrokers. *Why?*"

"It's our job. We're supposed to help the nobility—it's what we've always done. Provide power and wealth to the kings, the lords, the aristocratic elite. Make sure they stay elite." Marlen picked up his coaster and folded it into ever smaller squares. "So, in this wonderful modern age of ours, we continue to help various peers of the realm stay rich. We have a few minor spells which can affect the stock market. May not be as exciting as calling down lightning, which, by the way, we can't actually do, but I suppose it's something." He carefully unfolded the coaster and smoothed it out.

Nick finished off his whiskey. Alcohol did seem to help. He probably needed more of it. "It makes as much sense as anything else you've told me. I still think you're barmy. I mean, where am I supposed to fit into all this nonsense?" He paused as an errant thought struck. "By the way, is your name really just Marlen? With an 'e'?"

"My folks couldn't spell." He began folding the coaster again.

Nick shivered. "Must be weird, still having them around."

"Huh?" Marlen looked up from his task. "Oh, they're long gone. My parents were mortal."

"Mortal?" Nick scratched his head. "But how come—no, forget it. I don't want to know. Just tell me what you *want* from me."

"Nothing much," Marlen replied. "All you have to do is help me save civilization as we know it."

Nick nodded. "I had a feeling you would say something like that." He shoved his glass across the table. "Your round." Might as well get something out of this wasted evening. While Marlen disappeared into the throng at the bar, Nick considered how to test his story further. The only truth he could test it against was the dream. He had never consciously told it to anyone, and even if he did talk in his sleep it was unlikely he would blurt out the color of the horse or what he was wearing.

That dream was special, more vivid than any ordinary dream, more full of sound and smell, more tactile. He knew each detail intimately—the touch of coarse cloth against his skin, the odor of horse's sweat, the sound of the reins slapping, the feel of the early morning mist against his face. He knew every article of clothing, down to the small silver medallion round his neck. Nick rubbed his throat. Now there was a test. The dream began the same each time. He stood beside the horse, ready to mount. But each time, he paused to pull out the medallion and study its inscription. He saw it clearly. Ornate characters, spelling a Latin phrase—*memor mihi*. He had even found out what it meant. No one could ever know *that* minute detail. At least, not in a logical world.

Marlen returned with two more large whiskeys. "Prices are a bit steep here." He shoved one toward Nick.

Nick smiled, happy with the knowledge that he'd thought of a way to unmask this charlatan, pleased that he could soon return to his normal, sensible life. "Got a question for you." He took a sip of his drink. "And if you don't know the answer, you get to go back to jail."

"Is that right? What if I do know it?"

Something in Marlen's determined face made Nick's confidence waver. "You can't know it."

"Unless I'm telling the truth."

"Not possible."

"Go on then," Marlen's gaze remained steady. "Ask away."

Nick swallowed. "Fine. I will." He took another sip first, a feeling of anxiety gripping him. "All right. There's something I'm wearing in that dream. It's around my neck. Describe it."

The seconds ticked by as Marlen stared at him. "Take another drink," he finally said. "A big one."

"Why?"

"Because you're going to need it."

Nick didn't touch his glass. His hands were trembling. "Stop stalling."

"Fine. Have it your way." Marlen unfastened the top button of his shirt. He slowly pulled out a long silver chain.

At its end dangled a small medallion. "I gave it to you for your birthday. And I took it back before you were..." he hesitated. "Before the burial. Just as I always do." He lifted it over his head and handed it over. "You're welcome to keep it. It *is* yours."

The carefully constructed foundation of Nick's world-view cracked. "*No.*" He hesitated then took the medallion. Small, silver, with an ornate Latin inscription. An object from a dream couldn't take on real form. But this one had.

"It's not magical," Marlen said. "Just a memento. It says, 'Remember me.'" He raised his glass. "And I wish you would."

Nick had trouble speaking. His brain was too busy doing somersaults. "I don't understand this," he stammered.

"Didn't expect you would. Give it time." Marlen clinked Nick's glass. "But not too much time. I'm in a hurry."

Nick nodded dully, took his large whiskey, and drained it.

CHAPTER TWO

Duncan M. Phipps stared at the pile of sundry magical tools which threatened to topple off the ancient oak desk. The upper floor of his Mayfair home contained over a thousand years' worth of accumulated junk, most of it in a state of profound disuse. The objects he did use in his magical work, the few stones and jewels and talismans that remained practical in this modern age could easily be kept in one small leather pouch. He kept that with him always, neatly tucked away in his jacket pocket.

Up here, where he rarely came, nothing stayed tidy. One couldn't simply haul a load of ancient artefacts, magical or otherwise, off to the local antiques dealer without arousing some unwanted interest. He'd lived a long time, he'd kept hold of a great many objects. Over time, many lost their power, and some lost efficacy. A mage in the tenth century might use a conveying jewel to send a message through the ether to a fellow mage hundreds of miles away, connecting in a matter of minutes. Today, that same mage would simply pick up a phone.

He stared at the twelfth-century scrying mirror which had fallen off the pile onto the floor. Duncan picked it up and tossed it back on the desk. It wobbled atop a pyramid of faded visualizing stones, tipped over onto a frayed divining wheel, and came to rest between two bottles of musty power potion.

Duncan sighed. He wished he could hire a housekeeper whom he could trust to deal with this mess, but mortals were too risky to employ. Might be best to simply toss the whole lot into the Thames.

He brushed the dust off his pristine gray suit and headed downstairs to his clean, well-ventilated office. Here was a room he could live in, with its sleek black desk, swivel chair in padded leather, guest chair of a good but inferior quality to his own, glass and chrome bookcases lined with financial texts and annual reports, metal fireproof filing cabinets full of precisely labeled stock portfolios. He crossed the pale blue carpet to the window and opened the blinds to let in the morning sun. When he turned round, he found Georgina Pruitt sitting calmly in the guest chair.

"Ah. Miss Pruitt. Been practicing our hiding spell, have we?" Duncan spent a few precious seconds brushing back the sides of his perfectly well-brushed blond hair in an attempt to recover his sense of poise.

Georgina Pruitt was the newest member of the Immortal Society of Mages, having been given immortality in 1960. Physically, she had stopped the aging process at twenty-nine.

Mage-immortals were not easy to find. Once per year the Society's Inner Council members met to perform a ceremony to check for new ones, even though these were rare. They might locate one once in a decade. The members searched the etheric planes for specific psychic emanations, a mental signature possessed only by those individuals who had the potential to become mages. The emanations usually appeared after puberty, sometimes into the very late teens. Once the few who were found were properly identified, contacted, and thoroughly trained in the ways of the Society, they were then put through the ritual of immortality. Only a true mage could survive the ritual, which halted the aging process, most often in the person's twenties. Occasionally they found late-developers who completed the training in their thirties. He himself had not been able to go through the ritual until nearly forty, for a thousand years ago the mages were even fewer in number, much farther apart in distance. After the small band of immortals discovered his psychic signature, it had taken many long years before one of them could travel the hundreds of miles to find him. They were luckier these days. Though potential mages were still rare, at least they could be found quickly.

Duncan found Georgina's appearance faintly disturbing, as if she were continually planning to chastise him for some unknown affront. She always wore suits, dark blue today. She had a fondness for displaying heavy silver brooches on her white blouses. Her hair was kept in a carefully coifed bob, heavily sprayed into immobility. No makeup ever graced her stern features. Sturdy shoes and a practical handbag completed her ensemble. Duncan approved of tradition; conservatism was central to the mage philosophy. He approved of Miss Pruitt's attitude to her duties, which she pursued with a dedication and seriousness sadly lacking in some of his past students. Still, he never quite knew how to behave in the face of so much female domination. For Miss Pruitt was fond of dominating, there was never any doubt of that.

She reminded him unpleasantly of a mage he had known long centuries past, a woman who became his greatest enemy. He'd never completely trusted a strong woman since that time, and he didn't intend to start now. But he did like to keep them under close watch, the better to thwart them before they turned dangerous.

He coughed softly, sat in his leather chair, and leaned forward, hands clasped together on the desk. A few weeks ago, as head of the Society, he'd given her the task of spying on his former pupil, Marlen. That young man had never taken stocks and bonds seriously. He rarely did anything but laze around and get into trouble. Duncan, as head of the Society's Inner Council, had decided he bore watching. Miss Pruitt had taken up the job with relish.

"Well, Miss Pruitt, what do you have to report?"

Georgina sat primly in her chair, hands clasped on her plain black handbag. "That rascal is up to something devious."

"Is he?"

"Late last night he was arrested."

Duncan shook his head. "He's been arrested more times than I've had birthdays. What was it this time, drunk and disorderly again?"

"No. Breaking and entering."

"What?" Duncan sat up straight. That was unusual, even for Marlen. "Where?"

"The Memorial Gem and Mineral Museum."

Duncan felt briefly dizzy, even sitting down. He steadied himself with a few deep breaths. "He hasn't—he couldn't possibly—" He clenched the edge of his desk. "Where is he now?"

Georgina lifted her chin. "He escaped custody, after which I lost track of his movements. I presume he has returned to his flat, though I haven't had time for a seeking spell. One does need to sleep, after all. Tell me, why are you so disturbed by this news?"

"I am not disturbed. Whatever gave you that idea?" Duncan stopped clenching his desk and took up shredding the papers on top into confetti.

"Control yourself. If this is a serious matter, we must attend to it with haste."

Duncan nodded. He stopped shredding. "Do you know what was kept in that museum? Of course you don't. Only members of the Inner Council know where the three objects are. Of course, any intelligent mage would be able to find them, but they're not *supposed* to be looking for them, are they?" He bit his lower lip. She was right. *Control.* "Do you know what I'm talking about?"

"Mage History was one of my better subjects during my training. The three objects to which you refer were once the property of a mage named Vere. She was one of the originals, an extremely powerful woman." A ghost of a smile twitched across her upper lip. "Much older and more experienced than *you*, I believe."

"True. However, she—"

"She had an unpleasant streak. Quite. Apparently she was less than content to serve the wealthy, and expressed an unhealthy desire to help the poor." Georgina sniffed.

Duncan remembered all too well. He'd been intimately involved in the whole affair, on the side of the mages who opposed Vere's ideas. "Vere wanted democracy in the dark ages. Can you imagine?"

Georgina tapped her fingers on her handbag. "Please do not interrupt me."

"Sorry."

"This Vere woman," Georgina continued, staring levelly at him, "took to experimenting on dangerous new spells. She tried to learn how to make a mere mortal into an immortal. Not the mortals *we* choose, not the ones who already have our psychic mark, destined to become mages. No, she actually believed that *all* mortals should have the chance to live forever."

"An idealist. And a fool." Duncan took one look at the glare Georgina favored him with and went back to shredding paper.

"Ahem. Yes, she was a fool. Rather than express gratitude, the local populace branded her a witch. They tried to burn her, but failed. This unpleasant incident turned Vere wholeheartedly against the mortals, and she swore a terrible vengeance. She used her experiments to devise her most powerful spell ever, and this time, it was designed to destroy them all. This spell required the creation of three special objects which would focus power. She constructed these objects and was working out the spell when the other mages discovered her plans. Using the combined powers of the Council members, you were able to put a binding spell on her. Vere is still alive, but has been locked limbo, unconscious of the world around her. I believe this occurred over seven hundred years ago."

"Yes. We put her away in 1292." The first and only time they had taken such severe steps against one of their own.

"Unfortunately, the three objects of power could not be unmade. Therefore, they were scattered into separate hiding places, watched over and kept safe through the ages." Georgina leaned forward. "Didn't she also have a grimoire?"

"I was entrusted with that. It's safely hidden." Duncan glanced at the ceiling. Vere's book of spells lay somewhere in that mess upstairs. "As for the objects, they're not really hidden. The Council knows where they are, and any mage can detect their magical signature. Which is exactly what Marlen must have done. You see, one of the three objects was kept in that rock museum. A ritual stone. The curator is one of our own. Why would Marlen break into such a place, other than to steal the stone?"

"But why would he want it?"

Duncan had a good idea as to Marlen's motivation. "He's upset with the Inner Council. Not long ago, he came to us seeking a most unusual favor. He wanted us to perform a restoration spell, something to do with a mortal friend of his. Do you know about transmuted souls?"

"Naturally. It was part of my training."

"Marlen has kept company with one all his life, some fellow he met hundreds of years ago. This lifetime, the man's in an amnesia state. Doesn't know Marlen, doesn't remember any previous lives. Marlen's been through these stages before with this person, yet for some reason he acted abnormally upset this time. He wanted us to restore the man's memory. Marlen's not experienced enough for a spell like that." Duncan shook his head. "And it shouldn't be done in any event, as it goes against the natural order of things. So of course, we turned him down. Even if it could be done, we wouldn't do a favor for someone like Marlen. The man's a reprobate. He's never done a thing to further our mission. Not only did we turn him down, but I took the opportunity to do what I've wanted to do for centuries." He rubbed his hands together. "I talked the other members into threatening him. Either he shapes up and performs his duties, or we put him in limbo for a century." He smiled. "That's why I set you to watching him. We wanted to see how he was progressing."

"I see," Georgina frowned. "You might have told me."

"Ah, but we didn't wish to influence your reports. But now that Marlen's obviously gone mad, there's no point in holding back." Duncan made a clicking noise with his tongue. "It's sad, isn't it? We have so few failures in our Society."

"I confess," Georgina replied, "that his motives remain unclear to me. The point of obtaining the three objects is to use them to destroy the mortals, not to harm *us*. How would he use them to seek revenge against the Council?"

Duncan studied the small mountain of confetti he'd produced on his desk. "You never know with Marlen. I've had doubts about his sanity over the years. He might want to use them as blackmail. Hold us all to ransom, so to speak, to get whatever he wants. With those three objects he could do it. I mean, we really can't have him going around wiping everyone off the face of the Earth, can we?"

"Then we'd better call an emergency meeting of the Council."

Duncan adjusted his tie. "I'll call them. *You* are not a member."

Georgina raised her eyebrows. "Not yet," she replied.

Nick woke up on a strange sofa. Its worn green cover smelled of stale fish and chips. There was a throbbing pain behind his right eye, and his mouth tasted like month-old unwashed socks.

He sat up, and wished he hadn't. He slowly bent his head between his knees and moaned. What the hell had he drunk? Where was he? And that dream—he remembered a vivid dream about a strange fellow who claimed to be a real magician, and he'd known him for five hundred years. What a weird night.

When Nick raised his head, his eyes managed to focus on the coffee table, on an empty bottle of Scotch and two tipped-over glasses. The thought of alcohol made his stomach churn. Coffee, that's what he needed. A steaming mug of coffee, a shower, a shave. And he'd better make a call to the station before he got tossed off the force.

He crawled to his feet and managed to locate the kitchen. Uncertain of his ability to remain upright, he leaned his weight on the worktop while he searched the cabinets. There was only instant coffee. He filled a tea kettle and set it on the stove. Then he made the mistake of deciding to look for the bath. After a prolonged stagger down a short hallway he found a promising door. Nick pushed it open and ran straight into a naked man mopping a head of wet red hair with a large purple towel.

"Morning. It's all yours." The fellow wrapped the towel round his waist and padded off.

Nick leaned against the door and put his hands over his eyes. *Bloody hell, it was real.* Whatshisname... Marlen... he was real. Hell. His head hurt. He couldn't handle this while his head hurt. Reincarnation, transmutation, mortals, immortals.... "Why me?" he muttered.

Fifteen minutes later he emerged from the bath, showered, shaved, dressed, and feeling reasonably human. He carefully entered the living room. It was empty. He found the phone and dialed the station. He'd just gotten through to his superior, Detective Inspector Collins, when Marlen came up behind him.

"Left the kettle on, you berk." He shoved a mug of coffee at Nick. "Could've burnt the place down."

"Detective Sergeant Watson, sir." Nick took the mug. He was glad to see Marlen had put on a robe.

Inspector Collins shouted something about an escaped lunatic. Nick held the receiver away from his ear.

"We have to go to Wales," Marlen said. He sipped at his own cup of coffee as he paced in front of the window. "Right away."

"Nuts," Nick replied. He looked at the phone. "Not you, sir," he said, bringing it back to his ear.

"I should hope not," Collins replied. "Do you realize I've had half the force out all night looking for you?"

Nick was sure that was an exaggeration. "Sorry, sir. I've got the suspect, if that helps."

"It does not. You'd better have a good reason for your behavior."

"We have to steal a goblet," Marlen said.

"Not on your life, you maniac." Nick glared at him.

"I beg your pardon?"

"No, sir, I wasn't talking to you."

"I'm going to put you on suspension in thirty seconds if you don't start making sense, Watson."

"Yes, sir." Nick took one gulp of the watery coffee and set the mug down. "It's a bit complicated."

"Shouldn't drink so much," Marlen said loudly.

"Who the hell is that?"

"Er, the suspect."

"*What*?"

Nick tried to pull the phone across the room so he could kick Marlen, but it wouldn't reach. The cord was hopelessly tangled.

"Hang up," Marlen said. "We've got packing to do."

"That does it, Watson."

"Wait!" Nick yelled. "I can explain!"

"Call back when you're sober." Collins rang off.

"Terrific." Nick gave the phone cord a frustrated tug.

"Look, I'm going to get dressed and toss some clothes in a bag. When I get done, you'd better be ready to leave." Marlen set his half-full cup on the window sill and strode off toward the bedroom.

"Wonderful." Nick decided to ring the only other person who could help him, or even believe his story. His uncle Brian. They'd always got on well. Brian was a well-educated, widely traveled man with boundless curiosity and a calm, steady nature. It wasn't easy to surprise him, and he always had a ready answer to any question. Besides, Nick wanted some answers on the PIS nonsense.

Brian's alert, chipper voice came through the receiver. "Nick! Glad you called. Wanted to offer my congratulations—"

"Stuff it. You know damn well that PIS was my last choice of sections."

"Couldn't be helped, lad. We were the only DI6 unit with an active agent opening. If you'd gone elsewhere, you would've spent all your time training and waiting around. But I need an extra man right now. So as soon as you finish off your notice—"

"Won't come to that," Nick said grumpily. "Think I've just been given the boot there."

"What's that? You've lost your job?"

Dispensing with further preamble, Nick launched into a straight retelling of the previous night, in all its details. He ended with what little he understood of the morning's developments.

"I need your advice," he finished. "I've mucked things up with Inspector Collins, and now this fool wants to drag me to Wales."

There was a lengthy silence on the other end of the line, so long that Nick began to wonder if his uncle were using one of his "special" phones to trace the call so someone could come and haul him off to a sanitarium. He coughed. "Uncle Brian? What do you think I should do?"

"Go with him," Brian replied in his usual clipped tone.

That was decidedly not what Nick expected to hear. "Sir?"

"How would you like to go straight into active service with PIS? On probation, naturally."

"Isn't this a bit sudden?" Nick ran his hand through his hair. He had the ominous feeling that Uncle Brian knew more than he would say about this. "You didn't set this all up as a test, did you?"

"Don't be ridiculous. This mage business sounds important, and I need someone on the job. Find out what this Marlen fellow is up to. Find out how valid his claims are, and if he truly has any unusual abilities. Well? Think you can handle it?"

Nick sighed. He almost wished he hadn't made the call. He admired his uncle's intellect; at the same time, he knew Brian often used his intelligence to manipulate people, playing mental games with them to suit his own ends. But so far as he knew, it was never done maliciously, and Nick approved of the ends Brian achieved.

He turned at the sound of Marlen coming out of the bedroom, dressed in what looked like the same jeans and shirt from last night. The cause of all Nick's recent irritation tossed a backpack onto the sofa and headed into the kitchen. "Five minutes," he yelled.

"I'm waiting." Brian's voice snapped in his ear. "From what you've said, *someone* needs to check this out. Shall I send another agent instead?"

Nick considered the fact that he probably wouldn't have a job with the Met to return to. He considered the fact that he *did* want to work for the DI6, and Brian's section might be the only way to get a foot in the door. But mostly he considered the possibilities for exacting revenge against his "best friend" for getting him into this mess in the first place.

"I'll do it," he said.

"Good lad. I knew I could count on you."

"Thank you, sir." He hung up.

Marlen returned with a box of cheese crackers and a huge package of chocolate-covered doughnuts. "Who were you talking to?"

"My fiancee," Nick lied. He fished around for the name of his last girlfriend. "Gwen." Then he glanced down at his shirt front. He'd buttoned it wrong.

"Oh, yeah?" Marlen stuffed the food into his backpack. "You getting married?"

"That's what one normally does with fiancées." As he redid the buttons, Nick noticed an orange stain. On his favorite blue shirt.

Marlen grinned. "You've been engaged before without getting married. Usually you get too drunk the night before the wedding and can't find the church."

"Look, you get this straight right now." He strode over to poke his finger at Marlen's shoulder. "I am *not* the person you knew in the past. Or *claim* to have known." He jabbed the finger at his own chest. "I'm *me*. And I wouldn't do a thing like that." Nick looked at his shirt again. "What's this stain?"

"Spaghetti." Marlen began picking up sofa cushions. "You seen my jacket?"

"No." Nick couldn't remember eating spaghetti. Or anything else.

"Aha." Marlen pulled his brown leather jacket off the coat hook on the front door. "Come on, it's time we were off. Over to your place, pack a few things, and then, Wales." He slung the holdall over his shoulder. "You have a motor?"

Nick stared at him. "Don't *you* have a car?"

Marlen shrugged. "I temporarily mislaid it last week. I think it's somewhere in Skegness."

"Bloody hell. How did we get *here*?" Nick crossed to the window. His eyesight was still too blurry to make sense of the jumbled buildings. "Where are we?"

"Portobello Road. We hired a taxi."

Nick looked round for his coat and found it half falling off an armchair. He took out his billfold and counted the money.

"And you generously paid for it." Marlen lounged against the door frame.

"So I see." Nick tucked the billfold away. His hand brushed against something metallic in the pocket. He pulled out the long chain and ran his finger over the engraved surface of the medallion. It was a mystery, and there was nothing he liked more than solving mysteries. He put the chain back and looked up. "You're expecting a lot out of me, you know."

"I know." Marlen flung open the door. "That's what friends are for."

CHAPTER THREE

In the long history of the mages, more than one attempt had been made to gather together in a formal society. Factions formed, power shifted from group to group, charismatic leaders rose and fell. By early medieval times, the mages who dwelled within Britain came under Duncan's sway. Older than most of them, wiser and more talented in the use of magic, and more convincing in his arguments, Duncan bound them together in the Immortal Society of Mages. He formulated rules, created a hierarchy, and gave them a strong community. He formed an Inner Council of six mages dedicated to questions of law, for the Society had a strict code of mage behavior which held certain actions to be punishable. The Council's power over all British mages stood absolute.

For hundreds of years Duncan Phipps maintained his leadership over the Council. Occasionally one of the mages questioned his rule, or dared to challenge him outright. So far, none of these little disagreements proved serious, requiring no more than a slap on the wrist or at worst, a quiet removal from the Council of an upstart. Duncan felt comfortable with his control of the Society he had created, control he planned to wield for all time. Unfortunately, he now realized his comfort had turned into complacency. In the face of genuine threat, he would need to rediscover that skill, talent, and persuasion that had allowed him to form the Society long ago, to find those leadership traits that had fallen into disuse.

Marlen could very well become a threat, if Duncan failed to act quickly. But he needed Council approval, or at least, he wanted them to *think* he needed their approval. Maintaining power over his fellow mages always went more smoothly when they believed that power was equally shared.

He gathered the Council members in his home's library. Over the long mahogany table hung his portrait, admirably depicting his patrician features, his blond locks, his piercing ice-blue eyes, and his commanding presence, dressed impeccably in dark robes from the sixteenth century. Today of course, he wore his more customary three-piece suit, though nothing else had changed.

Duncan's chair at the head of the table was larger and higher off the floor than anyone else's. To his right sat his closest friend, Wulf. A wiry old warrior, he twisted nervously in his seat, never happy sitting still. To the left sat Isabel, their oldest female member. Duncan had never wanted to allow women onto the Inner Council, for he considered them emotionally unstable at best. However, strong leader though he was, the Council was a Council, not a dictatorship, and he had yielded to majority preference in the matter long ago. Isabel proved to be a brash, energetic woman with a mass of dark hair and a voluminous figure who didn't hold back on speaking her mind. Beside her perched Ed Kelly, a thin weasel of a man with a pale face and straggly brown hair, whose rumpled suit hung on him like a scarecrow's outfit. Across from Kelly, Lady Jane Foxborough relaxed on her seat, dressed in a riding habit, her wide blue eyes attentive, a playful smile rarely leaving her lips. At the end of the table, sprawled across a piano bench because no ordinary chair could contain his bulk, was the last member of the Council. Raymond Yount, at just over a hundred years, was the youngest Council member next to Kelly; he tended to observe the proceedings quietly, occasionally contributing an insightful comment.

They greeted Duncan's reason for calling them together with concerted disbelief.

Ed Kelly laced his long fingers together. "Are you sure about this?"

"I'm positive." Duncan disliked Kelly, a man not of his own choosing, but thrust upon his Council as a favorite of Lady Jane's. Duncan had at one time approved of Lady Jane, as she rarely questioned his decisions. But she had fallen out of his favor, as she had developed a mind of her own over the past century or so, with opinions that frequently diverted from his. He hadn't purged anyone from the Council in quite some time, so perhaps when this crisis had been dealt with, there could be another housecleaning.

For now, he had to deal with the current members, had to convince them to take the action he desired. "I'm quite certain that Marlen has stolen Vere's stone from the museum. The first of her three objects of power."

"So one of our own has turned against us," Lady Jane said. "That's twice in seven hundred years. What *will* the other mages think?"

Duncan frowned. He never could tell if she were being sarcastic or not. "The point is, we've got to stop him from getting the other two objects. He's probably on his way to Wales right now to get the goblet."

"You must have a plan," Isabel said. "You always have a plan."

He gave her a sharp glance. "Indeed. I suggest that this is best kept secret from the Society at large, and that we take action ourselves. We should immediately send Council members to guard each of the two remaining objects. The three objects must not be brought together again at all costs. I've already arranged for charter planes to leave at once. We can easily beat him to the locations." He rubbed the bridge of his nose. "We are fortunate in that Marlen is... well..." he hesitated. After all, he'd been Marlen's first teacher and mentor, and some might claim he should be held responsible for training the fool. "He has an impractical nature. I doubt he'll move swiftly, nor with great thought."

"You're being too kind," Ed Kelly said. "Marlen is a lazy, irresponsible, incompetent, and ungrateful ruffian."

His nose wrinkled. "He's spent hundreds of years hanging about with that disreputable, *mortal* friend of his, doing as little work as possible. He has outright refused to follow the mage path, for he has never even attempted to assist the powerful or the wealthy. And he recently had the gall to ask us for help." He slapped the table. "The man's a lunatic."

"By all means, don't hold back," Duncan replied. "Not on my account."

Kelly sniffed. "*You* trained him."

"I *tried* to train him!" Duncan suppressed an urge to throttle Kelly, who would be first on his list of candidates for his next council purge. "Marlen did just fine until he finished the training and went through the immortality ritual. He behaved himself until then, but as soon as he became immortal he spurned our mission and did whatever he felt like doing. How was I supposed to know?"

Kelly crossed his arms. "We shouldn't have given that miscreant another chance when he came to see us. We should have put him in limbo right then. In fact, we should have put him in limbo centuries ago."

Duncan sighed. He'd suggested that very idea more than once, only to have it fall on deaf ears. His influence on the Council went only so far when it came to the gravest punishment the mages could mete out. "We're getting off the point. We need to stop him. Agreed?"

The need for action seemed clear cut. He gazed round the table. Wulf and Isabel nodded, Lady Jane pursed her lips, Kelly frowned, and Raymond Yount made no sound or motion at all.

Duncan was glad he'd brought his gavel. He picked it up and rapped it soundly. "I call for a formal vote. All those who favor taking whatever measures are necessary to stop Marlen, raise your hand."

"Excuse me," Lady Jane put in. "But what tangible evidence do we have that he took Vere's stone?"

Damn. Why did she have to interrupt his desire for revenge against that troublemaker with something so irritating as logic? "We'll have the proof when we get our hands on him." Duncan crossed his arms. "Because it will be in his possession."

Raymond stirred. He shifted on the bench. "Jane has a point."

"I agree," Kelly said. "As much as I dislike Marlen, it sets a dangerous precedent if we go about waylaying fellow mages without restraint." He smiled as a murmur of approval went round the table.

"Very well, I shall reword my statement." Duncan glowered at Kelly. He despised having his authority as head of the Council challenged. "Raise hands, those who favor finding Marlen with all possible dispatch and questioning him about the museum theft." That should satisfy the upstarts.

"That's more reasonable." Lady Jane raised her hand. Isabel joined her. "Absolutely. Let's go find him."

"I'm with you." Wulf raised both hands.

"Yes, I think that's acceptable." Raymond added his.

"Yeah," Kelly muttered, "I guess so." He barely lifted his hand. "But I'd like to be there when you find him, so I can see for myself how things are."

"I'm glad to hear it." Duncan smiled. He had just thought of a suitable comeuppance for Kelly. "Now that we've agreed, we'll need to send members out to guard the two remaining objects from further mischief. The goblet and the ring. Ed, I believe you should guard the goblet."

"But it's in Wales," Kelly replied. "In the middle of nowhere."

Isabel prodded him with her elbow. "Not up to it, are you? I'm willing to look after the ring, Duncan. I can manage a little trip to Scotland."

Kelly bit his lip. "Fine. I'll go to Wales." He scowled at Duncan. "I hope you're happy."

"One of us should go directly after Marlen himself," Wulf put in.

"I'll do that." Duncan had no intention of leaving the most critical job to any of this lot.

"You?" Kelly cocked his head. "Aren't you too important for such tasks?"

Duncan fidgeted with his tie. "There are times when one cannot delegate. And as you politely pointed out, Marlen was my pupil. While I'm not admitting I caused his problems, I will do what I can to rectify the situation. Therefore, I shall pursue him."

"You'd actually leave London?" Lady Jane asked.

"Of course. Why not?"

"You haven't left the city in over a hundred years," Isabel pointed out.

"About time I went somewhere, then, isn't it?"

"Alone?" Kelly's eyes narrowed.

Duncan sighed; he hadn't wanted to tell them that Georgina would be coming with him. Once she had heard his plan, she had insisted on joining the chase. He had naturally refused, as she annoyed him. Then he remembered it was wise to keep your enemies close. Someday he would need to do something about Miss Pruitt, but in the meantime, he would allow her to think she was wanted.

The Council did not need to know this. He rolled the gavel between his hands. "I have my resources."

"Ha." Kelly grinned. "I'll bet you're taking Miss Pruitt."

Only as far as I want to, he thought. Aloud, he said, "We don't have time for further discussion. Shall we get moving?"

Marlen sat in the passenger seat, studying the road map. He'd never been any good with maps. Turning it right side up didn't help. Nick was doing all right, though. Marlen looked at his companion's determined profile, and past it to the rolling countryside. As long as they kept heading west and a little bit north, they probably wouldn't miss Wales.

He crumpled the map and tossed it on the dash of the Ford Escort. Then he leaned into the back seat and rummaged round in his bag until he found the doughnuts, taking three for himself before shoving one at Nick. "Here. Have some breakfast." Crumbs and bits of chocolate flew off.

"Terrific." But Nick stuffed it in his mouth.

"Is that your favorite word, then?" Marlen mumbled, his mouth full.

"Um. It is lately. You might try telling me what this is all about."

"I was getting around to that." Marlen wiped the chocolate off his hands, onto his jeans.

"Good. You can start now. What the hell is this goblet we're going after?" Nick glanced over. "You got any more of those?"

Marlen liked the fact Nick had used "we." That was a good sign. He handed another doughnut over. "It's a magical object. One of three which, when put together, could destroy all humankind."

"Terrif—sorry. Why would anyone want to do that?"

"A mage named Vere got out of control about seven hundred years ago. She got angry at your lot for trying to burn her as a witch."

"Thought you mages were immortal."

"We are. More or less. Back then, though, being burnt to a crisp was one of the few ways to kill a mage."

Nick grinned. "Tell me the others."

"You're not taking this seriously again."

"We're in *my* car, aren't we?" He tapped the steering wheel. "Using *my* money."

"I'll pay you back." Marlen finished off his last doughnut and brushed the crumbs off onto the seat and floor. "We eventually came up with protection spells against fire, so don't get your hopes up."

"Yeah, yeah. Okay, so this Vere got out of hand. What happened to her?"

"The other mages got together and put her into limbo. It's kind of like suspended animation. Where she couldn't do any harm."

"And she's been there ever since? Seven hundred years? That's nasty."

"So is she. Downright evil, in fact." Marlen wondered when would be the best time to tell Nick that Vere was on the loose again. He probably wouldn't take it very well.

"So what are these three objects?" Nick asked.

"Vere created them magically. They're power objects." Marlen found the seat adjustment and pushed it back until he could prop his feet on the dash. "She planned to use them to focus the energy she needed for her anti-mortal spell. After she was punished with limbo, the other mages found the objects in her workshop, but couldn't find a way to destroy them, not even with the strongest magics. Vere was one of the oldest mages. She was incredibly powerful, and incredibly dangerous. So the other mages decided to hide the objects in separate locales." He ticked off on his fingers. "One's the goblet in Wales that we're going after now, one is a jeweled ring which is hidden in Scotland, and the third was the stone from the museum."

The car swerved and Nick narrowly avoided a van and a motorcycle as he pulled off to the side of the road, bringing the car to a screeching stop. "What are you up to?"

Marlen sat forward and brought his legs down, rubbing his knees. "Why'd you do that?"

Nick narrowed his eyes. "If you're trying to get all three objects for yourself, we can turn back right now, because *I'm* not helping you."

"What are you talking about?"

"You've already got one of them!"

There were days when Marlen wished he hadn't got up; this whole week had been like that. "I told you before I didn't steal it. Somebody beat me to it. That's why we have to grab the others. So *they* won't get them all."

Nick studied him long and hard. "You'd better be telling me the truth."

"I swear," Marlen put his right hand on his chest. "I wouldn't lie to you."

Nick glanced down. "What are those crumbs doing on my floor?"

"Sorry."

"Christ." Nick started the car and pulled back onto the motorway. "Do you know who took it? The stone?"

Uh-oh, thought Marlen, *here it comes.* "They're called drones. They've been psychically taken over."

"You mean they're being ordered around by someone else?"

"Right."

"Hell." The car swerved again.

"Stop that! You trying to kill us?"

"*Are you?*" Nick managed to keep the Escort in its own lane. "It's this Vere woman, isn't it?"

"Yeah," Marlen admitted. "She got free."

"Terrific. And don't look at me like that. I'll say it if I bloody well want to." Nick waved a hand in Marlen's direction. "This is crazy. Why are you trying to deal with her by yourself?"

"Why don't you watch where you're going?" Marlen braced himself against the dash.

"Don't tell me how to drive. And answer the question. Why don't you call in the rest of the mages?"

"I figured they'd be a bit upset with me."

"Why?"

"'Cause I'm the one who set her loose."

"*What*?" Nick turned his head sideways to glare at him.

"Stop driving off the bloody road!" Marlen snatched at the wheel.

"Let go!" Nick swatted at him.

"All right! But will you *please* calm down?"

"It's not easy."

Marlen leaned back and rubbed his arm. "Try taking deep breaths and counting to ten."

"I have a better idea." Nick drove toward the shoulder again. "You can drive."

"Me? I'll get lost."

"No, you won't." Nick pulled the car to a stop. He got out, yanked Marlen from the passenger seat, and shoved him behind the wheel. Then he slumped into the recently vacated spot. "And if you get one scratch on this car, I'll tear your intestines out. Through your nose."

Marlen started the engine and slowly pulled out into traffic. "I used to like you."

"Shut up." Nick pawed around in the back. "Where are those cheese crackers? Ah ha." He found the box, ripped into it, and began munching crackers with abandon.

"I was only trying to be honest and open with you," Marlen said. He felt annoyed. When he held things back from Nick, he didn't like it. When he told Nick the truth, he didn't like it.

"No job is worth this," Nick muttered between crackers.

"What's that?" Marlen didn't dare take his eyes off the road. "You're mumbling."

"I said, we're going to bloody well die, aren't we?"

"Shouldn't bother you. You're used to it."

"Oh, great. That really cheers me up."

"Sorry." That had been a tad too cruel, and he hadn't meant to be cruel, but *this* Nick lacked a certain enthusiasm that the *old* Nick always had in abundance. If only he could get him to remember the past, he was certain Nick's adventurous nature would reappear. Not that he wasn't being a little adventurous. He was physically there, going along for the ride, but Marlen could tell Nick's heart wasn't in it, not the way it should have been. In the past, more often than not, it was Nick who dragged *him* off and got him into trouble. It was Nick who leapt wholeheartedly into any fray. That was the Nick he needed now.

Marlen remembered an evening when Nick had almost got them caught up in a duel. Even after two hundred years, the memory stood clear in his mind...

Marlen disliked Brook's, the gentlemen's club that Nick's father had founded some twenty years earlier. He didn't fit in with the Dukes, Earls, and Lords, nor did he enjoy donning the rich clothes necessary for admittance as Nick's guest. So he steered clear. Until the evening of the big cheat.

"You must come," Nick insisted as he straightened Marlen's cravat. "I need you to help me defeat Lord Chellingham at whist. That unmitigated son of a whoremonger has taken my entire allowance three months running, and I am convinced he is cheating."

"What can I do?"

"Help me cheat back, of course."

"You have a method in mind?"

"That little spell you do from time to time to find things, would it not seek out good cards? That, together with a few hand signals ought to do the trick, don't you think?"

"You'll get us both skewered. Chellingham is known all over London as an expert swordsman."

Nick boldly dismissed the danger. "Not to worry. I have my ways of dealing with swords."

In the gaming rooms at the club, he introduced Marlen as a cousin from the country who was new to cards. Lord Chellingham eagerly took them on.

"I do so love playing with you, Nicholas lad. Your ability to fill my coffers knows no bounds."

"My luck may be changing tonight," Nick replied. "My cousin is a lucky man, and it rubs off on those he likes. Naturally he shall play as my partner."

"If you feel lucky, perhaps we should raise the stakes. Let us dispense with these little hundred pound wagers. What do you say to a thousand a hand?"

Marlen furiously shook his head, which Nick utterly ignored, launching them into an evening of intense card-playing that eventually attracted the other club members to circle the table. They watched Nick and Marlen best Lord Chellingham and his partner trick after trick, game after game, shouting encouragement, tipping back glass after glass of port, until three hours later Nick had his quarry down to his final bet.

"Everything," Nick said. "Your estate in Sussex, your house in Marlborough, your horses, your wife's jewels."

"You ask too much." Chellingham whispered to his gaming partner, the Duke of Omnium.

Nick shrugged. "Only the estate, then. Surely you can spare one little mansion on a few thousand acres. I shall be gracious and not ask a thing of the Duke."

"It matters not what you ask," Chellingham replied. "What matters is how you play, and you have played remarkably better tonight than in the past. Your cousin has indeed been quite a charm."

"Are you suggesting something I won't wish to hear? I suspect it is something you yourself are most intimately familiar with."

Chellingham flushed crimson. "Are you insinuating that I am a cheat, sir? How dare you! You are the one who is winning every trick when before you could not track cards to save your life! You and your cousin have been sending signals, sir." He tossed all his cards at Nick's face. "I call you a cheat!"

We're going to die, *Marlen thought as Chellingham rose from the table and yelled to his valet for his sword.*

Nick calmly collected the money on the table, stood, and beckoned to him. "Come cousin, it's time we were away."

"My sword!" Chellingham bellowed. "Remain where you are so I may skewer you both!"

Marlen felt drops of sweat run down his forehead.

"Sorry, I'm afraid we cannot accommodate your wishes." Nick ushered Marlen towards the gaming room doors. "Some other time, perhaps."

"Where is that blasted valet! I must have my sword this instant!"

"Move faster!" Marlen urged.

Instead, Nick grinned as he paused to grab champagne from a passing waiter. "One for the road, I think. Lord Chellingham, I believe you will find your man in the alley behind the club, where he was lured earlier this evening, and improvidently provided with a bottle of gin, gratis. A pleasant evening to you all."

With the furious Lord waving his arms and impotently yelling for help, Nick and a much-relieved Marlen made their exit.

Marlen knew that Nick's adventurous nature was there, buried somewhere beneath the facade of disbelief and caution. All he had to do was to find a way to dig it out. But that would have to wait a while, at least until Nick relaxed a bit more.

Marlen focused on driving; he didn't want to do anything which would damage its pristine white coat. They'd been on the road about an hour and were just skirting past Oxford. It took all his concentration to stay on the right road, carefully watching the signs, so he drove in silence for another half hour, the quiet punctuated by the sound of cracker consumption beside him. At last Nick crumpled the empty cracker box. "Okay, I'm calm now."

"You sure?"

"Needed some carbs and protein. Had too much sugar this morning, didn't I?"

"That's true."

"Where are we?"

"I think we're nearing Cheltenham."

Nick snatched the road map. "What have you done to this?" He straightened it out. "Are we still on the A40?"

"Probably."

"What's the name of this place we're going?"

"Aberystwyth." Marlen easily rolled the Welsh name around on his tongue, trilling the 'r'. "It's on the coast."

"Hang about. I found it." Nick traced a line of the map. "You stay on 40 to Ross-on-Wye, then head north on 49 to Leominster, then west on 44. Simple." He waved the map in Marlen's face.

Marlen batted it away. "That's what you say." A minute later they passed a mileage sign. They were still on the A40. Good. He hadn't messed up. Yet.

Nick carefully refolded the map and popped it into the glove box. He leaned back and crossed his arms. "All right. I'm ready to hear the rest of it."

Whatever he decided to say, Marlen knew it would annoy Nick. "Maybe I'm not ready to tell the rest of it," he replied. At least he had control of the car now.

"What happened to being open and honest?"

"Nothing. I just don't want you getting excited at everything I say."

"I told you," Nick said. "I'm calm now. You're stalling. I want to know why you let this Vere woman loose."

"It was an accident."

"I've heard that one before."

"Well, it's mostly true." Marlen frowned as a sign for an upcoming juncture appeared. "Which way do I go? Cheltenham or Gloucester?"

"Gloucester."

"Are you sure? Don't you want to check the map?"

"I'm sure, and I already looked at it once."

"Yeah, but—"

"Some of us can understand directions, you know."

Marlen took the road to Gloucester. It was true that the old Nick had always been good at maps, a talent that often came in handy when Marlen inevitably got turned round. He idly wondered how many weeks of accumulated time he'd spent standing in car parks trying to figure out where he'd gone wrong.

"Hey," Nick prodded Marlen's shoulder.

"What?"

"You always get so easily distracted? How on earth did you manage to become a mage anyway?"

"Innate talent."

"Ha."

Marlen shrugged. "Well, that's how I was chosen. Then they trained me. More or less. I can't help it if my attention wanders."

"You were telling me about Vere."

"Oh, that."

"Yes, that."

"Can you hand me a doughnut?"

Nick sighed. He reached in the back seat and hauled out the box. "Here." He thrust a doughnut at Marlen. "Now get on with it."

"All right, all right. Do you know what a grimoire is?" He took a big bite.

"No."

"It's a book of spells," Marlen mumbled. "Vere had a special grimoire for her own spells and experiments. She had a rare gift for understanding magic. All of us can work spells—" he paused, knowing his own skills were subpar, "after a fashion, that is. But a few mages can also create spells, and some are better at it than others. Vere was bloody brilliant. Other mages were wary of her powers, even Duncan, who was no duffer himself when it came to inventing spells. Anything that makes a mage more powerful also makes them more dangerous. Other mages have two responses to those with great ability—either find a way to get rid of them, or make them their leader."

"Fascinating as all this is, what has it got to do with this grimoire thing?"

"It's still around. I borrowed it—"

"Borrowed? What, you mean you checked it out from the Mages' Lending Library?"

"Glad to hear your sarcasm's still intact."

"You stole it, didn't you? And stop spewing crumbs everywhere."

"Sorry." Marlen finished the doughnut and wiped his hand on his shirt. "I intended to put the grimoire back. But the drones took it from me before I was finished with it."

"I hope you had a good reason for wanting it in the first place."

There had been two good reasons, but Marlen didn't think Nick was ready to hear them yet. It might set Nick to asking all sorts of personal questions that he didn't particularly feel like answering, not while Nick didn't remember who the hell he really was. He opted for the reason less likely to cause problems. "I wanted to see if she'd come up with any spells for restoring memory. I did ask the other mages for help first, but they turned me down flat. The grimoire was the only other source I knew."

"A spell to restore memory," Nick repeated. "As in my memory?"

"Got it in one. Could you hand me another—"

"No." Nick dumped the box of doughnuts in the back. "You've had enough." He turned sideways in his seat to face Marlen. "Did you consider the tiny fact that maybe I didn't *want* my memory back? Did it even once occur to you that my life was going just fine the way it was? *Well?*"

Marlen's hands clenched the steering wheel; he consciously tried to relax them. "Yeah, I considered it."

"But you went ahead anyway."

"Couldn't help it." He took a deep breath, tried to shrug nonchalantly, and failed. "I missed you."

"You *missed* me?" Nick shook his head. "You've known me for five hundred years. I'd think you'd be sick and tired of me by now."

Marlen smiled. "Not quite. Besides, I told you, sometimes you remember your past, and sometimes you don't. All together, there were over two hundred years where you didn't know me from the postman."

Nick shifted round to face forward again. "You could try making new friends, you know."

"I know." Marlen wished he'd given out the other reason instead. Either one would probably have led to the same questions, though. Why did he care so much—that was the main one. He wondered how long it would be before Nick figured it out. That logical mind of his didn't seem to allow much room for emotion. Excitability, yes, but Nick had never been good at the deeper stuff.

They rode in silence for a while; Marlen waited patiently for Nick to break it. Which he did. "So did you find it?"

"What? Oh, you mean the spell. Well, I thought I had. It *looked* like it was meant to restore things. Deciphering the language and the handwriting proved a bit tough. I played around with it, and I guess that's where the trouble started. Apparently, I ended up restoring Vere."

"Why 'apparently'?"

"I haven't actually seen her." Marlen coughed. He wished he'd had something to wash the doughnuts down with; his mouth was too dry. "About a week after I started mucking about with that damned spell, these drones showed up at my flat. Two guys. They were wearing tour guide badges from St. Michael's Mount. That's where Vere was kept—in a vault on the island, under the castle. These guys demanded the grimoire, so I put two and two together and figured she was loose."

"You just handed it over?"

Marlen straightened up in his seat. "'Course not. I put up a fight. They were bigger than me."

"That wouldn't be hard," Nick grinned.

"Thanks. I thought the stone might be next on their list, and apparently it was."

"But you didn't bother to tell the other mages."

Marlen scrunched down in his seat. "Figured I would get the stone first, and then tell them. Thought that might make them a bit happier about the whole mess. I suppose I could always turn back to London and let them know all about it."

"You can let them know when we get to Wales." Nick chuckled. "You can use that handy spell of yours. 'Send messages hundreds of miles in less than a day.'"

"Very funny." Marlen saw a sign for a turn-off to Ross-on-Wye; the name sounded familiar. "Is that where we're going?"

"Yes."

"Good." He was getting much better at this. There was no telling, though, where he would have ended up if Nick weren't with him.

They rode on in silence, and as they got closer to Wales, it slowly and steadily began to rain.

CHAPTER FOUR

As the charter plane rolled to a stop on the private runway, Duncan gazed out at a land of gray drizzle. His umbrella was back in London, hanging on his office door, where it wasn't likely to do him a lot of good. Duncan sighed, picked up his small overnight bag, and watched Georgina Pruitt heft her impossibly huge carpet bag with practiced ease. He didn't ask if she needed assistance. Georgina Pruitt never required assistance.

They climbed down from the plane and hiked towards the taxi Duncan had hired. The stupid thing was parked at the other end of the runway. Georgina produced a voluminous umbrella from her bag. She did not offer to share it. The rain poured steadily, running in rivulets down Duncan's face.

"Has it occurred to you," Georgina said when they reached the taxi, "that we may be on the wrong track?" She shook the umbrella out before climbing into the car, effectively soaking the last few spots on Duncan's suit that hadn't already been drenched.

Duncan got in and told the driver to take them to Aberystwyth. "In what way?"

"Coming to Wales. We are assuming Marlen will go after the next nearest object. He could fool us by going to Scotland first."

She had put her bag and umbrella on the seat, taking up most of the room. Duncan squeezed against the door, his shoulders hunched. He made a little coughing sound. "And you're assuming Marlen is capable of being clever. Trust me—he is not."

Georgina took a handkerchief from the pocket of her blue suit jacket. "I should think," she said as she dabbed at the two or three drops of water which had managed to get past her umbrella, "that you would want to be certain of his movements."

"I am." Duncan smiled; he had got one up on Georgina. "I took the precaution, just before we left London, of performing a seeking spell on our young miscreant. It told me he was heading for Wales." He looked out at the miserable gray landscape, towards the forested hills in the distance. "Ed Kelly has already arrived ahead of us, and should now be in place to guard the goblet. All we need to do is find a comfortable spot in which to await Marlen's arrival." He checked his watch. Its face was smeared with water, but it still worked. "We can do another seeking in a couple of hours. He'll be getting close by then."

Georgina neatly folded her handkerchief and returned it to her pocket. "You haven't yet told me precisely where the goblet is." She turned to raise an eyebrow at him. "I believe it's time you did, in case something untoward should befall you."

"Untoward?" Duncan rolled his eyes. "You don't know Marlen well, do you?"

"I met him briefly at one of your birthday parties some years ago. He struck me as... indolent."

"Is that all? During the last party I saw him at, he drank four punch bowls by himself." Duncan wrinkled his nose. "Then he drove a Rolls which didn't belong to him through the middle of a nearby cricket match. Toward the end of the day, for some unknown reason, he attempted to climb a gazebo and fell off, breaking his neck. Took him three days to heal."

"That's the one," Georgina said.

"And you call that indolent? I call it insane." Duncan sneezed. Rain water dripped down his face from his hair. "We have nothing to worry about. We wait for Marlen to arrive, grab him, and take him to London. If the others have any sense, they'll agree to put the little bastard in limbo where he belongs."

"That sounds a tad extreme to me."

"Extreme problems require extreme solutions." He sneezed again.

Georgina promptly opened her bag, pulled out a package of travel tissues, and held them out. "I do hope you're not coming down with a cold."

"It's only an allergy," Duncan replied as he blew his nose.

Her eyebrows knit together. "To what are you allergic?"

"Rain."

"You should have brought your umbrella."

They entered the town proper. Georgina slid open the glass partition between them and the driver, and told him to deliver them to the best hotel in Aberystwyth. She slid the glass shut. "I do hope they've heard of private baths out here."

"Wales is a civilized country," Duncan replied.

"I'll believe it when I see it. Now tell me where the goblet is. There is no good reason not to."

Duncan had to reluctantly admit he couldn't think of one. "It's up in the mountains, about seven kilometers east of the town. Tucked away in a cavern by some waterfalls. A picturesque spot, I'm told."

"Doesn't sound as if it's a terribly comfortable place to be guarding."

Duncan envisioned poor Ed Kelly hiking about in the woods, out in the middle of nowhere, in the pouring rain. He grinned. "No, it doesn't, does it?"

Marlen propped his elbows on the table. "So. Tell me about this girlfriend of yours."

They were in Wales. They'd stopped for lunch at a small restaurant in an unpronounceable town. Nick poked at a plate of wilted salad. He tried to remember something, anything, about Gwen. All of his girlfriends tended to blend together. "Oh, you know, tall, blonde. Works as a secretary."

Marlen swept up a handful of crisps and chomped on them. "Doesn't sound serious."

There were peculiar bits of red stuff among the lettuce leaves that Nick didn't like the look of. "What do you care?" He carefully picked the mysterious bits out.

"Just curious," Marlen replied, a bit too quickly.

Nick raised an eyebrow. "Do mages have romantic entanglements?" he asked pointedly.

"Some of them do." Marlen's double cheeseburger and chocolate shake arrived. He rubbed his hands together and dug in.

Nick gave up that line of questioning for the moment. He prodded a cucumber. He loathed cucumbers. "I suppose you can eat whatever the hell you want and never worry about arteriosclerosis."

Marlen slurped at the shake. "Annoying, isn't it?"

"You can get hurt, though, can't you?"

"'Course we can. But we heal up pretty quick. Without benefit of drugs or doctors."

"That's handy."

Marlen didn't look up from his glass. "It's still not pleasant."

Nick wanted to ask more, but something in Marlen's expression forestalled him. Fine, it could wait. He had plenty of other questions to pursue. He watched Marlen take a large bite of burger. Juice dribbled down his chin. Marlen idly wiped it off with his sleeve. "Tell me," Nick said, "what exactly do you do?"

"What do you mean?"

"You have all this time, all these powers. What do you do with them?"

"Oh." Marlen extracted the last dregs of chocolate shake. "I just hang about, having fun."

Nick shook his head. "You're not my idea of a mage."

Marlen laughed. "If you don't think I'm much of a mage," he replied, "then why are you coming with me?"

"Curiosity." The last thing Nick wanted was to tell him about the PIS. That he was simply an assignment. Which wasn't entirely true, anyway. Yes, he was supposed to be spying on Marlen, but he also wanted answers to his own questions. "Curiosity's an advantage for police work, you know."

"Yeah? Is being a good climber an advantage, too?"
Nick frowned. "I thought we were going to Aberystwyth."
"Sort of. The goblet's hidden in the mountains outside the town. In a cavern."
Nick checked his watch. "By the time we reach Aberystwyth it will be too close to evening to go hiking about. Not to mention too wet. Stupid place to keep it, if you ask me. Too difficult to get to."
"That *was* the original idea," Marlen said as he finished off his hamburger. "We'll have to find a B and B nearby, and we can tackle the hike first thing in the morning. Simple."
"Simple," Nick repeated. But he didn't believe it for one minute.

The Lady of the Golden Woods they once called her, when times were good. The Dark Lady they called her, and the Witch of Penwith, when times turned bad.
All dead, each and every one of them, the men and women who called her those names. Seven hundred years dead.
Vere stood in the castle dining hall, gazing out the arched window. Across the water in the village of Marazion, the first lights of evening twinkled on. This was her favorite time of day in this new age she'd woken to, a time when every person could live as only the rich once lived, with light and warmth at their fingertips. She wondered if they, too, looked across the water to St. Michael's Mount, and saw the lights in the castle.
When she first woke from her ageless slumber, the changes in the world overwhelmed her. So much of the earth's beauty lay lost, consumed by this new mechanized civilization. Yet so many advances came to fruition that once she recovered her resilience of mind, Vere opened her eyes to a new life. One with comforts unimaginable in the life she'd been torn from so long ago. Light, warmth, ease of travel and communication, wondrous inventions and devices, medicines, goods, services beyond compare. What she slowly came to see was a new kind of democracy within all these strange advancements, a breaking down of the barriers between lord and peasant, between the haves and the have-nots which she had labored against

herself in those olden times, what she now saw as darker times when most men lived brutish lives. When she first wandered through the castle and found the strange projection on the wall, and pushed it upward, flooding the room with instant light—why, that moment had felt like... like *magic*.

The dining hall door opened. Vere turned to see one of her drones, a tour guide named Ron. He carried a large box into the room and set it on the long dining table.

"What a comfortable world we live in." She pulled the drapes closed.

"Yes, ma'am."

She hiked her skirts a bit and swept over to the table. She wasn't quite ready to give up the floor-length gowns she'd been so fond of seven hundred years ago. But that, and her waist-length black hair, were her only firm attachments to the past. Vere believed in the maxim that knowledge was power, and she had a lot of knowledge to catch up on. "Is this the computer?"

"As you ordered." Ron unpacked the components. "PC with monitor and color printer. Lots of software and manuals, too."

"Excellent. Did you have any trouble selling the paintings?"

"No, ma'am. They believed every word I said." He fingered a green amulet round his neck. "This must have worked."

The persuasion amulet was one of her more successful devices, designed to make people gullible. "Return it now." She held out her hand.

Ron lifted it over his head and dropped it in her palm. Then he looked round the room. "Where should I set the computer up?"

Vere studied the growing mess in the dining hall. On the antique oak sideboard lay an overflowing stack of newspapers; she had avidly read three to four a day since emerging from limbo. The formal dining table lay strewn with books she'd sent her drones to buy from the stores in Penzance; the castle library had already been thoroughly ransacked. Against one wall she had set up a row of three television sets, each turned to a different channel. They ran twenty-four hours a day. There were four more in the library, and two in the bedroom she'd taken as her own. All the time, every hour, she learned. Seven hundred years of learning in a few weeks. She had never doubted her ability to do it, for her learning was fueled by desire. She yearned to know everything about her new world, to absorb its ways so thoroughly that she would be prepared to face her enemies once more, on level ground.

The dining hall was her favorite room in the castle— roomy, and high ceilinged, with lots of light from the row of windows, and an enormous table to spread things out on. So what if it was a bit cluttered? She liked clutter; it stirred her creativity. She eyed a corner near the doorway and spotted an unused outlet. "Bring that big walnut desk from the study in here," she said. "Place the computer on it in that corner. Can you hook up a telephone line in here?" She'd been reading about computers nonstop for three days, and she knew what she wanted.

"I can do it." Ron headed off towards the study.

He made a good servant. Only nineteen or twenty, but smart and able to follow her instructions. She had turned all the tour guides into drones. It felt good to command again after all this time, and their assistance would enable her to gather strength while she studied and prepared. She also needed privacy, which the island provided. As her powers grew, she used them to fortify her isolation by keeping strangers away from St. Michael's Mount. Only her drones came and went with ease.

There were four of them. She kept two with her most of the time, sending one or the other on errands to the mainland. The two others she had sent to fetch her grimoire and the stone from London. They had returned both to her early that morning. She then sent them to get the remaining two objects she needed to complete the spell she'd begun so long ago, the spell she'd been so close to completing.

Vere wished there were someone around to whom she could tell her plans. Half the fun in working new spells came from sharing them with a person who could truly appreciate her efforts. Not the drones, of course. Someone who understood the mages. Someone who cared about them and their powers. Better still, someone who knew her prime enemy, Duncan Phipps.

She crossed to the window and pulled the drapes open again. "Seven hundred years that man took from me," she whispered into the night. "And for what? Exercising the power I was born with? He *will* regret it." More lights twinkled across the water. Vere smiled. No one would ever put *her* into darkness again.

She was going to see to that.

CHAPTER FIVE

They found a bed-and-breakfast a few miles outside of Aberystwyth, halfway between the town and the mountains. Because it was November, they were the only guests.

Nick let Marlen carry the bags up to their rooms while he went in search of alcoholic fortifications. Normally he wasn't much of a drinker, but something about being in Marlen's presence brought out a need to achieve happy oblivion fairly often. He returned to the rooms armed with a bottle of pure malt Scotch and two glasses.

Marlen sat cross-legged on the floor of his room, with a road map spread out before him. The entire contents of his backpack had been dumped out, and Marlen busily searched through the mess.

Definitely going to need a drink, Nick thought. Marlen had a look of fierce concentration which did not bode well. Whatever he was up to, it was bound to be something crazy. Nick sank onto the floor across from him. He uncapped the bottle and filled the glasses. "Scotch. Got it from the landlord." He handed a glass over. "What are you doing? Thought you were going to phone whatshisname. Head of the mages."

"I tried," Marlen said. "Duncan's not answering. So, in case you're interested, I am about to perform a real, live spell." His brow furrowed. "Provided I can find the bloody tools." He dug deeper through his pile.

"You could try a telegram." Nick leaned back against the bed. "Might be faster."

"This isn't for sending messages." Marlen produced a small leather pouch. He emptied out a pile of brightly colored stones. "This is for locating people. To tell us where Duncan's run off to." He picked out a blue stone and rolled it between his palms.

"Terrific," Nick muttered. "I get to see a real spell. I await with bated breath."

Marlen ignored him and began chanting words which made no sense to Nick. Then he set the stone on the map on top of the dot for London, and sat back with a little smile.

Nick started to say something rude, but stopped when he saw the stone wobble.

What the hell? As he watched, the damn thing moved slowly across the paper to the west. He blinked and rubbed his eyes. It couldn't have moved by itself. That wasn't logical. There had to be a trick involved.

He set his drink down. "How are you doing that?"

"*Shhh!*" Marlen glared at him. "I'm concentrating."

The stone continued its steady movement across the map. It crossed the borderline into Wales, drew close to their own location, then came to a stop directly on top of the dot representing Aberystwyth. "Bloody hell. He's here. Duncan is *here*. He knows what I'm doing. I'm in trouble, mate."

"But *how* did you *do* that?" Nick picked up the stone and examined it, checking its surface, even holding it up to the light. An ordinary rock. Nothing odd about it at all.

"I used magic, you berk." Marlen snatched the stone and put it back in the pouch.

"Yeah, but—" Nick shook his head. This was ridiculous. A hidden wire, perhaps? He picked up the map and turned it over a few times, running his hand over its perfectly untouched surface. No wire. "I don't get it. That stone couldn't move all by itself."

"Yeah, well, it did." Marlen grabbed the map. "And it told me that Duncan is in Wales. Which means I don't have to call him, 'cause he already knows. Question is, *how* does he know?" He randomly tossed the map and his belongings into the backpack. "I bet that pompous prick's been spying on me."

The wire must have been somewhere else. Nick got on his hands and knees, nose to the carpet. He carefully poked and prodded every inch of space where the map had been laid out. Still nothing. "Give me that bag."

"What? Why?"

"Just hand it over!" Nick snatched it and dumped the contents out again. A thorough rummaging, however, failed to reveal any apparatus whatsoever which could account for the stone's mysterious movement.

Marlen stared at him. "What are you doing?"

"Trying to stay sane." Nick stuffed everything back inside.

"Give up. It's a lost cause."

"Thanks." Nick returned to his cross-legged position, picked up his glass, and chugged it. He couldn't deny what he'd seen with his own eyes, try as he might. A shiver ran up his spine. Could everything Marlen had been telling him actually be true? *Everything?* Had he really been reincarnated, or whatever Marlen had called it—transmuted? Had he really known the idiot for five hundred years? *No,* his logical mind cried out. *Impossible.* And yet... this little thing called "evidence" kept popping up. What would Brian advise? Gather more information, probably. And keep drinking the Scotch.

Nick refilled his glass. He had to find out more, had to know everything, no matter how disturbing. "That was a real spell," he said.

"Yes."

"And it really worked."

"Yes."

Nick took a large gulp of his Scotch. "I don't think I like this."

"Neither do I." Marlen picked up his previously untouched glass and drank. "Looks as if we're going to have more company than we bargained for tomorrow, if not sooner."

"You mean Duncan?" Nick frowned. "But he'll be on our side. Won't he?"

"I don't honestly know," Marlen replied. "I hope so."

"What about those drones you said Vere had sent? Are they following us, too? Can you do one of those locating things on them?"

Marlen shook his head. "I tried it back in London, but it wouldn't work. Vere, if it is Vere, must have put a block against it." He smiled, "You didn't believe it before, did you? About my being a mage?"

"Of course not," Nick replied. "I'm a cop. I need proof." He leaned across to jab at Marlen's shoulder. "Maybe you can work a little spell, but I *still* don't believe you're immortal."

"You could find out," Marlen shrugged. "Just shoot me and see what happens. Not that I'll enjoy it much."

"Don't have a gun." Nick felt decidedly tipsy, but refilled his glass anyway. Then he held the bottle out. "Another?"

"Yeah. But that's it," Marlen said. "For *both* of us. And drink it slowly this time. We need to be in good shape tomorrow."

"How far are we hiking?"

"Oh, it's not that much. Seven or eight hundred feet up the mountain." Marlen uncrossed his legs and stretched them out.

"No problem." Nick patted his abdomen. "You have to keep in condition on the Force."

"Yeah, you always were athletic."

"You mean in those past lives you say I had?" Nick asked. "That's another thing I don't believe in." The existence of the medallion was intriguing, but reincarnation was far too incredible an explanation. Time to gather some more information. "How can I believe it really happened?"

"Well, I could tell you about your previous lives if you want," Marlen replied. "At least the highlights. Maybe it'll trigger something, ring a few deeply buried bells. You never know."

Nick looked at his watch. "How many are there?"

Marlen did some calculating on his fingers. "Ten. You're on number eleven now."

"Well, that's not too many." Nick grabbed a bed pillow and shoved it behind his back. He wished he had a tape recorder for all this nonsense. Brian would love it. "Go ahead."

"Okay." Marlen cleared his throat. "Life number one. You were born in 1478, to noble parents—"

"I like that part."

"Unfortunately, you were a fourth son. And your older brothers all lived to adulthood."

"Oh. Nothing for me to do, then?"

"Not on the family estate," Marlen said. "You took up fighting. Started out brawling in the local taverns. Managed to learn about swords and horses, and took to hiring out your services to any lord, prince, or king who happened to need fighters in a hurry."

Nick raised an eyebrow. "Are you saying I was a mercenary?"

Marlen nodded. "Everybody used 'em back then. Nothing to be ashamed of."

"Isn't ringing any bells yet. How do you come into it? When were you born?"

"1480."

"Yeah?" Nick grinned. "That makes me older than you."

"Technically. But don't worry, I've never held it against you."

"How kind."

"We met in a tavern in a village near London when you were twenty and I was eighteen. You accused me of cheating at dice, but then, you were pretty drunk."

Nick stared at his half-empty glass. "And I suppose you weren't?"

"Well, I was a little tipsy," Marlen confessed. "But I was *not* cheating. I was merely having an incredible run of good luck, and you were having an incredible losing streak. You got pissed off and attacked me. Leapt right over the table and tried to throttle me." He rubbed his throat for effect.

"Are you saying we became friends after I beat you up?"

"No, no, you didn't beat me up. We beat each other up. Broke nearly every piece of furniture before we finally got booted out. That didn't stop us—we kept fighting. It was spring, and pouring rain, and the local river was flooded. We rolled around in the mud and leaves all over the damn place until we got to this bridge, which we both managed to fall off. Got swept down river and nearly drowned. You never did have much luck with rivers."

Nick's eyes widened. The very vivid images of his nightmare flashed through his mind, images of drowning in the cold, swirling waters. He trembled. "Go on."

"We struggled to shore a good mile from the village. By then we were just interested in survival, so we helped each other across a field to a big farmhouse, where we stole some food and some very bad wine. Ended up passing out in the barn next to this massive sow. After that, we naturally started hanging out together."

"Naturally. Anyone would. Doing what?"

"The usual. You know—drinking, brawling, gambling—" Marlen hesitated.

"Whoring?" Nick asked. "We got to do that, too, didn't we?"

Marlen looked uncomfortable. "Yeah, we did that some-times."

"Why'd you hesitate before? Is there something you're not telling me?"

Marlen pursed his lips. "Yeah. We didn't do it all that much. We didn't always want women." He gave Nick an odd look. "Sorry."

Nick stared at him. *Didn't always want women.* That was far too close for comfort. He rolled his glass between his palms. "I think you just rang a bell."

"Yeah?"

"Yeah," Nick said softly. "I don't always want women in this life, either." There was no valid reason not to be honest. Marlen had been very open with him, and it wasn't as if he'd be in danger of losing his job over it, not on the word of a lunatic mage. Besides, all that was long since done with.

"Oh," Marlen let out a sigh. "Wasn't sure how you'd take that news."

"Correction," Nick said quickly. "I *didn't* always want women. That all happened years ago. Just one of those experimental phases one goes through. It's long since over, and I don't ever want to hear any of this repeated outside this room, is that clear?"

Marlen nodded. He concentrated on his fingernails, idly picking at them. "Don't worry. I'm not stupid."

"Good."

Not that there was anything stupid about caring for someone. It pained him that Nick dismissed so easily what had once been so important... had everything between them changed so much? Marlen closed his eyes, seeing another century, another night of drinking at an inn...

"'Tis *colder than a hag's tit, this inn." Nick rubbed his arms vigorously. "Landlord! Why is there no fire on the hearth?"*

"There is no more wood to be had in all the village, my lord."

"Hell. Then bring a tankard of ale." He looked to Marlen, who shivered on the bench beside him in the inn's tavern room. "Two *tankards!"*

"Fine establishments you choose to patronize," Marlen said through chattering teeth.

"Do you blame me for this unholy snow we've been enduring? There is none like it in all the annals. Be grateful we have but one more day on the road, my friend."

A goodly portion of ale soon warmed Marlen up. He gazed at his closest friend in all the world. One more day. Yes, and after that one day's ride, which would take them back to Nick's ancestral home, he would lose him forever.

Nick cocked his head. "You look saddened. You should be happy for me, should you not? An engagement is often considered a pleasant occasion."

"Normally, this is so. I do think your choice is a good one." He would not lie. The woman Nick had chosen for his bride was wise, kind, and beautiful. "I only hoped we would have more time... together."

"Ah." Nick's blue eyes, which Marlen once thought of as cheering as a summer sky, now pierced him like the ice-blue cold outside. "Such things cannot last. I have a title, an estate. I have obligations." He twisted the tankard back and forth. "A family is what is expected."

"I know," Marlen tried to smile. He drained the last of his ale. Suddenly he didn't feel so warm anymore. "I hate this winter chill. I'm going to my room."

"Wait—" Nick reached out as Marlen stood up. "We are friends. We will always be friends. That will not ever change."

"Everything changes. All relationships end. Some day."

He went on up to his room, climbed into the bed fully clothed against the cold, blanket pulled over his head. As the drink began pulling him into sleep, he felt something rather large climbing under the covers beside him. "Hello, there. I do hope you're Nicholas."

"Oh yes, it's Nicholas," his voice slurred. "Had another tankard. Had a wee think. My thought, should you care to entertain it, is that two bodies warm together better than one alone." He ruffled Marlen's hair. "'Tis pleasing, your hair. Lovely eyes, too."

"Idiot. You cannot see my eyes in the dark."

"True enough. Too true enough..." With which profundity, Nick promptly fell asleep.

Marlen touched his face in the dark, and sighed. All relationships end. He would see Nick soon as a married man, and then there would come children, and all his talk of friendship everlasting might be well meant but not truly possible, at least, not the way it had once been.

Of course, he had not known then that Nick would return to him again in a new lifetime.

He had said that everything changes. He simply didn't know how much it changed, over and over again.

Marlen looked up. "I can get through the rest of your lives more quickly if you want."

"Stick to the highlights. I think I can handle that."

"Well, you carried on with the occasional mercenary work, with frequent visits home to spend your money, and that covers the highlights of your first existence."

"Until I fell off a horse in a river and drowned." Nick shivered. Ice-cold water... he could feel it, washing over his head. "Not a pleasant way to die."

"No. But you'd had a long life for that era. Close to sixty years." Marlen shrugged. "No need to get morose about it. You said you didn't even believe in this stuff."

"That's right." Nick let out a burp. The Scotch was definitely getting to him. His head seemed rather muzzy. He tried to concentrate. "So I died. Excuse me, this person you say is me died. Fine. Let's see, 1478, sixty years, that would be 1538." Not so fuzzy as he'd thought. He could still add and subtract.

"No, it was 1536. I said nearly sixty. You were fifty-eight."

Nick frowned. "Well, get your facts straight."

"My memory's not perfect, you know," Marlen replied. "You were born the second time in 1536. But I didn't know you were a transmuted soul until I accidentally ran into you in 1556, after you'd just turned twenty. *You* recognized *me*. Of course, I hadn't changed any since the mages found me. Like I said before, they granted me immortality when I was twenty-five."

"So I knew you were one of them, didn't I?" Nick felt a surge of satisfaction at having figured this out, even in his inebriated state. "I mean, during the first life, I would have noticed you not aging."

"Yeah, yeah," Marlen said dismissively. "I told you all about it. You've never liked the Society of Mages. Said they were useless." He smiled. "Anyway, I'd heard about transmuted people before, but I'd never known one. You were pretty much the same, similar appearance, similar lifestyle. Didn't get to be a lord's son that time, though. Your father was a wool merchant. But you still took up gambling and drinking and fighting, just like before. You ended up getting yourself run through in a duel."

Despite its violence, Nick found this an easier "death" to handle, since he had no memories of it. "Never had any nightmares about swords. How old was I?"

Marlen did some figuring in the air with his finger. "Thirty-seven. You died in 1573. Your third life was a lot longer, the longest so far. Once I knew you'd be coming back, I went looking for you. Not right away, though. I always waited 'til you got through childhood and the teens.

That third time, I found you when you were twenty-two, but you didn't know who I was. It was the same as it is now. You couldn't remember."

"Then how could you be sure it was really me?" Nick asked as he eyed the Scotch bottle. His brain was obviously still working properly, and he wondered if it would be a good idea to rectify the condition.

Marlen sighed. "It's hard to explain. There's a psychic connection. I can *feel* it. Every time."

"But I don't. Not every time." Nick reached for the bottle.

"No. Usually I leave you alone when you don't remember." Marlen snatched the bottle from Nick's reach. "Hike tomorrow, remember?"

"Not fair," Nick complained. "*You've* still got Scotch in *your* glass."

"That's 'cause I haven't been slogging it back like you have." Marlen picked up his half-full glass and sipped some more at it. "Let's get this finished, all right? Right. I checked on you now and then during that third life. Did quite well for yourself—had a long military career, lots of honors, ended up quite prosperous. Went through three wives, tons of children. You know, you probably have descendants hanging about from that life."

"I don't want to think about it," Nick said.

"Could get complicated."

"I don't fancy meeting my great-great-great-whatever kids."

Marlen twirled the Scotch about then took another sip. "Probably a lot of 'em about. You made it all the way to eighty that time. Died in 1653. But when I went to search for you twenty or so years later, I found an eleven-year-old boy. I figured out that your fourth transmutation must have been too short. You must have died in childhood when you were around eight, long before I would have gone looking for you. Then you were born into lifetime number five, starting all over again, and I was too early. So I had to go off and come back again when you were older. I don't much like hanging out with kids. I checked on you again when you hit your twenties. You remembered again. It never fazed you, remembering that you'd been around before."

"I only get upset when I *don't* remember?"

"No," Marlen said softly, "you get upset when you can't remember and I come along and totally disturb your life. I've never done it before, honest. I've never told you about your lives when you obviously didn't know me." He stared into his glass. "I'm sorry, but I just couldn't help it."

"You'd think in five hundred years you could learn a little restraint."

"I said I was sorry."

"Yeah, yeah. Go on, then."

"Where was I?"

Nick sighed. "Life number five. Late 1600s."

"Oh, that one. It was quite a turnaround from your earlier times. Lower class, London slums. You were a petty thief, among other things. We didn't hang out together much that time. Your lifestyle was a bit rough, even for my tastes."

A thief? Nick refused to acknowledge the idea. "I find it hard to believe that I was ever a member of the criminal classes. Don't I ever get to be someone important? Famous statesman, perhaps?"

Marlen shook his head. "Sorry to disappoint you."

"I guess I'll survive. How did number five meet his end?"

"Got hanged. For stealing a bottle of wine."

"Great." Nick looked from his empty glass to the Scotch bottle. "I hope things improved."

"Don't know," Marlen said. "I found you again in the 1730s, but you had your amnesia again. That might have been a happy life. I do know you took up soldiering again, and died in 1745, during the Scottish uprising."

"Which side?"

"The English." Marlen finished off his drink.

"Some of my Watson ancestors fought on the other side. You reckon one of them did me in?"

"Please," Marlen said. "Don't make this more complicated than it already is. You died in 1745, and I don't want to know who was responsible."

Nick made a lightning grab for the Scotch. "One more."

"You've had enough."

"Okay, half a drink, then." He leaned over to fill Marlen's glass halfway, then poured his own two-thirds full.

Marlen rolled his eyes. "You always were a bit of a lush."

"Hey," Nick objected, "this is *very* unusual for me, I'll have you know. Can I help it if my entire world has been rearranged in the past twenty-four hours? It makes me nervous, okay? And when I get nervous, I drink. Which isn't very damn often. You got that?"

"No need to get your knickers in a twist," Marlen said. "Besides, you keep saying it's not *you* I'm talking about, anyway."

"Then don't say I'm a lush," Nick snapped. "Say, 'my old friend Nick who isn't really you was a lush.'"

"Oh, hell." Marlen chugged down his Scotch. "Forget I said anything. Christ, you're touchy. You never used to be."

Nick scowled.

"I mean, this friend of mine who bears a remarkable resemblance to you didn't used to be so touchy," Marlen amended. "You're much more fun when your memory's intact, you know. Or he is. Whoever." He took the Scotch and refilled both their glasses. "Hell with it. Where was I?"

"Damned if I know," Nick said, happily drinking away. "Bonnie Prince Charlie, or something."

"Oh, yeah. You got it in the uprising. Right. Well, next time around, you remembered. And thank goodness. We spent the rest of the 18th century mucking about Europe. Your father was a wealthy diplomat and you never had to work. You just spent his money, and got terribly fat in your middle age. 'Course, back then, that was looked upon as a good thing. Sign of wealth. You popped off when you were fifty-five, barely making it to the new century. Heart trouble."

"So that brings us up to... um, 1800. Not much left, is there? I haven't heard any more bells yet." And Nick was very glad he hadn't. The whole thing sounded like so much piffle. Marlen had probably read too many bad novels in his time, and he certainly had a much too vivid imagination.

"Maybe life number eight will do it," Marlen said confidently. "You got to join Robert Peel's new police force."

That made Nick grin. "I was one of the first Bobbies? That's much better than those early bits. Catching criminals." About time something interesting happened in his, or rather, the other Nick's many lives. "Fighting injustice, uncovering the truth. That's me, all right. Did I remember you that time?"

Marlen nodded. "You told me that you were somehow making up for life number five, when you were on the other side of the law."

"Must have been boring for you, hanging out with a cop." Nick envisioned a bold young police officer, newly appointed to mete out punishment to the unlawful, striding briskly through quaint Victorian neighborhoods, protecting the upright, decent citizens therein from vicious cutthroats and hooligans.

"Wrong."

"Huh?" The vision faded. "Why?"

"'Cause you still knew how to have a wild time. Didn't even slow down when you got older. Made it into your seventies. Found dead of natural causes in a brothel."

"Good Lord." So much for decency and uprightness. Nick let out a long-suffering sigh.

"One of London's finest."

"Thanks."

"Any time."

"That gets us to number nine," Nick said, glad they were nearing the end of this nonsense.

"I don't know much about that one. You had amnesia again, and the few times I checked up on you, you didn't seem terribly happy. Forced to follow your father's footsteps into banking. Wrong profession for you. And I think you had an unhappy marriage, though I can't be sure. You lived into your seventies, but died a suicide."

"You could have skipped that one." Nick finished his drink and set the glass down.

"Probably. There's only one more. The one before this
one." Marlen paused far too long. "Born in 1948. I found
you in 1970 when you were twenty-two. Your memory of
the past was back intact. You'd just been thrown out of
college. You were trying to be a professional undergraduate,
but you had trouble attending classes. Soon after, you went
to bet on the horses and made a small fortune. We had a
lot of fun spending it."

"Must have been a short life, though. 'Cause I was born
in 'seventy-eight. Which means he must have died then.
Right? When he was only thirty years old. What happened?"

Marlen eyed the bottle of Scotch. "Motor accident," he
said quietly. "Got hit by a drunk driver who ran a red light."

Nick shook his head. "I've never been a good driver.
But at least that one was the other fellow's fault."

"That's what everyone said. Didn't make it any easier.
And you weren't driving. You were just a passenger."

"What?"

Marlen hesitated. "I was driving."

Nick's eyes widened. "Bloody hell."

Marlen unclenched his fingers from his palm, where
the nails had made deep indentations.

Not knowing what to say about something that
obviously still caused Marlen pain, Nick looked down at
his own hands and mumbled, "You must have been badly
hurt yourself."

"Oh, I would have been dead, if I could have been
dead." Marlen rubbed at his palms. "I ended up in hospital,
of course, and managed to stir up a few inquiries. They
couldn't figure out why I was alive, and then, a few days
after entering the casualty ward, why I was trying to get
up and walk around. There was one bloke—this young,
hotshot researcher, who kept coming around, highly
suspicious. Asked lots of questions, poked a lot of needles
in me. It was all I could do to escape before they locked me
away in a lab somewhere. Left the country for a few years."

Nick heard him talking, but not completely. A red light
was flashing through his mind, a light from nowhere. He
rubbed at his eyes, trying to make it disappear. Instead,
it rapidly changed to white, then blue, then back to red.

Somewhere, a siren sounded. *No,* his mind shouted, *I don't want this.* He shook himself, but it didn't help. An image hit him hard, of broken glass, metal crunching against metal, blood everywhere—it wasn't a dream, and it wasn't a hallucination. He was *there.*

He drew his knees up to his chin and covered his face with his hands. "No," he moaned, "make it go away."

He felt Marlen's hand on his arm. "What is it? What's wrong?"

"Stop it!" Nick angrily slapped his hand away. "It's you—you're doing this to me! You put this in my mind!"

"I don't know what the hell you're talking about!"

"Yes, you do! The wreck, the sirens, the blood—it's all here!" Nick tapped at his own head. "Make it stop, dammit!" He put his hands on either side of his head and groaned as stabs of pain lanced through him.

"Oh, great," Marlen said. "Of all the things for you to remember, did it have to be that?"

Nick vaguely heard him rummaging about, and as more cascading images of pain and fear and death invaded his mind, he heard Marlen chanting something, and felt a cool, flat object against his forehead. Just as suddenly as the nightmare had started, everything fled, returning him to sanity. He looked up to see Marlen putting a white, flat stone away. "What did you do?"

"Tried a mental healing spell. Seems to have done the trick."

Nick tried to control his rising anger. "Why did you put those images in my mind in the first place?"

"I *didn't.* They're memories. Your memories—"

"*No.* It wasn't *me.* I don't *want* your friend's lives, I don't want his memories. Just let me be *me.* Do you understand? *Leave me alone.*" He rose unsteadily, wanting only to get away from Marlen, get to his own room. This whole damn thing was going all wrong. Screw Brian and the PIS.

"Wait!" Marlen staggered after him. "It doesn't have to be this way. You have plenty of good memories, too—"

"I said, leave me *alone.*" Nick shoved Marlen aside and stormed out the door, slamming it shut behind him. Christ, no job was worth this.

He found his own room and fell across the bed, exhausted.
His mind whirled with visions of battles, duels, thieves and
policemen—all those lives, all those struggles. None of it
seemed real, yet it still unnerved him greatly. And despite
the protests, Marlen *had* to have done something to put
those images of the car wreck in his mind. That wasn't a
part of him either, had never been a part of his memories
or his dreams or his nightmares. No, none of it was *him*.

Then why, he wondered as the room spun around him,
did the tale Marlen had told bother him so strongly?

He lay there for a long, long time, waiting for the whirling in his mind to come to rest, unable to do anything but
wish for the sweet oblivion of sleep.

CHAPTER SIX

"No," Georgina said. "We wait."

"But why?" Duncan put his seeking stone and map away. "We know where he is. It's only a few miles from here. We can go get him tonight."

"And then what?" She sat primly at the hotel room's tiny table, her hands clasped. "I doubt if he has the stone on him, and he won't go after the goblet until morning. If we take him back to London *now*, what can we prove? That he came to Wales? He could say he was on holiday."

"What about the museum? He broke into that."

"True. But unless we find the stone in his possession, we can't prove he took it. But if we can catch him in the act of stealing the goblet, *then* we have him."

The argument was well-reasoned, which was why it annoyed Duncan. Perhaps he should ditch Georgina so he could do what he wanted. Which was to find Marlen and pummel the little miscreant into oblivion.

"We can follow him tomorrow," she said. "If he goes anywhere near the cavern, then we can grab him."

"And what if something goes wrong? Have you thought of that?"

Georgina sniffed. "What could possibly go wrong? Counting Ed Kelly, there are three of us. Three against one—he is clearly outnumbered. You said he isn't competent enough to pose any danger."

Duncan nodded. He *had* said that.

He just hoped it was true.

Nick woke up shouting.

He opened his eyes, confused, his body trembling. The shout must have happened only in his dream. After a few moments of staring at the sparsely furnished room he remembered where he was. He slowly sat up.

Moonlight flickered through the thin curtains as storm clouds rolled across the sky. Fragments of the dream came back to him, shifting in and out of memory. Nick struggled to hold on to them. Steel against steel... two swords clashing. A glimpse of a muddy field and men in ragged uniforms. Feet slipping around, trying to stay upright. A horse whinnied. A scream, a flash of blood. Rivulets of blood running through the mud. The sound of swords clashing, a glint of metal... the polished surface of a shield reflecting a familiar face... dark hair, blue eyes... the shield was thrust aside and a sharpened blade found its way home to a stranger's throat, the blood spattering his arm... *his* arm.

Nick threw the bed covers off, got up, and grabbed his robe. He dashed down the hall to the bath, but couldn't find the light. So he left the door open, using the dim yellow glow from the hall to find the sink. Parts of the dream faded as he splashed cold water over his face. He gripped the edge of the sink and slowly looked up at the mirror. Light from the moon streamed through the tiny window, clashing with the light from the hall, giving his face a ghostly waver. There were other faces in that face. Nick closed his eyes. So much for the oblivion of sleep.

He grabbed a towel and rubbed his face vigorously before slowly walking back to his room. As Nick carefully climbed into bed he heard snoring through the thin wall from Marlen's room. At least he hadn't disturbed anyone in the place. He pulled the covers tightly and curled up, hugging the pillow, unable to quell the feeling that something was horribly amiss. And no matter what he tried, sleep wouldn't come.

In the chill of dawn, Ed Kelly stood shivering on a narrow mountain path, wiping his runny nose on the sleeve of his jacket. He wrapped his arms round his chest and patted himself in a futile attempt to warm up. There was no point to staying inside the cavern to keep dry. The ceiling was too low and the ground too damp. All night he'd been in there, never once finding a position he could sleep in. So now he stood just outside the entrance, staring down the path that led to civilization, which at that moment meant nothing more than a hot breakfast.

Ed stared at the layer of frost blanketing the ravine below. He stared at the nearby tree, where a raven perched, preening itself, no doubt the same raven that had cawed incessantly all night. Then he stared at the empty coffee thermos lying by his feet.

Why the hell was he suffering? He didn't have to stay here. His mission was to guard the goblet, but did he really have to guard it in this forsaken piece of miserable real estate that only tourists would be insane enough to visit? Why couldn't he just take the thing to a warm, cozy hotel room and guard it there?

And where was Duncan? Had he caught up with Marlen yet, or not? When was that bastard going to contact him? Ed looked at his watch. Six a.m. Not only six in the morning, but six in the morning and freezing, and not likely to warm up any time soon. Ed stared up at the sky: it also looked like it was going to rain again. Worse, his supply of bagels, tinned caviar, and chocolate bars, was all gone.

So were his tissues. Ed felt a sneeze coming on, and looked for a clean spot on his jacket to wipe his nose. Just as he found one, the raven took flight from its tree branch, flapped overhead, and shat on his sleeve.

One minute later, Ed was hiking down the narrow path toward civilization with the goblet in his food sack, banging noisily against his hip.

Marlen swore as he tripped over a branch. He had never developed a fondness for the great outdoors. Especially in the rain. He had lived too many centuries without central heating, and all he really wanted to do now was to take as much advantage of it as he possibly could.

Nick straggled up beside him, looking as wet and bedraggled as Marlen felt. "That's the third time you've nearly fallen off the path," Nick observed. "Are you sure you're cut out for this sort of thing?"

"I'm not usually awake at seven in the morning," Marlen rubbed his eyes and yawned. "Being mostly asleep does affect coordination, you know." He slapped half-heartedly as his cheeks in an attempt to inspire alertness.

"You're also hung over."

"So are you." Marlen took a closer look at his friend. "You look half dead. Didn't you get any sleep?"

"Strange bed," Nick replied.

"Uh-huh." Marlen didn't believe him. There was something more than haggard circles under Nick's eyes. Something unsettled. "Are you sure you're feeling all right?"

Nick sighed. "You've been asking that every ten minutes since we got up this morning. I'm *fine*."

Marlen sensed this was far from the truth. Whatever memories Nick had experienced last night, memories of the car crash, had disturbed him greatly. But as usual, Nick wasn't about to admit it. If there was one thing Marlen wished he could change about his best mate's basic personality, it would be his ability to express his emotions. Nick was okay on the surface stuff, and whenever things were going well he had no problem being happy and carefree. Nick was always fun to hang out with during his lighter moods. But when it came to the darker stuff, the deeper stuff, he tried very hard to keep his feelings tightly locked away, would pretend that nothing could touch him, wouldn't dare risk letting anyone get in close. And that hurt. You'd think, after five hundred years of friendship, that they could trust each other enough to reveal anything and everything, including the things that made them most afraid.

"You've got that distant expression again," Nick said, prodding him in the shoulder. "Are *you* all right?"

"No," Marlen replied, risking honesty. "But since when did you ever care?"

"Oh, Christ." Nick gazed briefly upwards as if to ask some higher authority what he'd done to deserve this. "What are you on about now?"

"Nothing. Forget it." Marlen wiped fat drops of rain from his forehead. "Let's just get going."

"Fine. And which way do we go?"

Marlen looked ahead to where the path forked. He'd spent some time studying the tourist map he'd found at the B and B, but it hadn't been this detailed. They had to keep going up, he did know that. Both branches of the path seemed level, but he detected a slight incline in the one to the right. "That way," he said, with more confidence than he felt.

"Are you sure?"

"'Course I'm sure." Marlen trudged off to the right.

"Can you see them?" The rain had gotten in Duncan's eyes again. He wiped his face with a thoroughly damp handkerchief.

"I'm not trying to see them," Georgina replied. "If we can see them, then they can see us. We wouldn't want that, would we?"

Duncan knew what he wanted. A steaming bath, a hot toddy, and to be about a thousand miles away from Georgina Pruitt. Keep your enemies close, indeed. What on Earth had he been thinking?

"They're about ten minutes ahead of us," she went on. "They'll reach the cavern first, and either Ed will handle things, or he won't. If they do get the goblet, they'll have to come back the same way, won't they? And then we'll have Marlen red-handed." She paused to brush an errant leaf off her tweed jacket.

"Where the hell did he round up reinforcements, that's what I'd like to know." Duncan had been unpleasantly surprised when he and Georgina had found the B and B that morning, and secretly watched Marlen heading out with his accomplice in tow. He hadn't expected Marlen to be so resourceful.

Georgina arched an eyebrow, "Afraid we can't handle them?"

"Of course not," Duncan snapped. "Any friends of Marlen are probably as incompetent as he is. Come on." He slogged on up the path, brushing the dripping tree branches out of his face, until he came to a juncture.

"We go left," Georgina said.

Duncan knew better than to question her.

"We're lost!" Nick shouted.

"Nonsense," Marlen replied with absolutely no confidence at all. The path had climbed upward for quite a long way, then gone round a curve and suddenly plunged downward. They were headed straight toward a ravine.

Nick plodded up alongside him. "Don't you know where you're going? Where's this cavern? You said it was by a waterfall. I haven't seen any ruddy waterfalls."

All Marlen could see were trees, mud, and steep declines. He idly wondered how long it would take for his soaked trainers to dry out. "I'm sure it's around here somewhere."

"We should have gone left back there," Nick said. "We should be going up, not down. Correct?"

Marlen sighed and leaned against a damp tree trunk. "I've never been very good with directions."

"Terrific." Nick started to head back the way they'd come.

"Wait," Marlen held his arm. "We've gone too far. It would be quicker to cut through the ravine and climb up the other side. We're running parallel to the other path. I can just make it out through the trees."

Nick studied the steep drop of the rocky, brush-and-tree strewn ravine. "We don't know what's down there."

"A river?" Marlen guessed.

"Could be," Nick muttered. "If there *are* waterfalls around here, they have to empty out somewhere. You're right, that's what's down there. A big, nasty, dangerous river—"

"Nah, probably just a stream." Marlen began scrambling down the hillside then stopped to look back at his friend. It belatedly occurred to him that Nick probably wasn't all that fond of water in general and rivers in particular. "You can go around the long way, if you like. Meet me there."

Nick seemed hesitant then abruptly squared his shoulders. "No, I'm coming. I'm not afraid of a little water." He joined Marlen in the downward climb.

"Ed? Edward? You there?" Duncan pulled aside the branches which partially hid the cavern entrance, and crawled inside. He brought out his torch and flashed it round the small space. The light illuminated nothing but bare stone walls.

He crawled out to face Georgina. "Empty. No Ed. And no goblet."

"Impossible. Are you sure this is the right spot?"

Duncan walked up the path a few yards, round a bend, and saw, up ahead, a waterfall cascading into the chasm below. He walked back, checking the hillside and the brush, but there were no other caves. When he returned to the entrance to the hiding place, he found a crumpled candy bar wrapper in the bushes. He straightened it out. "Mars Bar. Ed's favorite."

Georgina peered into the cavern herself. She straightened, shaking her head. "It's still impossible. They couldn't have waylaid Ed. Surely we would have heard. And where *is* he?"

Duncan gritted his teeth. "I told you we should have grabbed Marlen back at that B and B." He couldn't believe this was happening. Not to him. He hadn't been the most powerful mage in the Society for a thousand years only to see that power threatened by one irresponsible lunatic.

"Hindsight is easy," Georgina said. "There's no point in arguing now. We need to think. They must have gone on ahead."

"Doesn't go anywhere. It's a dead end. Besides, that would presume they knew we were behind them."

"They might have heard us. They could be hiding up ahead somewhere, waiting for us to turn back. We should check."

"Very well, I'll show you." Duncan strode up the path, Georgina on his heels. "But it's a waste of time. They could be anywhere." He waved at the steep drop beside the path. "They could have climbed down into the ravine."

"We would have heard the noise."

"The point is, this is a large, wooded area, where someone could hide for hours and never be found. And where we could spend hours searching while they could double-back and get a head start to Scotland."

"We could do a seeking, then."

"Not here," Duncan said. "We don't have a map this detailed. But we could get back to the hotel and do one there. Find out if they're still in the area or if they're already on their way north. And we should send a warning to Isabel in Scotland." Duncan came to a halt at the dead end. The only thing in front of them was a waterfall. "I'm telling you," he said, "there's nothing we can *do* here."

Georgina stared at the waterfall for a minute, then sighed and turned round. "What about poor Ed? Shouldn't we at least search for him?"

"That bastard lost the goblet." Duncan stormed down the path, kicking random stones out of his way. "As far as I'm concerned, he can rot." He didn't look back.

Nick slid down the smooth surface of solid rock on his bum a good twenty feet, until the ground leveled out. He stood and rubbed his hands together, trying to ease the soreness of his palms. Scraping his hands on boulders in the middle of a rain-soaked forest was not his idea of fun. Better to be walking a night beat in Soho. He found a big fir to stand under, attempting to stay dry beneath its canopy of branches, at least for a few minutes. His peace was soon disturbed by the sound of Marlen calling his name.

Nick spotted him and reluctantly waved, "Over here."

Marlen ducked under the branches. He didn't look any better than Nick felt. Mud spattered Marlen's clothes, there were rips in his jeans and jacket, and a few twigs were snarled in that mass of bedraggled hair. "Do I look that awful, too?" Nick asked.

"Yeah. Did you know you've got dirt smeared all over your face?"

"I fell. More than once. Guess I'm not good at climbing."

"Fine time to mention it," Marlen said.

Nick waited another minute to catch his breath, then he and Marlen tackled the next decline. Nick staggered about between the trees, using the rough trunks for balance as he half-hiked, half-slid downward. At least the rain had finally lightened. Just as Nick wondered if the ravine really had a bottom, he heard the sound of gurgling water. The trees thinned out, the land leveled off, and he slogged down the last bit of slope to stumble onto the edge of a bank. The water proved to be a harmless looking stream. On the other side, partway up the hill, he saw movement. A man sat by a tree, waving frantically.

Marlen skidded up behind him, nearly knocking him down. He grabbed Nick's shoulder for support. "Listen," he said between gasps, "next time I say it's faster to go across a ravine than around it, don't pay any attention."

"Okay." Nick was too exhausted to move. "I found something." He nodded up the hill.

"Who the hell is that?"

"Dunno. 'Spose we'd better find out."

"Yeah." Marlen took off across the stream.

Nick followed, and when he reached the other side he heard Marlen shouting for him to hurry up. He clambered up the hill to join him.

Against a tree trunk sat a man of about thirty, who was rubbing the back of his neck. Nick knelt beside him. "Are you badly hurt?" He tried prodding the fellow's ribs, but was brushed aside.

"Just help me up this ruddy hill."

Marlen squatted nearby. "Kelly? It *is* you, isn't it?"

Ed Kelly stopped rubbing his neck and looked over at Marlen. "You!" He lunged at Marlen's throat. "You bastard!"

He knocked Marlen off balance, and they rolled together, grappling, ending up halfway back down the hill before Nick caught up with them. He grabbed Kelly by the shoulders and dragged him away from Marlen.

"Who is he?" Nick gasped.

Marlen sat up, sputtering dirt from his mouth. "Ed Kelly. He's a mage."

It was all Nick could do to keep control of Kelly as he
flailed his arms and tried to twist out of his grasp.

Marlen came over to help. "Knock it off, Ed. What are
you doing?"

"What am I doing? What are *you* doing? You've gone
mad, you have! Stealing the stone, coming here—"

"Hold on. *I* didn't take the stone. Vere's behind it."

Kelly's jaw dropped. "You *are* mad."

"Is Duncan around?"

"He'd better be. And I hope he finds you and wrings
your bloody neck. And your friends' necks as well."

"*I* haven't done anything," Nick protested.

Kelly squinted up at him. "Not you. The other ones.
The two blokes who took the goblet and knocked me down
this bloody hill. Are you going to try to tell me you didn't
send them?"

"Hell." Marlen slumped against a boulder. "They've
got the goblet, too. Damn."

Nick stood glaring at him. "Vere's drones?" Of all the
stupid, idiotic... slogging around out here in the mud and
rain for a good reason was one thing, but slogging around
only to find out their quarry had beaten them to it was too
much. He should have known better than to let Marlen
handle the details of this little adventure.

"Has to be her drones," Marlen replied. "They got here
before we did."

"Obviously."

Kelly looked from one to the other then shook his head.
"You're nuts. You *do* remember that Vere's in limbo?"

Marlen studied his shoes intently. "She got loose."

"Since when?"

"Since I accidentally restored her."

"Oh, come on." Ed rolled his eyes. "You don't expect
me to believe that, do you? Very sneaky, trying to invent
a scapegoat, but it's not going to work. Vere on the loose.
Right. I'm not that stupid."

Marlen blinked at him. "You really think *I'm* after the
objects? What the hell would I want with them?"

"Revenge," Kelly said, eyeing him warily.

"Nonsense. Don't you understand? I'm trying to keep them out of her hands." Marlen stood and brushed off his clothes. "Forget it. We're wasting time. We've got to get after them. When did they knock you down?"

"Hour, hour and a half ago."

"Terrific," Nick muttered. He gave Marlen another fierce glare. "So we trudged all the way up here for nothing. The goblet's gone, and they've got a head start on us. You got any more brilliant plans, or are you just going to get us lost again?"

"I'm doing my best! I'm not used to taking action—it's not my strong suit."

"What *is* your strong suit, pub-crawling?" Nick let out a long-suffering sigh. "You're useless. I know why you dragged me into this. Because you're barely capable of tying your shoes on your own."

"Please," Marlen said. "Can we argue later?"

"Absolutely," Nick replied. "I'm sure there'll be plenty of opportunities." He got Ed Kelly to his feet, and helped him up the hill.

Marlen trudged behind them, keeping his distance, which was fine by Nick. His first assignment for the PIS wasn't exactly running smoothly. *Go with him*, Brian had said. Find out more about these mage blokes. On the surface, it sounded simple enough. He knew how to infiltrate, how to work undercover, how to pretend he was something he wasn't. It seemed easy enough to gather details about the mages, since Marlen had no qualms about talking his ear off on that particular topic. And he could easily pretend to be Marlen's friend, act as if he were there solely to help him out of a spot of trouble. Not that he'd been making a good job of that so far, what with all his complaints and accusations of incompetence. Perhaps he ought to work on rectifying the situation, try being companionable for a while, before all his complaining made Marlen suspicious as to why he kept sticking with him. Simple.

Nothing in his training, however, had prepared Nick for a revenge-crazed mage freed from a seven-hundred-year-old limbo, a magical stockbroker, or a sodden eight-hundred foot hike in Wales to chase after a goblet accompanied by someone who didn't know up from down. What the hell should he do now? Just keep on going along for the ride? How much crazier would this get, and how long was he expected to put up with it before going round the bloody twist?

"Idiot," Nick muttered, though whether he meant himself or Marlen, even he didn't know for sure.

"I beg your pardon?"

Kelly, keeping pace alongside, apparently thought it a reference to him.

"Sorry," Nick said. "It was more of a general comment." He took a closer look at the lanky, dour-faced fellow. "Who are you, anyway?"

"Ed Kelly. Used to work for John Dee. You ever heard of John Dee?"

Nick frowned in concentration, "Not really."

"Doesn't matter," Kelly replied glumly. "Long dead anyway. Have to do Duncan's bidding now. The egotistical, overbearing, ungrateful sonofabitch. You don't see the likes of *him* being knocked down ravines, *do* you?"

"Well, no."

"Of course you don't. Self-satisfied, smug, patronizing old bastard. Thinks he can snap his fingers and we'll all come running. And we do, you see, 'cause he's the big shot, isn't he? Head of the stupid Council, been around for bloody ever, thinks he knows everything just 'cause he made up the protection spells all those centuries ago, I ask you, what has he done lately?"

Kelly happily rattled on, listing his boss's shortcomings with great glee. Nick only half listened, and wished Marlen would catch up with them. At least Marlen's brand of nonsense was entertaining. Kelly's was boring.

They finally reached the top of the ravine and clambered onto the path. Nick waited to help Marlen up.

"What were you two nattering on about?" Marlen asked as they hiked back towards civilization.

"Your friend Duncan."

Marlen turned on Kelly. "You can tell Duncan from me that he's got it all wrong."

"Why don't you tell him yourself?" Kelly sneered.

"Because I'm not suicidal, that's why. He's had it in for me for years. If he gets hold of me now, and I haven't got any way of proving I'm innocent, he'll talk the rest of you sheep into putting me in limbo, won't he?"

Kelly grinned. "It *has* been mentioned. Good idea, if you ask me."

"Nobody's asking you," Marlen snapped.

"Look," Nick put in, trying to make some sense of the mess, "what can Duncan prove against you? You haven't got the stone or the goblet in your possession."

"He'll just say I hid them somewhere, that I had accomplices. No, what I've got to do is get hold of the third object. The ring. And then take it straight round to HQ and hand it over to the Council. I've got no reason to hand it over unless I'm innocent, right? Right. And afterwards, we can all go out to Cornwall together to deal with Vere."

"Good luck," Kelly said. "You'll need it, if you want anybody in their right mind to believe that story."

"Ed," Marlen replied, "I've never liked you."

"You know what?" Kelly said. "It's mutual."

The three of them fell into an awkward silence that lasted all the way down the mountain.

CHAPTER SEVEN

They dropped Ed off a couple miles outside of
Aberystwyth to fend for himself before driving back to
their B and B. A quick freshening up was in order before
packing, and to that end, Nick had immediately appropri-
ated use of the one bath in the place.

Marlen found this a tad inconvenient and, after rinsing
off what dirt he could in the owner's kitchen sink, decided
enough was enough. He needed a good scrubbing. Before
breaking into the bath, however, a peace offering might
be wise. Nick hadn't seemed terribly pleased with the
adventure so far. A hot cuppa might do the trick.

Some minutes later, he tapped gingerly on the bath
door, having stripped off his soaked, muddy clothes and
donned a robe. He bore two steaming mugs in hand.

"What do you want?" Nick called out.

"Not to be damp and cold," Marlen shouted. He
tried the door. It wasn't locked. Fancy that. He waltzed
inside. Warm wafts of steam hit him, instantly inducing a
feeling of drowsiness. He sank down against the wall
beside the tub.

Nick lolled in the steaming water, head back, eyes
closed. "Some people like privacy when having baths,"
he said lazily.

"Some people are greedy with the hot water, too. You've
filled that right up to your chin, you know. Didn't save
any for me, I suppose?"

"There's always the sink."

"Tried that downstairs," Marlen said sullenly. "Nobody in the family seemed to want to see me undress, though. All I could do was clean behind me ears." He set one of the mugs on the tub rim. "Made you a cuppa, if you're interested."

"Oh." Nick opened his eyes. "How kind." He lifted his head and took up the mug, cradling it between his palms. "What brought this on? Pangs of guilt?"

"A bit," Marlen admitted. "Didn't know things would go so badly today. Sorry."

"It's okay. What are mates for, if not a little abuse?" Nick sipped at his tea. "Mm. Perfect. How'd you know I only take milk, and no sugar?"

"You've always had that peculiarity." Marlen drank his own sweetened tea. He added, with a tinge of sadness, "Or rather, that person named Nick whom I used to know always did."

Nick looked at him for a long moment. "You really do miss him, don't you?"

More than you'll probably ever know, Marlen thought. *Or will ever want to know.* "Yeah," he said simply. He looked away, unable to handle Nick's penetrating gaze. "Sorry. Maybe I shouldn't have got you involved in all this. Maybe it was wrong of me."

"No, not wrong," Nick replied softly. "Somewhat careless, but it wasn't wrong. It's only natural to go to your best mate for help."

That's what they had always done—tackled problems together. Never mattered who wanted the help, either...

When Nick had been one of the first police detectives back in the 19th century, he had been the one to come to Marlen for help.

"We've got a high-class jewel thief working in Mayfair," Nick explained one day. The thief operates practically in the open, during parties. I'm going undercover tonight, and I want your help—an extra pair of eyes and ears."

"Sounds like work to me."

Nick grinned. "Idle as always, aren't you mate? Listen, this is important to me. I've not had a promotion in ages, and I deserve one. The case could make or break my upward climb. It's not as if I've had many opportunities for a real career in my lifetimes, you know."

"So get one of your lowly constables to help. Why me?"

"The party is at Sir Stuart-Clark's home. They've already invited you to attend. Seems you know them."

True enough. Over the centuries, Marlen had steadily amassed a good deal of wealth by hoarding objects that weren't expensive in their day but he would sell for much higher prices a century later when they became "antiques." Lately he'd been selling off Louis XIV chairs to Stuart-Clark, who liked him, and had invited him many times to his home.

"Right, then. What's the plan?"

There was no plan, as usual. They merely mingled, each taking different sections of the massive ballroom where the gala was held. Nick moved smoothly among the upper crust, Marlen noted, no doubt retaining lessons in manners from his previous life as the son of a wealthy man. They met up after two hours of careful observation.

"Well," Nick asked, "do you think our thief is here?"

"He ought to be if he isn't. There are enough diamonds in this room to fund the national treasury for the next century."

"He? What would say if I said the thief was a 'she'?" Nick bounced on his heels.

"Excited, are you?" Marlen smiled slyly. "I'd say you're a very bright boy with great promise on the Force."

"Oh," Nick deflated a bit. "You figured it out, too?"

Marlen glanced towards a corner where a certain Miss Carstairs nibbled on a biscuit. "She hasn't stopped cramming hors d'oeuvres down her gullet all night."

"Nervous, perhaps?"

"It's more than nerves."

"Too right. She's been upstairs to the powder room five times to repair her face because of all those crumbs that keep flying. A handy excuse for casing the bedrooms."

"And their jewelry boxes. Besides, in all my visits here, I've never seen her, nor heard talk of her before."

"I've asked around," Nick said. "No one seems to know who she is."

"She's getting up. Shall we?"

Nick nodded. "Yes."

They followed Miss Carstairs as she slipped off upstairs. She bypassed the powder room to go on to Lady Stuart-Clark's bedroom, where they surprised her in the act of rifling through the jewels.

And where she surprised them by producing a wicked-looking knife.

"By her rather fierce expression, I think she knows how to use that," Nick said.

"Agreed," Marlen winked at him. "Should we use the Dixon ploy?"

Dixon had been an old acquaintance of theirs who liked to whelch on his bets by threatening them with broken wine bottles. Until they devised the "Dixon Distraction."

Miss Carstairs circled between them, keeping them both at bay with wide swipes of the knife. "Let me go, or I'll cut you!"

"Not nice," Nick said. "So unladylike. But a gentleman should incline to a woman's wishes." He went to the door and held it open. He waved for her to go through.

"You first!"

"Indeed." Nick stepped into the hallway.

"Now you!" She swiped at Marlen. "I'll be right behind you with the knife, so don't plan on going far. You'll be my way out of this house."

"My pleasure." Marlen walked through the doorway, and as she followed after, he suddenly tripped and fell to his knees. She stumbled over his backside to fall unceremoniously onto the floor, where Nick promptly secured her.

"Nicely done," Nick said. "Just like old times."

Not long after, Marlen was able to congratulate Nick on his promotion.

Yes, it was natural for best mates to help each other out. Marlen gave Nick a steady look. "You *are* him, whether

you believe it or not. There's no mistaking a psychic signature, trust me."

Nick focused on his tea. "Well, even if it is true, and
I'm not admitting it is, maybe I'd like to keep having my
own life. Maybe I don't like being totally confused about
who I really am."

Marlen nodded, but didn't reply. "Careless" was the
right term. Here he claimed to care deeply about his closest
friend, and what did he wind up doing? Making a huge
mess of Nick's life, that's what. All the mental turmoil
Nick was suffering was his fault, and it was quite true that
he'd been abusing his "best mate" privileges, whatever
those were.

"You know," he said at last, "it's good of you to keep
putting up with me." He tried a smile. "Thanks."

Nick was silent for a moment then he smiled back. "It's
no problem. Really. I mean, at least it's never boring."

"You got that right," Marlen said. "Suspect it'll get worse
before it gets better, too. You sure you want to go on?"

"Be hard to walk away now," Nick replied. "Despite
being utterly confused, I do want to know the truth. All
of it. No matter where it leads."

"It might be dangerous."

"It's already been that," Nick pointed out. "Could've
killed ourselves in that bloody ravine."

"Sorry."

"Will you stop saying that? It's getting on my nerves."

"Sor—" Marlen sputtered.

Nick laughed, sending little ripples along the bath water.

Marlen grinned. "You're not mad at me anymore, are
you?"

"I think 'continually irritated' would be closer," Nick
replied, still chuckling. "But I'm getting used to it." He
paused, calming down a bit. "You really think we're in
danger? From Vere?"

"Oh, yes. I never met her, of course. Before my time.
But the stories are legend. Cheer up, though, it's not only
us. She has good reason to hate all humans and mages,
so pretty much the entire world is in danger from Vere."

"Then I hope we never meet face to face."

"Or Duncan, either. He has it in for me too, in case you hadn't guessed."

"I had, as a matter of fact, sussed that out. And it's not just because he thinks you're a thief, is it?"

"No." Marlen bit his lower lip. "It's because he thinks I'm an irresponsible, lazy, disrespectful fool who isn't pulling his own weight. Which is perfectly true, but I don't see why he has to get worked up over it."

"Can he really put you in limbo?"

Marlen felt comforted by the fact that Nick sounded genuinely concerned. "Oh, yeah. He could convince the Council it was necessary. They don't like me, either."

"You're universally beloved by mages everywhere."

"Ta very much."

"You know, I'm surprised Ed Kelly isn't on our side," Nick said. "Back there on the hillside, he said some pretty harsh things about Duncan. Made him sound downright full of himself."

"He's that, all right. Always has been."

"Why do you lot put up with him?"

"'Cause he's powerful, invented more spells than the rest of us. It's rumored he keeps the best ones secret. Besides, he's still riding on his reputation as the Savior of Humankind, thanks to putting Vere away all those centuries ago. That really cemented his position as head of the mages, that did. Well, okay, that and the Spell of Protection."

Nick cast him a puzzled look. "The what?"

"As you know, it's a bit hard for a mage to die—smash us up, and we tend to bounce right back. Wasn't always so. The Old Ones— the first mages, thousands of years ago, used to actually die. Fire, flood, injuries, all sorts of things if they caused so much bodily harm that our healing powers couldn't counteract it. A few of the old mages came up with spells here and there against specific dangers, but Duncan was the most brilliant mage to turn up in centuries. He created the best of the spells that protected against most every means of death, and then combined them all into one. Since then, every mage performs the Spell of Protection when they turn immortal, and once a year after to enforce the effect."

"Handy. And he's been riding that fame ever since?"

"That, and being the oldest mage left, at least in Britain."

"How old?"

"A couple of years ago I went to a huge party to celebrate his 1,500th birthday."

Nick whistled. "Bit long in the tooth. Nobody's older?"

"Accidents happen, especially before he invented the big spell. And even Duncan couldn't come up with ones against everything. Complete obliteration of the body, for instance. Only last year a mage in Wales vanished in a natural gas explosion. Me, I always choose flats with electric or steam heat."

"I'm surprised your caution doesn't extend to the possibility of falling down ravines."

"I can recover from a fall."

"I can't."

"Sorry."

"Stop saying that. Better yet, stop hurtling us headlong into trouble and you won't have to say it."

"Oh, come on." Marlen did not hurtle. "I didn't *mean* to get us lost in the woods. Look, the thing is, Duncan worries me, but Vere downright terrifies me. Fear can addle the mental faculties, you know."

"Oh, you have mental faculties, do you?"

"Why, you ruddy great—"

Nick reached out to ruffle his hair. "Only teasing."

Marlen instantly warmed inside. "You do it well."

"Thanks."

"Anytime. As for our real problem, I was going to do another seeking before our next move, so we need to get going." He eyed the bath with relish. "You getting out of that soon? Is it still warm?"

"Yeah, yeah."

Nick climbed out and began toweling himself off. Marlen disrobed and sank into the water, still wonderfully hot, though a bit murky from the mud. He didn't care, so long as he could get the chill out of his aching bones. As he lay there soaking up the warmth, Nick casually got dressed. Then he tossed a clean flannel at Marlen, hitting his face dead on. "Hurry up and get washed off. We haven't got all day."

Marlen groaned. "Just because I said we had to get moving doesn't mean you have to turn into a taskmaster."

"It suits me," Nick replied.

"Too right," Marlen agreed. He reluctantly took up the flannel and started scrubbing away.

Ten minutes later he was clean, dressed, and sitting in his room with his map spread out on the floor and his seeking stone in hand. Nick perched on the edge of the bed, watching intently. "Who are you tracking?"

"The goblet." Marlen did his incantation and set the stone down.

"But it was taken by the drones. You said you couldn't track drones."

"Quite so. But the goblet has its own power signature, and I *can* track that." He watched the movement of the stone across the paper. "It's on a direct line to Cornwall. The drones must be taking the goblet back to Vere."

"Has it occurred to you," Nick said, "that you might be attacking the wrong end of the problem?"

"How so?"

"You could go to Cornwall to try to stop this at the source. And if say, we split up, then I could continue on to Scotland to grab the ring. A double-pronged attack."

"No thanks," Marlen replied. "Vere is too damned dangerous, and I don't fancy going anywhere near her."

"But she's been in limbo for seven hundred years. Won't she be weak? She's been sending these drone people to do all her work for her. Maybe you can deal with her before she gets stronger."

"I'd rather not find out."

"You're the one who freed her." Nick gave Marlen an accusing look.

"So? It was an accident." He felt whatever tenuous hold he'd had on this expedition rapidly disappearing.

"Look, you'll probably have to face her sooner or later, right? To help put her back in limbo?"

"Probably." Marlen picked up the seeking stone, tossing it in the air. "But *if* I can keep just one of the three objects out of her hands and in a safe place, she'll be about ten times less dangerous to deal with." He glanced at Nick, wondering what had brought on this sudden strategizing on his part. Taking his taskmaster role too seriously, was he? "The way I see it, if she gets all three objects back in her possession, she can complete that anti-humanity spell of hers. I'm not going to Cornwall until I've tried the easier way to stop her. Besides, St. Michael's Mount is an island fortress—I'm sure she's secured it. *I'm* going to Scotland." He tapped the map. "The drones are on their way south. Before they have time to drop off the goblet and head out again, we can get to the third object first."

"Unless *they* split up, of course." Nick cast him a look of exasperation. "Or she's using more than one set of drones. You've been alive for five hundred years? Didn't anyone bother to teach you to think logically in all that time? No, never mind. I suppose someone might have *tried*. There are always masochists around."

Marlen threw the map and stone into his bag. He should have known their recent camaraderie wouldn't last. Nick just couldn't stop when he got going on the topic of Marlen The Fool. Maybe splitting up wasn't such a bad idea. He'd gotten into this mess by himself, and he could bloody well get out of it by himself. And prove he wasn't so utterly useless. But he sure as hell wasn't going anywhere near Cornwall. "Fine. You're right, as always. Vere could already have drones heading for Scotland. *Someone* should try to get the ring before they do, and that someone is me. If you, however, really think attacking Vere first is such a dandy idea, you go right ahead. Have a nice time." He angrily stuffed his socks and underwear in his backpack.

Nick straightened his shoulders. "What are you doing?"

"What's it look like? I'm packing. We were supposed to check out half an hour ago."

"Yeah, but where are you going?"

"I told you. I'm going to Scotland." Marlen stood and grabbed his comb and billfold from the dresser and packed them. "You can do whatever you want. I was right before, I shouldn't have gotten you involved in this, but now you are, you ought to go ahead with your own plans, right? Right. Why should you listen to me? I'm incompetent, you said so yourself. *Fine*." All he needed was his jacket, which was nowhere in sight. He searched through the drawers.

"Hang on a minute," Nick protested. "Going to Cornwall was only an idea. I'll go to Scotland with you."

"Yeah? Why?" Marlen slammed a drawer shut. "Why would you want to? Why do you want to risk going anywhere with someone as useless as you think I am? Why not just go back to London?"

"You're forgetting one small detail."

Marlen spied a piece of familiar blue cloth underneath Nick. "You're sitting on my jacket, you berk." He tugged at it, pushing Nick's shoulder to get him to move.

"Don't shove me around." Nick pushed him back hard, and Marlen stumbled against the dresser. Nick started to rise, but Marlen leapt on him, knocking him back onto the bed. They rolled over, wrestling for control. Nick was stronger, but Marlen was quicker; he slipped away from an attempted arm-pinning move, and got an elbow jab to Nick's stomach. Nick rolled onto his side, clutching his abdomen. Marlen got on top, straddling him, and tried to wrench Nick's right arm behind his back. Nick scissored his legs around Marlen's, twisting hard. Marlen found himself flat on his back. Nick pounced on him. He got a strong grip on Marlen's wrists then yanked them above Marlen's head.

"I just wanted my jacket," Marlen gasped.

"And I just wanted to explain why I'm going to Scotland with you, you idiot."

"*Why?*"

"Because it's my bloody car, that's why!"

"Oh. Forgot about that."

Nick released Marlen's hands and rolled off him. "You're a bit temperamental, you know that?"

Marlen sat up, picked up his jacket, and shook it out. "Thought you didn't trust me anymore. Just 'cause I got lost in the woods—"

"Forget it," Nick smiled. "Have you always made a habit of driving me nuts?"

"Yeah," Marlen smiled back. "And it's mutual." He shrugged his jacket on, suddenly feeling much better. "Scotland?"

"This ring isn't tucked away in a cave, is it?"

"No, it's in a castle."

"Well," Nick said as he got up from the bed, "that's all right, then." He trotted off to his room to pack.

Marlen sat there waiting, not quite certain what had got into them both back there. One moment they were busy practicing warmth and understanding in the bathroom, and the next moment they were nearly at each other's throats. They'd always had a fairly intense relationship over the years, though, so he wasn't all that surprised. Or perhaps it was simply the fear of being left alone that had triggered his anger. The fear that Nick would really go off and leave him to his own devices... he hadn't wanted that to happen, despite what he'd said. He shouldn't have let it get to him so quickly, shouldn't have been so volatile. But sometimes he couldn't help himself, because his feelings for Nick were too strong.

He was going to have to watch that. Or he'd risk driving Nick away, and that was the very last thing he needed, after all he'd been through lately. No, he needed Nick with him now, more than ever.

Someday, of course, Nick would find out what he had *really* been up to when he'd stolen Vere's grimoire. And he didn't like to think what might happen when he did.

Duncan studied Ed Kelly's haggard face. He hadn't expected the fool to turn up at the hotel in Aberystwyth. But then, he hadn't expected to still be stuck in the stupid place himself.

When he and Georgina first returned to the hotel, he immediately did a seeking spell, but his blue stone refused to budge from the immediate area. So he traipsed all over town for hours, searching for a more detailed map. He finally succeeded, and returned to the hotel to find Kelly there, telling his woes to Georgina. And telling her what Marlen had said.

"Vere? On the loose?" Duncan felt his gut wrench. "He's lying. He has to be."

"That's what I said." Ed sat hunched in a chair, nursing a steaming mug of coffee. "It's a wild story he invented to pass the blame. He's a nutter, plain and simple."

"And you think he has the goblet?" Georgina said.

"Of course he does. I know he set those drones on me. I told you, he's lying about Vere."

Georgina raised an eyebrow at Duncan. "He seems to be smarter than you thought."

"Is he? I wonder." Duncan laid out his new map and brought out his seeking stone. His first incantation directed it toward the goblet. The stone moved south. He picked it up and did a second incantation for Marlen. The stone headed in the opposite direction. Duncan pulled out his older, larger map and performed the two spells again.

"No doubt about it," he said. "The goblet is being taken south, toward Cornwall. But Marlen is heading north." He bit his lip. "It can't be possible. *She* can't be free again." He quickly folded the map and gathered up his other belongings. "I must know. I'm going down there."

"What about Marlen?" Ed set his mug down. "I want another crack at that bastard." He made a fist and smacked it against his palm. "Don't care what you think, he's still a lying little shit."

"Good," Duncan replied. "Feel free to go after him." He smiled. "Why don't you take Georgina with you?" He was thoroughly done keeping an eye on her. Especially if Vere was on the loose.

To his surprise, Georgina nodded. "An excellent plan. Cornwall is a wild goose chase. You'll find Vere exactly where you left her. In limbo. Catching Marlen is more important."

For the first time since this all began, Duncan felt things were going his way. He slapped Kelly on the back. "Take good care of Miss Pruitt, Ed."

Ed Kelly put his face in his hands and groaned.

Light snow fell as Nick drove north. The word "terrific" started to form on his lips but he caught it in time. Silence, that's what he needed. A peaceful, quiet drive. No need to start any convoluted conversations with the nutcase beside him.

Nick took a quick look at Marlen. He was engrossed in a Scotland guidebook, studying a section of brightly colored maps. Good. Maybe the idiot would learn what they were for.

Five hundred years, and he couldn't even read a map. Five hundred years of hanging about, having fun. If *he'd* been alive that long, he would have done things, learned things, explored the world. Of course, according to Marlen, he *had* been around that long. But what good was the experience of all those past lives if he didn't remember them? On the other hand, judging from the nightmare he'd had last night, not all of it was worth remembering. Not the fighting, not the battles, not the deaths. Had he really spent most of those past lives as a soldier? A mercenary? A policeman? A fighter, no matter what the occupation. Was he like that still? It was true he enjoyed running down criminals, enjoyed the adrenalin rush of confrontation. He had a temper, no doubt of that, either. And even off-duty he tended to seek out excitement—car races, soccer, sailboating. And he liked to bet on the horses, but who didn't? None of that made him the man from his dream last night. The images of swords and blood stayed with him, no matter how hard he tried to erase them from his mind. He wasn't like that. Yes, he would defend himself, but he wouldn't hurt anyone unnecessarily. Nor did he ever want to have to kill anyone.

The person Marlen had told him about—the Nick that Marlen had known—was that really him? There were some things about him that sounded familiar, things that *were* a part of him now. But there were other things which didn't feel right. People changed over time, and he'd had plenty of that. If all of this was true.

Nick looked over at Marlen again. He'd given up on the guidebook to stare vacantly out the side window. If Marlen was searching for the friend of his youth—

the wild, brawling, irresponsible one—then he was searching for someone who didn't exist anymore. And, Nick thought, as he focused all his attention on the roadway, who probably never would.

They stopped for lunch in Liverpool. Nick invented a trip to the gents and took the opportunity to call Brian. He gave his new boss a brief report.

"You're on your way to Scotland, then?" Brian asked when he'd finished.

"Yes. Marlen says the ring is on the Isle of Skye, in Dunvegan Castle. We probably won't get there 'til this evening."

"And the goblet is being taken to Cornwall."

"Right. Might be a good idea to send someone out there, Sir."

"Yes, Nicholas, that did occur to me."

"Of course it did. Sorry."

"Tell me, have you observed anything so far which lends credence to this fellow's story?"

"He did a spell." Nick briefly described Marlen's use of the seeking stone. "I suppose it could have been a trick, but I didn't see how it was done. He used it to locate both people and the goblet."

"Intriguing."

"I better get back, sir. Any instructions?"

"Yes." Brian's voice turned harsh, "I want that ring. If you two do get hold of it, then I want you to bring it straight back here."

Nick didn't like the sound of this. "Marlen wants to turn it over to this Society of his, to something called the Inner Council. Then they can keep an eye on it until he gets this mess with Vere straightened out." He hesitated. "I can't exactly ask him to take it to the PIS instead."

"Don't be obtuse, Nicholas." Now Brian's tone had turned patronizing. "We don't want him to *know* about the PIS, do we? People don't like being spied on. It's so much easier on them when they don't know it's happening. No, my boy, if you succeed, then you simply accompany him back to London as if everything were fine. When you reach town, *then* you steal the ring from him and bring it to our HQ." He waited, but Nick didn't respond. "Is that understood, Nicholas?"

"Yes, but—"

"Don't argue with your superiors. One more thing. Find out where this mage council hangs out. They must have a headquarters somewhere."

"I have to go—"

"You've been given your orders. Follow them."

"Goodbye, sir." Nick hung up. He stared at the receiver, wondering why his stomach felt so tight. It wasn't as if he owed Marlen anything. It wasn't as if they were best friends. Marlen was an assignment, nothing more. He knew, though, that Marlen needed to turn that ring over to the other mages, to try to convince them he hadn't gone bad, that he hadn't wanted it for himself. Trying to explain his actions to the council, and having them believe it, would be hard enough *with* the ring; without it, he would face disaster.

Duplicity came with the job. He should be used to it— duplicity came with police work as well. You always tried to befriend the criminals who might do you a favor one day. Informants were a policeman's lifeline. And he was used to investigating people, watching them, chatting up their friends and family for information. Yes, he was quite familiar with pretense.

But that didn't mean he had to like it.

As they headed out again on the long drive into Scotland, Nick fiddled with the radio for a good half hour, giving up after hearing nothing but static-filled news reports and classical music. He let out a long sigh. This self-imposed silence was starting to get to him.

In the end, Marlen broke it. "It's a long drive, you know. I can take over if you get tired. I promise not to scratch anything."

"But can you promise not to get us lost?"

"No." Marlen smiled. "Afraid I can't promise that."

Nick shook his head. "Five hundred years, and what have you learned?" So much wasted time perplexed him.

"Five hundred years, and what have you got to show for it? What have you accomplished? Have you ever even held a job?"

Marlen crossed his arms and stared straight ahead. "I've had jobs. I worked most of the 16th century."

"Doing what?" Nick glanced over and caught the flush as it rose on his cheeks.

Marlen squirmed in his seat. "I was an artist's model. I was quite popular with the late Renaissance painters. There are a couple of works in the National Gallery with my face in them." He grinned.

"What'd you do after, take the next few hundred years off?"

"Certainly not. I worked. Occasionally. Mainly in antiquarian bookshops. I know a lot about old books. Used to set aside interesting volumes here and there, add them to my personal collection. Then, in the early 1800s, I auctioned most of them off. Made a small fortune. Had the Society invest it for me, and I've been living off the proceeds ever since." Marlen uncrossed his arms and picked at his fingernails. "Anything wrong with that?"

"It doesn't sound terribly productive."

"Who cares? I did what I wanted to do. Maybe that's selfish, but so what? Everybody is selfish. Most people just won't admit it."

"Including me?"

"Probably." Marlen looked at him. "I don't know why you're still going along on this trip—maybe it's curiosity. Maybe it's masochism. But it isn't altruism, I know that. You've got a reason, and I'll lay odds it's a selfish one. I know you're not sitting there driving to the Inner bloody Hebrides out of devotion to someone you can't even risk calling a friend."

Nick kept his eyes steady on the road. "I don't call you a friend because I don't *know* you."

"Yes, you do, dammit."

The road was really quite fascinating, Nick thought. So fascinating that it required all his concentration. Even conversation would be too distracting. He waited, knowing it wouldn't be long before Marlen broke the silence again. He wasn't wrong.

"Why do we always have to argue?"

"We don't," Nick replied. "I wasn't. I guess what I really wanted to know was why you keep going on. What's the point of living forever if you never accomplish anything worthwhile? Why bother?"

Marlen shook his head, as if he couldn't believe anyone would ask such a question. "To avoid dying, of course."

Nick considered this. It did have a certain simple logic. "Don't you get bored, though?"

"Are you mad? Of course I don't get bored—how could you possibly get bored of life?"

"You must have had a few depressing decades here and there," Nick said.

"Yeah," Marlen replied. "I did. But I told you, anything beats the alternative."

"You're really that afraid of death?" Nick glanced over and saw Marlen shiver.

"I'm afraid of oblivion. And that's what it is. Don't tell me *you* don't mind dying, either, 'cause I know you do. You've told me that, in the past. Even when you knew you'd be coming back."

"Maybe so," Nick conceded. "But at least when I get to the end of my life, I'll be able to look back and remember the good that I did. Would you be able to do the same?"

"I wish you could remember more of your past, mate. Then you might not be so snarky."

"And I wish you would stop trying to make me into someone I'm not."

Nick waited for the comeback, but Marlen kept quiet for once. And he stayed quiet all the way into Scotland.

CHAPTER EIGHT

They hit Glasgow around tea time. Marlen had spent enough hours with the guidebook to finally figure out they couldn't afford to stop again, or they'd miss the last ferry from Lochalsh to Skye. But when they reached the outskirts of the city, something came over Nick, a feeling of strong familiarity. He found himself turning off the main road and driving into town, slowing down when they reached its center. Something tugged at the back of his mind. He didn't care for the feeling at all, since it bore an unpleasant similarity to the one he'd had right before the images of the car wreck. He tried to push it away. No more memories of someone else, no more intrusions... but it refused to budge, and the longer he drove around the city streets, the stronger it became. He had been here before.

Yet Nick had never set foot in Glasgow in his whole life.

Marlen's puzzled voice broke into his thoughts. "What's up? You hungry? We might just have time to grab a take-away meal."

"No, I'm not hungry." Nick continued his prowl of the streets, scanning the buildings.

"Look, we can't stop here. The ferry doesn't run late in November, and we're a good three hours from there."

Nick abruptly turned the car down a narrow side street, and came to a stop. A battered sign swung above the door of a run-down pub. He could make out a painting of two severed limbs streaked with red, and the name of the place—The Bleeding Arms. But he saw the pub in his mind as vibrant with life and activity, the sign new and freshly scrubbed.

"Someone had a sick sense of humor," Marlen said.

"Late eighteenth century," Nick replied. "This was a very rough neighborhood." He paused, not understanding where his knowledge came from. "I've never been to Glasgow." He stared at the boarded-over pub door. Why did he know this place so well? Not just the sights of ragged men drinking, gambling, fighting, not just the sounds of revelry, but even the smell—a faint but distinct odor of sweat and ale and urine—wafted up out of the past to haunt him.

Marlen let out a low whistle. "I remember now. We came to Glasgow around 1780, to spend your father's money. You wanted to buy a racehorse, and heard there was a good stable up here. We also found some gaming action in the local pubs." He studied The Bleeding Arms. "Don't remember this one, though."

"You didn't come here." Nick leaned back, rubbing his forehead, trying to drive the images away. "Why do I remember this? That spell—the one you were doing that restored Vere—originally you directed it towards me, right?" It was starting to make a horrible kind of sense now. Marlen had done something, maybe unwittingly, but *something* had been done to make him see these things.

"Yes," Marlen said. "But the spell was ancient, in a language I didn't entirely understand. I didn't think it had worked. After it all went wrong, I had a little think, and figured out Vere must have had another spell embedded within it. I'd completed that spell without realizing what I was doing. And *that* was the one that worked. On *her*. The memory restoring spell—that was the part I was trying to get to work on *you*—seemed incomplete, so I gave up on it."

"Dammit, it *is* working." Nick squeezed his eyes shut. "Only it's not coming back all at once." All those lives, all the memories, were coming back a little at a time. He couldn't deny their reality, as much as he wished to. "I had a nightmare earlier. Worse than a nightmare, because it was so vividly real. A battle, with people dying all around me.

It ended with my putting a sword through a man. I don't *want* to remember those things. Don't you understand? I don't want a past full of so much pain. Why did you want to bring that all back to me?"

"I didn't." Marlen put a hand on Nick's arm. "When everything is added up, the good times outweighed the bad by a long shot. That's what I want you to remember."

"Well, it isn't working out that way." Nick opened his eyes and gazed at the pub. "I can't believe this... but it's so *real*. I can see it." He closed his eyes again, his brows furrowed. He had been in that pub. Its dimly lit, crowded interior stood plainly before him, tight, stuffy, and packed with dangerous men. And he had been one of them.

"This is another bad one, is it?" Marlen gently squeezed Nick's arm. "Something happened here... we've been through a lot together, let me think a bit."

"There was a fight," Nick said. "Not here—another place. A private home, people with money... I think there was a card game—"

Suddenly Marlen's hand tightened in a painful grip.

"Hey—you're hurting me—"

Marlen loosened his hold. "Sorry."

"You know what it is? You remember it now?"

Even as he asked, the image of a knife flashed in Nick's mind. And Marlen, taking the blow. The details of that night, so long ago, broke through in pieces which he snatched at like fragments from a dream. A very bad dream. He saw himself and Marlen inside a wealthy home, then the scene shifted to a dim corner, a plush settee... a woman with blonde hair. Nick shook his head. All the strands twisted together in his mind, and he struggled to untangle them. The blonde woman flirted with him, then he heard an angry shout, a man with a knife. Somehow he knew it was her husband. Nick cringed inwardly as he saw the man lunge for him, with deadly force and accurate aim... the image swirled out of focus. Nick shut his eyes even more tightly. *Concentrate.* There—what was that? An image became clearer—a figure—it was Marlen, shoving him out of harm's way. Marlen took the jab himself, directly in the gut. Nick could feel his friend falling backward into his arms, saw blood gushing onto his white shirt. Someone running away.... More images flickered in and out. He was outside, carrying Marlen to their room at an inn. Marlen lying on the bed, the wound closing up by itself. Then outside again in darkness, searching, stopping random people on the streets, asking questions. A pub, where he saw the man with the knife. A wild attack... Nick shivered, not wanting to relive the vengeful fury he'd felt. The woman was there, pleading for him to stop.

Marlen glanced over at The Bleeding Arms. "I remember waking up in our room, but you weren't there. You came back early in the morning, but refused to tell me where you'd been." He paused. "Is this where you went that night?"

Nick opened his eyes, and nodded. A dull ache settled within him. There was no going back, no more lying to himself about all this, no more denial. These memories were his, becoming more concrete by the moment. "I tracked a man down here." He looked at Marlen, the friend who had saved his life. "There was a woman, and her husband... I got into a fight. This fellow would have stabbed me, but you got in the way."

"You know me." Marlen gave a nonchalant shrug. "I must've tripped. Incompetent, as always."

"Sure you were." A wave of guilt hit Nick. "You did that a lot, didn't you? I mean, acted like my personal body-guard. Took blows meant for me, because you knew you'd survive them."

"You're getting off the subject. Besides, I told you, we don't have time to stop here."

"Marlen—"

"What?"

Nick smiled. "Thanks," he said softly.

"You're welcome. Can we get going now?"

Nick took another look at the pub. "I just want you to know that I went after him."

"Did you? You never told me before."

"Must have been too upset at the time. It wasn't pleasant. I can see most of it, like a too-vivid dream. And I can feel what I felt then. I went out looking for the bastard. Tracked him here." Nick took a deep breath. "I can see myself with a knife. He's staggering around, must have been drunk. I cut his face. Must have scarred him for life."

Marlen nodded. "You weren't into fighting much during that lifetime. Weren't used to that sort of thing."

"I don't ever *want* to get used to it, either." Nick gunned the motor. As he pulled away, he said, "Two days ago I would have said this was impossible." He turned onto a main street. "What's happening to me?"

"Think of it as a bad case of amnesia."

"Oh, that really helps."

"Sorry," Marlen sighed. "Maybe I really should have left you alone."

"No," Nick said firmly, and he meant it. "I *do* want to know who I am. But it scares me—when I remember these things it's as if there's someone else inside me. And I don't want to be anyone else. Always liked myself just fine." He refrained from adding, *and I don't want to be your best mate*, which was what his refusal to accept his past lives added up to. Marlen wanted his old friend Nick back the way he'd always been, but even with the memories trickling back, *this* Nick didn't feel like cooperating. And yet he couldn't help but feel a soft spot for the idiot beside him, not after what he'd remembered today. So far, what he'd seen of Marlen's personality hadn't been terribly impressive—he was irresponsible, far too carefree, and a champion layabout. But now, for the first time, Nick had gotten a glimpse of someone he might actually like a bit better, someone who was willing to make sacrifices for those he cared about. Which didn't exactly make him feel good about continuing his pretense. Under other circumstances, he and Marlen might have become good friends. As it was, he was already starting to like the fellow too damn much to be useful in his PIS assignment.

"So what you're afraid of," Marlen said, "is that you'll change."

"Something like that." All his life, Nick had stood on solid ground. He always knew who he was, what he wanted, where he was going. He didn't want to feel lost on such unsteady shores, yet he couldn't stop the shifting, couldn't keep his hold on anything solid anymore.

Marlen sat quietly for a while then said, "You've already changed, as far as I'm concerned. I don't know why, but in this lifetime, you're different from the friend I've known all these centuries. Not completely different, not even mostly different. But you *have* changed. I'm not used to you being so devoted to being a hardworking, responsible member of society, for one thing. Might not be such a bad thing for you to try lightening up once in a while."

"I'm not all that boring," Nick protested. "Can I help it if I've been a bit stressed lately?"

"Guess not. Still, you're more fun when you're in one of your teasing moods. Practice that more often, okay?"

"I'll try," Nick agreed. "That's a change I can live with." The rest of it, though—all the other aspects of his "old" personality—well, he'd just have to wait and see. He certainly had no intention of turning into a brawling, boozing gambler with wanderlust, which was what, on the whole, that Nick seemed to be. No, maybe some of his traits were ones he could accept, but he was never going to become the good old adventurous mate that Marlen was searching for. "Like I said, though, I prefer to keep being *me*, if you don't mind."

"Yeah, well, you'll still be you," Marlen replied. "But when you get the rest of your memories back, just think of the advantages—you'll have five hundred years of experience to draw on. Could come in quite handy."

"Yeah." Nick smiled. "I might become as incredibly resourceful as you are."

"Very good," Marlen said. "Keep practicing."

Nick turned the car onto the motorway, heading north.

Vere watched the brightly colored computer screen. Modern technology was quite amazing. She tapped at the keys, pleased by how quickly each tap brought an immediate action. There was so much to learn, so much that science could teach her.

The hours she had spent at the machine were, however, taking their toll. Her fingers and wrists ached, and a nagging pain had developed in her back. As she paused to rub her eyes, Vere realized that she should have been spending this time with her grimoire. She needed to study it, to reacquaint herself with its contents. The computer fascinated her, but it took up all her time. If she wanted to complete the spell she'd devoted so much effort to, she'd have to dispense with all this modern learning and get back to the ancient ways.

On the other hand, as she continued to study the numbers and figures on the screen, she realized something. Those devious mortals had invented games out of warfare. She'd found several among the software her drone had delivered. The ability to learn strategy from these so-called games might be critical to the success of her plans. Vere decided the grimoire could wait just a bit longer. Her enemies might very well know these strategies, and anything they knew in this new world, *she* would need to know also.

Marlen stared at the dark gray water as he leaned on a railing at the end of the dock. He watched the lights of the ferry grow smaller as it made its last run to the Isle of Skye. They had missed it by precisely five minutes.

Clouds hung over the distant island, solidly enshrouding the land. Marlen wrapped his arms round his chest against the evening chill. A few minutes later Nick strode up to stand beside him. "Found out when the next one is. Seven o'clock in the morning. I'm sorry. Shouldn't have stopped in Glasgow."

"It's not your fault." He gave Nick a light punch on the shoulder. "After all, we could've left Wales five minutes earlier if I hadn't wrestled you for my jacket."

Nick grinned. "Yeah. You ought to watch that temper."

"Me?" Marlen shook his head, thinking back to their first encounter in London. "Who was it that went and slammed me against a brick wall not long ago?"

"You were resisting arrest," Nick smiled.

"Well, it hurt."

"So did that kick in the gut, mate."

Marlen sucked in his breath. Mate. Nick had called him *mate*. About time. Now all he had to do was not mess things up again. Don't draw attention to it, he decided. Act nonchalant. He slowly let his breath out. "Sorry." He coughed and rubbed his hands together. "Bit chilly. Better find a place to stay." He turned and headed briskly back to the car.

CHAPTER NINE

Georgina Pruitt made Ed Kelly stop in Glasgow long enough for her to purchase a guidebook to the Inner Hebrides, thus causing them to miss the last ferry to Skye by exactly ten minutes.

Ed's mood did not brighten when they discovered that only one guest hotel in tiny Kyle of Lochalsh was still open for business at that time of year. Nor did he cheer up when the owner informed them that one room was available, with one bed. The only other room had been taken a few minutes before.

"It doesn't sound entirely suitable," Georgina said. "But I suppose we must make do."

The owner, a hefty woman whose face closely resembled a mutton chop, pushed the register at them. "T'other room's only got one bed as well. So there you be."

As Ed carefully wrote down false names, he checked out the two names on the line above. "This Mr. Brown and Mr. Green—what did they look like?"

"T'isn't none of your business." She slapped a meaty hand on the register book and closed it with a bang. "T'isn't none of mine, neither." She thrust a key at him. "So there you be."

The room turned out to be minuscule, its tiny bed crammed against the wall. One hard-backed chair and a tiny chest of drawers squatted beneath a slanting attic roof.

"Naturally I will have the bed," Georgina pronounced. "You will sleep on the floor." She gave Ed a scathing once-over. "Fully clothed."

Ed nodded dully. "You know, I think I spied a pub down the block—"

"No. The first thing we do is find out where everyone is." She tossed her carpet bag onto the bed and dug out her bag of stones.

"Only if we can do Duncan first."

"But we know where he's gone—to Cornwall."

"So he said. I don't trust that toad farther than the end of his nose. We do Duncan first."

Georgina shrugged. "Then let's get started, shall we?"

Nick sat on a hard-backed chair, staring first at the one small bed in the room, then at the thin, dusty carpet. He stared at Marlen, who'd already taken his shoes off and now sat in the middle of the bed, digging through his bag. He wished they had had enough money to take both available rooms. But his charge card had been rejected, and if they wanted money to eat with, buy petrol, and pay the ferry fee, they were left with just enough for this one tiny room with its one bed.

"Think I'll sleep on the floor," he said.

Marlen didn't look up. "Bed's big enough for two. Barely. Why suffer?"

"I feel like suffering."

"Fine. It's your back." Marlen hauled out his map, his guidebook, and his stones.

Nick frowned. He'd expected Marlen to argue more. "What are you doing? Checking on your friends?"

"Duncan and Ed haven't been terribly friendly of late." Marlen did the incantation and set the seeking stone on the map. "This one's for Duncan." He followed the stone's movement southwest. "Looks like he's going to Cornwall."

"Damn. Does that mean Vere truly is restored?"

"She must be. Duncan wouldn't waste energy going to Cornwall if he hadn't confirmed it."

"What's he up to? Would he try to stop Vere himself?"

Marlen shrugged. "He's the one who stopped Vere the last time. He's powerful enough."

"Kelly must have told him what you said. You think Duncan believes you're on the good side of this after all?"

"I doubt it." Marlen picked up the stone and did a new incantation for Kelly; he set the stone down, but it didn't budge. "Looks like Ed didn't believe me. He's right here."

"How close?"

"Too close to tell how close." Marlen bit his lower lip. "Didn't the landlady say this was the only hotel open in town?"

"Hell. You don't think—"

"Shhh." Marlen got up and put his ear to the wall. "Movement next door. And voices. Two of 'em."

"Terrific. What do we do?"

"Nothing. What can he do here?"

"Try to kill us, for starters." Nick stood and paced the entire eight feet of the room.

Marlen leaned back against the wall. "He can't kill me. As for you, well—" He grinned, "*I'll* protect you."

"Oh, thanks a bunch."

"Look, Ed's here to make sure the ring's safe. We come second on his list, I'm sure of it. Even if he does get the ring, that's not so terrible. *Someone* needs to keep it out of Vere's hands, though I prefer it be me." Marlen crossed back to the bed and sank onto it.

Nick waved his hand at the wall. "Suppose that's not Ed? You said there were two people next door. It could be a pair of those drones."

Marlen shook his head. "No, it's Ed. I can't track drones. Besides, drones wouldn't be stopped by the lack of a ferry. *If* they missed it."

Nick stopped pacing. "What, are they going to swim across?"

"Of course not." Marlen stuffed the map and his stones into his holdall. "But drones are single-minded, and they don't let social niceties get in their way. *If* they missed the ferry, they would find a boat somewhere, and rent it or steal it to get across. And then find a car on the other side and do the same."

Nick resumed pacing. "So why are we letting the social niceties get in *our* way? We could steal a boat."

"You?" Marlen raised his eyebrows. "You ever steal anything before? Thought you were a law-abiding police officer."

Nick hesitated. He couldn't tell him that he wasn't exactly a policeman anymore. Nor did he fully understand why he was suddenly volunteering to steal boats. It wasn't normal for him to be so reckless. Oh, Christ—surely his old personality wasn't busy taking over whether he wanted it to or not? He fought back a sudden urge to bolt, tell Brian to go find another agent, and then return to his nice, uncomplicated life as a policeman. "I'm not reckless," he said with more conviction than he felt. "But I figured we were in a hurry."

"True. But given our combined lack of experience in things criminal, we're more likely to get nicked than anything else. Which would slow us up considerably."

"Lack of experience? I thought you spent five hundred years engaged in nothing *but* dubious activities."

Marlen straightened his shoulders. "I've never been a thief."

"You broke into that museum."

"That was different. Proves my point in any case—I got caught, didn't I?"

"Yeah." Nick brightened. "You did." He stopped in front of the chair. The logical thing would be to prop it under the doorknob to keep out intruders. That, of course, would leave only the bed to sit on. He sighed and did the logical thing, then sat on the edge of the bed.

Marlen propped up the pillows and leaned back. "You worried about Ed attacking in the middle of the night?"

"Well, I'm pretty sure we could handle him. He didn't look that formidable. But he's not alone, right? We don't know who he's got with him. Or do we?"

"I don't know. The other voice was female."

"A woman?"

"Many females are women, yes," Marlen replied with a completely straight face.

Nick rolled his eyes. "But *who*?"

"Don't know. Another mage, no doubt, probably one of the Inner Council members. No, wait. It has to be someone Duncan would trust, and he doesn't trust anybody. I'm surprised he's let Ed in on the job, in fact. He's got to be the last person on the Council who Duncan would trust. They hate each other."

"Why?"

"Ed thinks Duncan's been Head too long. He'd like to have a shot at the job."

Nick considered this carefully. Politics had never been his strong suit, but he managed to come up with a theory. "So maybe Duncan allowed this Ed chap in on this venture in the hopes that he would foul things up, which would make him look a right ninny with the other mages, thus buggering his chances at a coup."

Marlen pursed his lips. "But this is far too important a mission. Duncan wouldn't risk such a thing."

"Which is why he's on his way to Cornwall." Nick felt he was getting the hang of this theorizing stuff. "He has to make certain that Vere is taken care of, whether Ed succeeds or not. And secretly, he's hoping Ed will fail. But there he'll be, perfectly placed to defeat Vere when Ed does fail, which will make him look like a true hero. Right?"

"Maybe," Marlen said. "I don't know. I've known Duncan a long time, and I've never figured out how his mind works. He does like having contingency plans, though."

"In that case, we can posit he'd want to have one, just in case he can't handle Vere on his own after all. He'll need to have someone in place at this end to keep an eye on things, someone who can rush in to save the day if needed." He was definitely warming to this. "See, his plan is, Ed fails to get the ring, and Duncan succeeds in stopping Vere, thus making Ed look bad and Duncan look good. But suppose Ed fails, and Duncan also fails. Then he needs someone else who's ready to make another attempt at grabbing the ring, someone who's more competent than Ed is. And that's the other mage with Ed, the woman. It has to be someone he trusts." Nick beamed triumphantly.

Marlen frowned. "Sounds convoluted enough to be true."

"So who could that be?"

"Georgina," Marlen said instantly. "It could only be Georgina Pruitt. His latest pupil."

"What's she like?"

Marlen's lip curled. "Georgina is the sort of person from whom lint runs away screaming. She's perfect, and nothing imperfect ever touches her. And she never makes mistakes. The word 'formidable' comes to mind."

"Terrific."

"We might be able to handle her," Marlen said. " Provided we take a Chieftain tank along. Or two."

"You're making me so enthused about this," Nick replied.

"Sorry."

Nick thought Marlen ought to have the word tattooed on his forehead to save time. He wondered what steps he should, or could, take against Ed and his cohort. They were bound to meet up in some kind of confrontation, what with being so close on the same trail to the ring. He wished Brian hadn't thrown him into this without at least a little training in the ways of the PIS, or of its parent, DI6. How much authority did he have as an agent? He knew, in general, that most DI6 agents had fairly extensive powers—to search without warrants, to seize without proper cause, to use both psychological and physical intimidation on suspects. What if things got sticky, and the question of deadly force came up? You just never knew.

He decided this required another call to Brian. Stretching elaborately, he said, "Think I'll find some food. How about takeaway? Thought I saw a place down the street. I can pick something up for both of us."

Marlen's eyelids drooped, and he let out a huge yawn. "Sounds good. Get something with sweet 'n' sour sauce." He failed to offer any monetary support for the venture.

Nick leaped up and grabbed his jacket. "Fine. I'll be right back." He shoved the chair from the door and headed off in search of a phone.

"I think they're right next door," Georgina said. She pulled away from the wall. "Quick, check the hall. Someone just slammed a door."

Ed gently cracked their door open and peeked out, in time to catch a glimpse of a dark head disappearing down the stairway. "It's that other one. Marlen's friend. I'll follow him."

"No." Georgina pushed him aside. "He knows you. He hasn't seen me before." She scooted out the door.

Ed watched her dash down the hallway in pursuit. He looked at the door of the next room. Marlen was in there. All by himself. Be easy to go in and thump him around a bit. Get a little revenge for setting those goons on him in the forest.

On the other hand, what if the little bastard had told him the truth? What if he hadn't set the drones on him? In that case, if he did beat Marlen up, he'd have to do some explaining to the Council. They frowned heavily on mages attacking each other.

On the other hand, if Marlen really had gone bad, he'd be doing the Council a favor by beating him to a pulp. They'd undoubtedly praise him. Who knew what evil machinations Marlen was up to? And *he* would have stopped him.

On the other hand... Ed sighed. He was running out of hands. He looked at the door again, and remembered that Marlen could be a scrappy fighter. Maybe it would be best to leave him to Georgina. After all, she could render him unconscious with one swing of her carpet bag.

Ed shut the door and sat on the bed to wait.

The hotel's public phone stood at the end of a dim corridor, and it wasn't terribly modern or prone to clear connections. Nick's throat felt hoarse from shouting down the receiver through the static.

"So you see, sir, it's two against two, not counting the drones, which would make it four against two or something like that, depending on who attacks who. And I'm concerned about our ability to fend them off." He waited for Uncle Brian to reply. There was a long pause, and a lot of mysterious whistling on the line. "Sir? Are you there?"

"Still here, Nicholas."

"Should I try to arm myself?" All he got in response was a wave of static. He made out the words "Cornwall" and "go there". "Sir? What's this about Cornwall?"

"I've decided to go there in person." Brian's voice came through clearly. "You'll be on your own, Nicholas. I trust you to handle this with the efficiency and level-headedness for which you were hired."

"Um, thank you, sir. It's just that I have a feeling this is going to get very tricky, and I wanted to make sure I didn't do anything I wasn't supposed to do. I know you're very keen on getting this ring, but if it comes down to actual violence, how far should I go?"

More fuzz filled the line. Nick played with the position of the receiver, turning about, standing in different spots. Out of the corner of his eye he saw a flicker of movement at the other end of the corridor. Someone was watching him. He couldn't let anyone overhear. "I have to go."

"Wait. There's something I want to tell you—"

"I know what you're going to say." Another reminder about his mission, Nick thought, about getting the ring back to HQ, no matter what. He didn't need to hear that again. "Someone's listening. Goodbye, sir." He hung up, and ran down the corridor towards the mystery spy. He skidded round the front desk into the tiny lobby. The place was empty.

Georgina slipped into the room and quietly closed the door. She gave Ed a disapproving look. "Get off the bed."

"Yes, ma'am." Ed reluctantly returned to his chair. "Well? What happened?"

"Nothing." Georgina brushed off the bed covers, as if some of Kelly had stuck there. "He made a phone call, then went back to his room."

"You didn't hear what he said?"

She devoted her attention to a completely unnecessary re-arrangement of the pillows. "No," she replied. "I couldn't get close enough." Georgina dug into her bag, pulled out a mystery novel, and sat back against the pillows to read.

Nick woke up with his nose buried in a mass of wavy red hair. He vaguely remembered starting out his sleep the night before scrunched up as close to the wall as he could get, with his back to Marlen. Sometime during the night he must have rolled over, because he now had his arm across Marlen's bare chest and his face in the crook between Marlen's neck and shoulder. Thus the hair in his nose. Soft snores emanated from the other man.

Another flash of memory hit him—a different bed, in a different time, but with the same occupants. Only they weren't just sleeping. Nick jerked and shook his head, as if he could physically banish the image. And then a familiar sensation hit his groin. "Bloody hell," he muttered. Part of him denied it; part of him wasn't surprised at all. In the back of his mind he'd known, at least from the time Marlen had told him about his first life. And had told him that they hadn't always been interested in women. He hadn't wanted to dwell on the implications. But he'd known. Question was, what was he going to do about it?

This wasn't the time to figure it out. Marlen stirred, and Nick froze. The last thing he wanted was to wake him. He waited motionless until he was sure Marlen was still asleep. Nick couldn't see how to get out of bed without dislodging him, but he had to try. A trip to the washroom and a shower were definitely in order.

He slowly pushed his half of the blankets aside and managed to sit up. Moving as carefully as the small space allowed, he twisted his body until he was on his hands and knees; then he lifted one leg over Marlen. His foot found the floor. He shifted his arms a bit, then raised his other leg over, got both feet balanced on solid ground, and finally shoved off with his arms and stood up. Success. Now all he had to do was find his robe in the gray morning light. After some precious wasted minutes, he found it under the bed.

Nick put on the robe and opened the door, banging into the chair he'd put against it. He cursed, and looked to the bed. A tremendous snore erupted from the area of the red hair. Nick gently moved the chair to one side, slowly opened the door, and tip-toed out.

He returned fifteen minutes later to find Marlen still snoring away. It was already six, and he wanted breakfast before catching the ferry. He could handle an awake Marlen now; enough was enough. Nick got dressed as noisily as possible, even opening and shutting the chest of drawers, which didn't have anything in it. Marlen slept on. Finally Nick traipsed back to the bath, where he soaked a towel in cold water. He headed back to the room and what he hoped would be a rude awakening.

When he opened the door, it was to find Marlen sitting up, scratching his head. Nick studied the towel, wondering if he should still fling it at him.

Marlen stretched and hopped out of bed. "Mornin'. That for me? Thanks." He snatched the towel and rubbed his face. "Bit cold." He tossed it back at Nick before grabbing his bathrobe and trotting off down the hall.

Nick stared after him, shaking his head. Then he sat down on the chair, the wet towel in his hands, and laughed.

It was inevitable that the four of them would meet up on the ferry. On that morning there was a grand total of seven passengers. Nick drove on board right behind Ed. He and Marlen considered staying in the car the whole way, but eventually decided to go on up to the lounge and face their nemeses.

They joined Ed Kelly and a young but stern looking woman at one of the tables. "You going to try to strangle me?" Marlen asked as he sat down. Nick scooted in beside him.

"Not yet," Ed said.

"I don't believe we've met." Nick directed this at the woman, then glanced at Marlen. Marlen shrugged.

"*Your* name," she replied in clipped, upper-class tones, "is Nicholas John Watson. *My* name is Georgina Pruitt. I am a mage." She looked at Marlen. "I met *you*, briefly, at the last Society party."

"Don't remember that," Marlen said.

"I said it was a brief meeting."

"No, I mean, I don't remember the party."

"That's because you're an idiot," Ed said.

"Shut up," Marlen snapped. "I've had my abuse quota for the week."

"Good manners have sadly deteriorated in our modern age," Georgina said. "There is no reason why we cannot conduct our business pleasantly and politely."

Marlen drummed his fingers on the table top. "And what business is that?"

"I believe we all know why we're here. The ring. You want it, ostensibly, to keep it from Vere."

"Thought I'd turn it over to the Council," Marlen said. "Be safer with them."

"We would like to get the ring as well," Georgina continued. "To keep it from you. We really can't take the chance that you might be lying to us."

"Why would I concoct a story like that? I'm sure I could have come up with a more valid reason if I'd spent a few minutes on it. And that reminds me—how did Duncan find out what I was up to in the first place?"

"Ah." Georgina laced her fingers together. "A little bit of spying, I'm afraid."

"I knew it." Marlen ran his hand through his hair. "That bastard had no right—"

"You're wrong," Ed put in. "You heard the ultimatum the Council gave you. Start behaving like a real mage or else. How would we know if you were complying if we didn't keep an eye on you?"

"What's he on about?" Nick said.

"I'll tell you later," Marlen whispered. He turned back to Ed. "Look, I don't care what you believe or not. As long as the ring stays in safe hands, you do whatever you want."

"Fine," Ed said. "Why don't you just turn around and head back to London, then? We'll get the ring, and we'll deal with you later."

"You'll have to deal with Vere, too."

"The idea of Vere running about again only exists in your imagination."

"Then why has Duncan gone to Cornwall?"

Ed looked flustered, but Georgina smiled. "Merely a precaution." She rose. "Come along, Ed. We don't have anything more to say to these two."

"I do." Ed stood, leaning over the table until his face was inches from Marlen's. "Don't get in my way. You'll regret it." He strode off after Georgina.

"Tough, isn't he?" Nick smiled.

"Maybe they're right."

"About what?"

"Going back." Marlen rubbed his eyes. "What difference does it make if they get the ring? We don't need to waste time competing with them. We could turn around, head straight to Cornwall."

"What? We can't do that." Nick thought furiously of some way to keep Marlen on track. He needed to get that damn ring, that's what he'd been ordered to do. He felt unusually torn. Part of him wanted Marlen to get the ring so he could turn it over to the Council, so they might finally believe his story. And part of him wanted them to get the ring so *he* could turn it over to Brian, to prove he should stay with the PIS. If he failed his very first assignment, they wouldn't be likely to keep him on. And it wasn't as if he had a job with the police to return to.

"Why not?" Marlen looked puzzled. "Helping to stop Vere will make me look good in the eyes of the Council. And it just occurred to me that I can prove she was the one who took the stone and the goblet, 'cause they'll be down there with her. I could tag along behind Duncan, keep out of his way, wait for him to nobble Vere and retrieve the objects, and then he'll see I was telling the truth about it all."

Nick racked his brain for a plausible response. "Yeah, but we're much closer to the ring then to St. Michael's Mount. Why not just go on? I'm bloody tired of being on the road. Besides, I've always wanted to see the Isle of Skye."

Marlen scowled. "Boring old rock, that's all it is. And when we reach it, we'll have to deal with whoever's guarding the ring, plus Ed and Georgina if they get in our way, not to mention Vere's drones. Not good odds, if you ask me."

Nick pondered this. What he needed was a reason for them to continue their pursuit of the third object despite the odds. He suspected Marlen had a wide streak of cowardice, and was simply getting cold feet now that they were getting nearer to possible danger. It wouldn't be any different if they headed back towards Cornwall. Marlen would get nervous as soon as they got there, and think of some excuse to turn tail and run. Tag along with Duncan, indeed. Duncan would no doubt throttle him on sight.

He considered the problem carefully. If he could convince Marlen that Cornwall held the greater danger... shouldn't be that difficult. Not with someone who appeared to have the mental acuity of a dormouse. Nick spent a few minutes concocting a grand new theory to confuse his companion with. "You know," he eventually said, glancing over at Ed and Georgina, "those two don't trust you."

"I figured that one out myself."

"Right. Question is, why should *we* trust *them*?"

"What do you mean?" Marlen frowned. "We're not at cross purposes, except that they'll try to get in our way if we do go on."

"But has it occurred to you that they might want the ring for some other purpose?"

"Those two? You must be joking."

"They're just working for Duncan," Nick said quickly. "Doing whatever he tells them. Suppose he's been manipulating events all along? Suppose he wants those three objects for himself? Who wouldn't?"

"*I'm* the one who started this, not Duncan."

"Are you sure? Maybe he *knew* you would go after the objects." Nick started to enjoy himself. This fabrication business was quite fun. Elaborate as much as possible, that was the key. "They already admitted he was spying on you. Suppose he's been using you as a cover, a scapegoat. He gets the objects and you get the blame."

"But he couldn't have known that I would work that restoring spell in Vere's grimoire."

Nick relished the challenge of inventing logical answers
to Marlen's objections. He was becoming quite fond of his
new theory. "All right, let's think this through. Why did
you steal the grimoire in the first place?"

"I told you, to find a spell—"

"No, no. I mean, what specifically inspired you to take
it at that particular time?"

"Well, the Council turned down my request—"
Marlen paused. "Hey, you might have something there.
It was Duncan who swayed them into it. I asked for their
help in finding a memory restoring spell, going through
proper channels first, so to speak. Duncan convinced them
to refuse. Not only that, he's the one who got them to
threaten me with limbo. A hundred years of it unless I
straightened up."

Nick clapped his hands. "Perfect. He set you up. He
knew you didn't have much respect for authority, so after
the refusal from the Council, it would be natural for you
to go 'outside the proper channels'. Thus, the grimoire.
Where did you steal it from?"

Marlen's eyes widened. "From Duncan's attic."

This was working out beautifully, Nick thought. It was
so beautiful it could even be true. "You see? He could have
planted that restoring spell in the grimoire, and waited for
you to steal it, knowing you'd try that spell out. Then *he*
sent the two drones to your flat, suitably attired in their
Cornwall tour guide outfits, letting you assume you'd
accidentally restored Vere. He calculated your every move.
He probably stole the stone himself before you got to the
museum. And he convinced the other mages that you were
on some kind of revenge plot. Simple."

"Sounds extremely complex to me," Marlen replied.
"People don't think that way, do they? Tell me why he's
on his way to Cornwall then?"

"That's where the goblet was headed, wasn't it? He
arranged that, of course. To keep you and the other mages
believing in this 'restored Vere' story. And when Kelly and
Miss Pruitt deliver the ring to him, he'll be unstoppable."

"Yeah, but—" Marlen rubbed his forehead. He looked suitably confused. Perfect. "Why would Duncan *want* the three objects?"

"You tell me. He's the head of your Society, right?"

"Right."

"How long?"

"As long as I can remember. Longer."

"And are the others all happy about his long hold on power? No, they're not. You told me yourself that Ed didn't care for it much, right?"

Marlen studied the ceiling for a few seconds. "Yeah. And he's not the only one making rumbling sounds of late. There are definitely those who would like to see a change."

"So Duncan has a sense of irony. Using his own enemy, Kelly, to unwittingly assist him." Nick rubbed his hands together. "It's brilliant."

"Is it?"

"Absolutely. Ed doesn't have a clue what's really going on."

"*That* I can believe. The rest of it, though... I mean, what's the point of it? If Duncan does plan to use the objects to secure his power, he'd have to do it by threatening the others. By telling them he'll use the objects against them if they don't follow him. And if he does that, they'll know he stole them in the first place. So why go to all the trouble of setting me up?"

Nick perceived a crack in his carefully constructed facade. "Well, you were meant to be a temporary scapegoat. Someone handy to cover his tracks and provide him with an excuse to go to the various hiding places."

"But he could have simply grabbed the objects without all this subterfuge. He could have taken the stone, gone to Wales for the goblet, and to Scotland for the ring, and had all three in his possession before anyone figured out what he was doing."

The crack widened, decidedly in need of patching. "Does he travel a lot, then?"

"That's a point. Duncan hates leaving home."

Nick snatched at it. "When did he last leave London?"

"Near as I can recall, around 1840."

"Ha. There you go! Duncan couldn't go off to Wales or Scotland without a good reason. That's too unusual for him. People would talk. You were there to provide the excuse." Nick grinned, happy with the complexity of the plot he'd invented. It truly was a work of art. "You still want to turn back? You want to take the risk? Do you honestly trust Duncan?"

"Well, not entirely."

"Of course you don't. It would be far too dangerous to confront him. He no doubt has cohorts in this grand scheme of his, people who are still loyal to him. We have no idea what he's really up to down there, we'd be going in totally blind. No, we have to go on. And get the ring before they do." Nick looked over at Ed and Georgina sitting on the other side of the ferry. He smiled and waved at them.

"Of course," Marlen replied, "if you're right, we should be going after Duncan no matter what. Stop it at the source. Even with comrades, he won't be a major threat until he gets that ring. If there's really no Vere in Cornwall, then going there isn't half as dangerous as I thought. And if we headed off now, we'd be able to reach him long before Ed and Georgina get hold of the ring for him."

Nick's argument came crashing down, crumbling to dust before his eyes. "Oh. Hadn't thought of that." He slumped in the seat. Bloody hell. What now? He'd expended all his mental energies on that contrivance. He'd gone to all that trouble, succeeded in putting doubts in Marlen's mind, and ended up with the opposite result of what he wanted. It wasn't fair.

"Never mind," Marlen said. He patted Nick's shoulder. "We'll go on here."

"What?"

Marlen shrugged. "Ed and Georgina are closer to hand. It would be just as easy to stop this by stopping them."

"Really?" Nick straightened. "You mean it?"

"'Course I do. It doesn't really matter. Was only feeling a little despondent before, that's all."

Nick swallowed hard, letting his relief show.

"What's wrong? You're acting as if your life depended on it."

"No, no... that's great. We'll go on." He strove to compose himself. This business wasn't as easy as he'd imagined. Marlen might not be able to thwart him with intelligence, but he was quite capable of thwarting him by being utterly scatterbrained. Things were going well again, though. Barely. They were still on their way towards Dunvegan, he could still grab the ring for Brian.

Nick remembered the other piece of information his boss wanted. Mage HQ. Should he risk it after that last confused interchange? Taking a steadying breath, he opted to go for broke. "By the way, what should we do if something goes wrong, and we become separated for some reason?"

"Hm?" Marlen had been staring out the window. "Separated?"

"Yeah, you know, suppose one of us gets the ring, but during whatever turmoil ensues, we wind up having to make our way to London separately, or one of us winds up being held back. How will we find each other again? What if I've got the ring and you get held up? I'd want to rush it to safety at your whatever it is—Council office?"

"ISM headquarters," Marlen replied. "That's the safest place for it. But why worry until it happens?"

"Because we might not have time to discuss it then, that's why. Because I believe in being practical, and in making contingency plans."

Marlen tapped his fingers on the table top. "You never used to have contingency plans."

"Well, I've got them now." Nick crossed his arms. "And it's not as if things have gone smoothly so far."

"Point taken."

"Then tell me where this place is."

"Mage HQ? But it's a secret."

Nick rolled his eyes. "Of course it's a bloody secret! I know that!" He uncrossed his arms and leaned forward. "Listen, the last thing I'm going to do is *tell* somebody, especially anybody I'm interested in impressing with my sanity, that I know the place where a load of immortal magicians who like to play with the stockmarket hang out, am I? Besides, it's merely a precaution. I'm sure we'll wind up going there together with the ring. In which case

I'll find out where it is anyway. Unless, of course, you don't trust me to go with you."

"You're my best mate," Marlen said. "I trust you."

Nick decided this was not a good time to feel pangs of guilt. He ruthlessly shoved them aside. "Fine. If we do get separated, and I happen to have the ring, I'll take it right to your council for you. That's a promise. So where is it?"

Marlen glanced round the ferry then leaned close to whisper. "Underneath St. James Park near Whitehall. An underground room built during the First World War. You go to the statue of Edward Jenner, walk fifty feet north, turn right at the stone bench with the series of minute cracks on the back which resemble East Anglia, walk ten feet east to the rather large willow that has 'LSE' carved on the trunk, and after making sure no one is watching, you press your thumb hard into the center of the 'S'. Then hum the first two lines of 'God Save the Queen', tug your left earlobe three times, and wait for the false door in the tree trunk to open."

Nick burst out laughing.

"What's so amusing?"

"You're putting me on, that's what."

"Am not." Marlen looked affronted. "It *is* in an underground room by Whitehall."

"Through a tree trunk in St. James Park. Right. What's 'LSE' stand for?"

"London Stock Exchange, of course."

Nick shook his head. "How do I really get there?'

Marlen sighed. "You're just no fun anymore, you know that?"

"Sorry."

"All right, so there's no tree and there's no map of East Anglia. But the ISM headquarters *is* where I said it was. You have to go down this alley, there's a door marked 'members only'. Oh, here, let me just draw a map." He grabbed the ferry time schedule and began doodling bits of London which didn't look much like the area around any government offices Nick was familiar with.

"A map. You're drawing a map." He wondered why Marlen didn't immediately sense the absurdity of this idea. "What's that street there?"

"Oxford."

"And what's it doing near Whitehall, pray tell?"

"Um... well, it's for reference purposes."

"And this little blob of ink here, what's that?"

"Nelson's Column. I thought it might come in handy."

"Marlen, give it up. You couldn't draw a map of your own flat while you were standing in it. Give me a general idea and I'll work it out for myself, okay?" He pulled out the road map they'd brought with them from London and pointed to the bit which contained an inset of the city. "This might help."

Marlen looked at the map. "Oh. I guess it might."

"Whereabouts do I look for this 'members only' door?"

After a good ten minutes of intense study, Marlen pointed the tip of his pen at one particular block, making a tiny mark. "Between this block and this next one over here, there's a very narrow alley. The door's on the west side about halfway along. It's green, and it'll be locked. Just knock once. Don't ever knock more than once. Got it?"

"Got it." Nick folded up his map and tucked it away. "Won't they want to know who I am?"

"Find out the stock exchange closing quote for a company called Arthur Lance Realties for the day before. Give it to whoever answers. Don't tell them anything else."

"Arthur Lance," Nick repeated. He groaned. King Arthur. Lancelot. "Do some of you mages go all the way back to Merlin?"

"Of course they do. He was a real person."

"Right." Nick rubbed his hands together, feeling much more in control of the situation now that he'd managed to succeed at part of his mission. He had the all-important address of mage HQ. Brian could hardly fail to be impressed. Now, he simply had to make certain he secured the ring as well. "How long before we dock?"

Marlen checked his watch. "Quarter hour or so."

"Good. You stay here. Don't want them to get suspicious. I'll be right back." Nick stretched and stood.

"Where you off to?"

Nick smiled, "I'm off to nobble their motor."

CHAPTER TEN

Vere looked up from her book as Mark, the second of the two drones she'd sent north, walked into the dining room. He stood a few feet from the desk, a short, weedy youth lacking in brain power which made him easy to control.

"I put the goblet in the study," he said in a reed-thin voice. "As you ordered."

"Very good. You will now explain why you were delayed in your return from Wales."

"I got a puncture," Mark said.

No matter how much she read, Vere could never completely comprehend the peculiarities of this modern language. She gave the young man a once-over, not seeing any obvious holes. "Explain this further."

"The tire," he replied, as if this would make everything clear.

Vere tapped her fingers impatiently. "You are saying you had trouble with your automobile?"

Mark nodded vigorously, causing unattractive things to happen to the mangy thatch he called hair. "Had to fix the puncture. But the spare'd gone flat. Had to find a garage. Long walk."

Vere gave up interpreting his meager attempts at English. "Very well." She glanced down at the text she'd been studying, then back at Mark. He certainly seemed to be the type of person who would understand mindless violence. "Do you understand explosive devices?"

"Bombs and mines and things? Not real ones. I only see them on TV and in computer games."

Yes, she had seen explosions when she had studied warfare strategy on the computer. They intrigued her so she had gone searching for more information from the castle library, which was sadly inadequate. The one book she'd found seemed hopelessly out of date. "When you play these 'games' on the computer, you can use these bombs to destroy your enemies?"

"Yup. You can blow 'em right up good and proper."

As she had thought, yet she had learned that television and computers were not reliable indicators of what happened in the actual world. "What about in the real world?" She had seen what were called "documentaries" about real wars, in which real men, not just figures on a screen, were killed. "Do they truly cause obliteration of the body?"

"Yes, ma'am. My great uncle was in the War. His buddy stepped on a mine and got blown to bits."

Interesting. She waved him off. "You are dismissed."

He obediently trotted out. Vere rested her chin on her hands to contemplate. She *did* have two of the three objects she needed for her spell, but it never hurt to have a backup plan. Now who could get something like that?

Mark was fairly useless, but Ron had been quite industrious in acquiring her other supplies; she wondered if he knew where to find items of a more deadly nature. Something which would make Duncan, or anyone else, think twice about disturbing her plans.

"I just thought of something." Marlen looked back as Nick drove off the ferry and onto the road. Ed and Georgina were still on board, making futile attempts to start their car. Marlen looked at the distributor cap on the dash. "Suppose they nobbled us, too? Suppose they did something we won't know about until we've reached a good, fast speed out in the middle of nowhere?"

They came to a stop sign. Marlen twisted round to look back again, resting his hand on Nick's shoulder. The contact felt comfortable, but Nick shrugged him off. Then he gunned the motor.

"We should go slowly," Marlen said. "In case they did do something to the car."

"The element of danger," Nick replied as he drove on, "gets the adrenalin flowing. Makes life more exciting."

They left the small ferry town behind. Nick punched the car into high gear. A blur of brown and gray whipped by the windshield, hills alternating with moors. Marlen wished Nick would take that adventurousness of his and put it back inside whatever corner of his mind he'd hauled it out from. "Slow down."

"Why? It'll only take us an hour to reach Dunvegan at this rate."

"Alive?"

"Stop worrying, I'm not going to wreck the car. I'm very attached to this car."

"It's not the bloody car I'm worried about," Marlen said. He saw the determined look on Nick's face and gave up. He slowly pulled his seatbelt on with great deliberation.

The stark countryside continued to whip past. There was very little traffic; Marlen had seen only a couple of cars pass by. At least, he thought they were cars. They could have been anything, since they zipped by too fast to tell. As the hectic drive continued, he constantly cast his gaze behind them, watching for any sign of pursuit. His neck was developing a painful crick from looking back, looking forward, and being wrenched about by the way Nick careened around the curves.

"Why do you keep checking behind us?" Nick said. "They can't catch up."

"If it were only Ed, I'd agree. He's not that resourceful. But Georgina Pruitt is another kettle of fish entirely."

"I'm surprised you didn't recognize her. I figured all you mages would know each other."

"Yeah, well, she's new. Watch out for those sheep—"

"I see them." Nick swerved the car around the pack of sheep that had started across the roadway, narrowly avoiding a very fat ewe. "Go on, then."

"What?" Marlen was still shaking from the near collision. "Georgina is a new mage, you said. How's that work? I mean, I take it you don't hold auditions."

Marlen took a breath, counted to ten, and let it out. "The Council gets together once a year and performs a search. It's a magical ritual. They look for what's called a signature. Every mage has one; so does every potential mage. They search for unknown signatures, ones they don't recognize. It's rare to find one, maybe once every twenty years. And the physical distance they can search is limited. When they do find a person who's got the signature, they send someone to check it out. Watch the person, do a few simple tests to make sure. Ninety-nine out of a hundred potential mages know there's something unusual about themselves. When we do approach them and tell them about the Society, they tend to be ready for the news."

"Were you?"

"More or less. That's a village coming up—"

"I know." Nick slowed down, but not by much. "What happens then? They get to be mages?"

"First they go through a training period." Marlen clenched his teeth as Nick screeched past a pedestrian, wheeled round a donkey cart, and then found open roadway again and sped up. "When they're deemed ready, they're made members of the Society and the immortality ritual is performed."

"Very interesting."

A lorry loomed up ahead of them, going the same way. It had slowed in its climb up a small hill. Marlen had a feeling Nick wouldn't like staying behind it. He shut his eyes as Nick pulled out to pass. "Tell me when it's over."

"Stop getting so worked up. There's nothing coming... oops."

Marlen opened his eyes in time to see the car coming from the other direction, and to see Nick speed up even more. They pulled even with the lorry and zipped in front of it at the last possible second. Nick grinned. "Told you I've never been a good driver."

"I believe you," Marlen said as he continued to grip the dash.

"Relax. We'll make it. And don't say 'alive?' again."

"It's an important distinction." Marlen looked at him, thinking back nearly three decades to the night of the car wreck. The night he'd lost Nick yet again. "I'm not going through this any more, you know," he said.

"What are you on about now?"

"I'm not putting up with this transmutation nonsense any more, that's what. No more waiting, no more tracking you down, no more explaining things. I'm tired of you dying on me."

"I don't have much choice," Nick replied.

"You *could* stop driving like a maniac with a death wish, for starters. What is *wrong* with you?"

"Nothing." But Nick slowed the car's speed. "Nothing's wrong with me."

"Is that so? First you don't want anything to do with all this, then decide to come along, then you just complain about everything I do, and now you're more eager to get on with it than I am. It's almost as if you're—" Marlen stopped. He'd been about to say "two different people" when he realized how close he was to the truth. Nick really didn't know who he was anymore.

"As if I'm what?"

"Forget it. It's probably just stress, right? Thanks for slowing down."

Nick didn't answer. He stared ahead, driving steadily toward Dunvegan Castle. Marlen kept quiet, not wanting to irritate him.

The silence continued for an hour. Then, out of the blue, Nick said, "So how do you destroy a mage?"

Marlen had nearly nodded off; the question made him jerk awake. It took him a moment to work out what Nick meant. "You mean Vere? If it comes down to that?"

"No, I mean mages in general. You're not truly indestructible, arc you? Back in Wales, you told me the mages didn't have those protection spells against *everything*, just most things."

Marlen rubbed his eyes. "True. We can recover from most injuries provided the body's more or less intact. I do know that a mage wouldn't survive being crisped to

cinders in a fire, if he let the Spell of Protection lapse.
That's how Fred bought it." He shivered.

"Fred?"

"Mage named Frederick the Elder, one of the Old Ones.
He got caught in the Great London fire. Never did find
him again. That was before Duncan devised a protective
spell against being burnt. An explosion wouldn't do us
much good, either."

"Yeah, I know. Never rent a flat with natural gas. So
tell me,
can mages destroy other mages?"

"That's against the code."

"How would they do it if they decided to break the
code? By magic? Strip them of that protection spell thing?"

Marlen shook his head. "Not possible. No, you'd have
to do it physically—like I said—try a bomb. That should
work. I suppose that's the only way to really threaten
one of us."

"One more thing—"

"Better be." Marlen yawned. "You're making me tired
with all your ruddy questions."

"I want to know how the line of mages originated. I
mean, you're obviously not entirely human."

"Oh." Marlen shrugged. "We're not sure. 'Spose it
could've been an alien race visiting the planet long ago,
mucking about. That's always a popular theory. Ancient
mage history is as much myth as anything else. But
according to our legends, we're descended from a union
between a human and one of the fairy folk." He smiled.
"'Course, nobody believes in the fairy folk these days. Mind
you, being Irish, I have to admit a tendency to believe in
them myself." He gazed out the side window, thinking
of the land he hadn't been back to in a long, long time.
"Strange things happen in Ireland."

Nick glanced over. "You never told me you were Irish."

"Well, I left when I was fifteen. Lived here ever since.
Lost the accent about four hundred years ago." He propped
his arm on the window, resting his head against it. "I lied
about not having a last name."

"I figured you had."

"It's O'Neill."

"Why is that such a secret?" Nick asked.

"It isn't. I just don't like explaining my first name. Once people find out my last name, they always want to know how a nice Irish lad ended up with a name like Marlen. So I avoid it by not telling them my surname to begin with."

"You realize you're going to have to tell me now."

"I know. That's why I brought it up. I was supposed to be named Merlin."

Nick laughed. "You serious?"

He nodded. "My father was overly fond of the Arthur legends. That's what he wanted to call me. But the priest was new, had just come over from England, and didn't understand the accent. My father probably said something like this—" Marlen spoke with a thick Irish brogue. "'I'd like to name the wee lad Merlin.'"

"It did sound as if you said 'Marlen'. At least to my ears."

"I know." Marlen returned to his usual, middle-of-the-road English accent. "That's how the priest wrote it down. Even *I* didn't realize the error until years later. My folks were horrible spellers, so they never noticed it either. By the time I figured it out, I was used to it."

"'Marlen' suits you just fine," Nick said. "You shouldn't worry about being an O'Neill, either. Look at me. Do you have any idea how much taunting I've had to put up with? In my profession? I mean—Nicholas *John Watson.* You know how many times I've heard, 'where's Holmes, then?' Or, 'been in Afghanistan recently, Watson?'"

Marlen grinned. "Elementary—"

"No! Don't say it!"

He laughed softly. "Relax. Since I've known you, you've had a lot of different surnames. I only think of you as plain old Nick."

"'Old' being the operative word."

"Yeah." Marlen gazed at the blur of low hills out his window. Their repetitiveness made him sleepy. "I do feel old sometimes." He yawned again.

"You falling asleep on me?"

"Told you before, I'm not used to getting up so bloody early. It's not natural."

Nick shook his head. "You're a five hundred year old, immortal mage, and you're discussing what's natural?"

Marlen decided to ignore that. "I'm not going to sleep. I'm just resting." He shrugged out of his jacket and bunched it against the window as a pillow. "Try not to go too fast round the bends, all right?" He closed his eyes.

"Lazy bum," Nick muttered. But the next time he came to a curve, he took it slowly.

Ed reluctantly handed over a wad of bills to the garage mechanic. "Highway robbery, this is." The mechanic grumbled something in Gaelic and sauntered off. Ed slammed down the bonnet of their hire car. He was tired of Scotland. He was tired of the rain. Most of all, he was tired of Georgina Pruitt.

He drove back to the ferry dock, where the object of his discontent stood beneath her umbrella. "Car's fixed. When's the next run?" Ed tried to squeeze in beside her, but stepped back at her disapproving glare.

"New plan," she announced.

"Is that right? Who put you in charge?"

"You will wait here at the dock. There's no point in going across. If they get the ring, this is the way they'll come back. All you have to do is watch everyone who comes off each ferry."

Ed sniffed, unwilling to admit that it made sense. "And what will you be doing?" He hoped it was something far away.

"I shall be returning to London."

"What?" Ed surprised himself by being offended that Georgina was doing precisely what he wanted her to do. "You're abandoning me?"

"I am confident you can handle things here."

"But why are you leaving? You're not taking the car." He was attached to that car. He liked the way it kept the rain off him.

"I have made my own transportation arrangements," Georgina said. "I will return to London and make a report to the Council."

Ed wiped the rain from his forehead. "There is this thing called the telephone."

"I wish to make my report in person." Her tone of voice brooked no argument. Ed decided he'd better just accept his good fortune. "Yes, ma'am." He watched Georgina walk away. As Ed returned to the warmth and dryness of the car, he wondered what the hell she was really up to.

Duncan tossed his overnight bag on the bed and sank into an armchair near the hotel window. *Rusty, that's my problem.*

He'd been out of the game for too long, resting on his laurels. He'd been letting weaker mages, newer mages, even *women*, push him around when he should be ruling over all of them with a will of iron. This modern age with its myriad comforts had turned him soft. He'd adopted its ways, as he always changed with the times, the better to move through society without notice, the better to serve the rich well enough to become so wealthy himself that he no longer needed to serve anyone.

For hundreds of years he'd been the quiet power behind the scenes, working his magic when needed, and calmly guiding the others to follow his example. They'd done well, all of them. Yet there were some who questioned his methods, a few mages here and there, now and then, who bristled under his touch. For he could be harsh when harshness was called for, when the tasks no one else liked doing had to be done.

What did it matter if he answered to no one, so long as the Society ran smoothly? Who cared if a few upstarts were put down, or if ungrateful mages were shunned by all if he willed it so? He made the Society work. The Inner Council bent to his will, and everyone knew that he held the real power, only he controlled the Society, and that was as it should be.

Under his rule, the trains would always run on time.

Still, he'd gone lax. Comfort did that to a man. In the old days he would never have gone haring off to the back of beyond with a mere pupil in tow to chase after a miscreant like Marlen. He would have simply called up his private army to deal a swift, merciless justice and be done with it.

But no. He had shoved his past far away, up in the attic along with his ancient memorabilia. Stored away too long, grown dusty from disuse. Could he even remember his most potent spells anymore? Could he work them as swiftly as he would need to? Could he bring Vere down again, was she as rusty as he was?

He sighed and patted his jacket pocket, where he kept the cracked leather pouch with his magical tools and powders. The time had come for the return to the old ways. His enemy had been dead to the world for seven hundred years. She would not know how to fight any other way. Ancient tactics against an ancient enemy. He would meet her on her own ground, and he would win.

From his hotel window Duncan could see the bay, and the hulking form of St. Michael's Mount, shrouded in trees, the tiny harbor village ringing its rocky beach, the blocky stones of the castle jutting up from its crest. No one could get to the island. The opening to the wide flagstone causeway that made a dry path to the island during low tides had been blocked off with a chain-link fence. He'd been to the beach on this side, in the town of Marazion, and seen the sign claiming the entire island had been shut down for 'renovations'. He had tried to hire a boat to take him over, with no luck. No amount of money, not even his best persuasion spell, would convince any villager to make the attempt. In fact, all the people who lived in the island's tiny harbor village had left, holed up here in Marazion, uninterested in returning. All her doing. He could sense it in the frosty air; he could feel her powerful signature chilling the wind itself.

Vere. The woman he'd condemned to limbo, his most hated and most feared opponent, free once more. Marlen had no idea what he had done.

Duncan rose, stretching his back and arms. Time for a little planning, a little prep work. Maybe he couldn't hire a boat, but he felt fairly certain she hadn't put spells on all the DIY shops in the area. One large pair of wire cutters ought to take care of that chain-link fence barring the causeway. The townsfolk might have fallen under her spells, believing the renovation lie, but he remained unaffected. Theirs were weak, mortal minds. She would find him much more formidable. And as soon as the tide went out, which the desk clerk kindly informed him would happen around five that evening, he would be ready.

Dunvegan castle rose up before them, a faintly dull, blockish building squatting atop a rocky, brush-covered crag. Nick had parked the car a quarter mile away; they were taking the final approach on foot. As they walked along the base of the crag, Nick stared up at the castle, unimpressed. "You reckon anyone's home?"

"According to the guidebook, the family spends its winters in more hospitable climes."

"What about tourists?"

Marlen rolled his eyes. "In November? The place is closed up, trust me."

Nick started to make a sarcastic comment, but decided, for once, that this wasn't the right time or place.

"Doesn't mean it'll be empty, of course," Marlen added.

"Servants?"

"Maybe. Maybe not." Marlen kicked a stone out of his path. "But Ed was guarding the cave in Wales, right? So Duncan probably sent someone up here to guard the ring."

Nick had to admit, that even coming from Marlen, the statement was logical. "The drones might have got here before us as well."

"True." Marlen followed the path as it curved round the crag. It joined a narrow roadway which led up to the castle entrance. He stopped. "I don't think we should walk up and knock."

"Why not? Whoever's in there won't have a sub-machine gun trained on us, will they? Come on." He strolled past, heading briskly up the road.

"No, wait!" Marlen sprinted to catch up. He grabbed Nick's arm to hold him back. "There's a danger—"

Before he could finish, Nick jerked away, said, "Nonsense," and strode on. He'd had enough driving around, enough hanging about hotel rooms, enough failure. He was ready to go get that ring. Two strides later, with absolutely nothing in front of him, Nick ran straight into what felt like a brick wall, a wall with a jolt in it. The force of it threw him backwards a good six feet. He lay flat on his back; a tremendous tingling ran through his entire body and his head buzzed. He blinked as the blue sky above suddenly went black.

When he blinked again, he saw Marlen leaning over him, rubbing something oily on his forehead that smelled faintly of cinnamon. He instinctively brushed Marlen's hand away then realized the buzzing and tingling were fainter.

"Stop that," Marlen said. "This is helping." He dabbed a few more drops on Nick's forehead. "How're you feeling?"

"I've been better." Nick raised his head, staring at the spot where whatever it was that had hit him had hit him. Roadway. Perfectly empty roadway stretched a hundred feet to the front steps of the castle. There was absolutely nothing in it. "You know," he said, "I liked it when my life was logical."

Marlen put the bottle of oil back in his bag. He put his arm round Nick's shoulders and helped him sit up. "Someone's put up a defensive series of magical wards. I did try to warn you."

The fog in his brain started to clear. "Why do you say it's a series?"

"They always work that way. A simple ward on the outside, a more complex one inside that one. The most complicated ward will be used around the ring. It could be worse."

"I'm so glad to hear that."

"How's your head?"

"Buzzing's gone." Nick rubbed his legs and feet. "And I can almost feel my toes again. What do you mean, it could be worse?"

"Wards are just defensive. If you can manage to hold back, I can detect them first and we can get past them, no problem. But there could also be magical traps set. Those are offensive. Can get you before you know they're there, unless you know what to look for."

"Terrific." The energy with which Nick had started the day was rapidly fading. "Think I can stand up now. How do we get through this stupid thing?"

Marlen still knelt over his backpack, rummaging through it. Nick put a hand on his shoulder to lever himself up, staggered, and nearly knocked Marlen over. "Watch out. Are you sure you're all right?"

"I'm fine. What are you looking for? Magical anti-ward powder?"

"Something like that."

Nick watched him pull out a small leather pouch. Marlen shook a handful of red powder from it then sprinkled it on the ground. He knelt and waved his hands over the area while speaking words Nick didn't understand.

"That's done it." Marlen put the pouch away.

"But nothing happened."

"What do you want, a flash of light? Go on, try it."

Nick took a few tentative steps forward. The barrier had vanished. "Won't whoever's in there know you've done this?"

"Not unless they're checking on the wards at this particular time." Marlen pulled something new from his bag; as he stood, Nick saw it was a long chain with a familiar looking silver medallion.

"Hey, that's mine." He stumbled towards Marlen; his brain didn't seem entirely reconnected to his leg muscles.

"No, it's not."

Nick grabbed it from Marlen's hand. He looked at the engraved surface. Something about it looked a bit different. He checked his coat pocket and found his own chain inside. "Oh. You're right. Sorry." He looked at his own medallion, then at the other one. The only difference was the Latin inscription on his. Nick handed the other medallion back. "What is it?"

"Something I should have put on earlier." Marlen slipped the chain over his head. "It's a warning device. If we get near another ward, I'll get a tingling sensation around my neck."

Nick put his own medallion on. "Thought you told me it wasn't magical."

"Well, you can wear it if you like, but it won't work for you." Marlen slung his backpack over his shoulder. "Only works for mages."

"Why'd you give it to me, then? Originally."

"You came by to see me the day I was making that one." Marlen pointed at Nick's medallion. "You took a fancy to it, so I added the quote and turned it into a gift. Then I had to make another one for me, to use for what it's supposed to be used for. Which is finding wards." He tugged at Nick's arm. "Come on, we're too exposed out here."

Nick ignored him. He continued to study his medallion. "Why this quote?"

"Why not?"

"You gave this to me in my first life. You didn't know I was a transmuted person then, so why did you put 'remember me' on here?"

"It's a long story." Marlen headed off. "I'll tell you later."

"You're always going to tell me later." Nick sighed, tucked the medallion under his shirt, and followed him.

They made it past another external ward. Ignoring the main entrance, they crept round the walls until they found a small door. It was locked, but that didn't stop them long; Nick had learned a lot about locks from his time on the force.

Inside, a pantry led into a huge, empty kitchen. Nick led the way between a row of cabinets and a large, spotless worktable. The three stoves looked unused, the sinks were clean. At the end of a long counter stood a trash can stuffed with Chinese takeaway boxes. Marlen took one look and said, "Isabel."

"Who?"

"She's a mage. She eats a lot, and she hates to cook."

"Very good." Nick picked up a carton and sniffed it. "Still fresh." He dropped it. "Keep this up and we'll make a detective out of you."

"Thanks."

They cautiously moved into a long hallway. At one end stood a small table littered with pamphlets. Nick opened one up. "'Welcome to Dunvegan Castle's Self-Guided Tour'." Inside were drawings of each floor with a key for the highlights. "Looks like your fairy folk have influence here, too."

"What's that?" Marlen studied a pamphlet, his brow furrowed in puzzlement.

"'The famous fairy flag of the McLeod family can be found in a glass case in the main hall.' You think your little friends left these pamphlets for us?"

Marlen turned his map right side up. "You never know."

"This place is enormous."

"Most castles are."

Nick sighed. "Right. Come on, let's check out the main hall."

In the large entrance hall they found only a few tapestries, a guest register, and the glass case containing the faded fairy flag. "We need to find Isabel," Marlen said. "I'll bet she's keeping the ring with her."

"What's she look like?"

Marlen put his arms out. "Big." He moved his hands up to either side of his head, holding them a foot or more from his ear level. "And she's got this hair..."

"Not easy to miss, then."

"Nope. And obviously not in here."

Nick looked at the pamphlet. "Let's try these bedrooms upstairs." He headed up a wide stone staircase leading off the main hall.

"Hang on." Marlen bounded after. "When are you going to let me go first? I need to detect the wards."

But Nick had already reached the landing, and he'd started down the long corridor when he suddenly came up short.

Marlen nearly stumbled into him. "What's up?" As he moved beside Nick, he stopped as well. "My neck's tingling," he said. "There's a ward here."

Nick stared blankly at the empty hallway, his fingers touching the chain around his neck. "So is mine," he replied softly.

Marlen stared at him. "That's not possible." He reached for the medallion, but Nick pushed him away.

"I'm telling you, it tingles, dammit." Nick swallowed. He clutched the medallion tightly. "If this is your warped idea of a joke—"

"I haven't done anything. It shouldn't work for you."

"Then why the hell is it tingling?"

"I don't know!"

"You must have done something!" He poked a finger at Marlen's chest. "And don't you dare say you'll tell me later."

Marlen ran a hand through his hair. "I can't tell you later. It doesn't make any sense. The only way that thing can work for you is if you're a mage, and you're not a mage, so it *can't* work for you."

"Well, this isn't a bloody muscle spasm." Nick rubbed his neck. "It's that damn grimoire you were mucking about with. *That's* what messed me up."

"Can't be. All I did was play around with a couple restorative spells." Marlen frowned. "More or less."

"You little bastard." Nick felt every ounce of patience drain away. He grabbed Marlen by the front of his jacket. "What the hell did you *do*?"

"Calm down." Marlen tried to shake loose, but Nick kept a firm grip. "Okay, so I did try one other spell. That still wouldn't explain anything."

"*What* spell?"

"One designed to break psychic blocks."

Nick loosened his hold. "Why?"

"'Cause I figured it couldn't hurt. Some people have mental blocks against certain things. You've always had this thing about logic, how everything had to make sense all the time. Even when you remembered that I was a mage and that you'd lived before, you always had to make it fit into some pattern that made sense to you, that fit your little world view. Only this time, from what I'd seen of you, it was a hell of a lot stronger than before. So I tried the anti-block spell, hoping it would weaken your sense of disbelief a bit. Thought it might help trigger some past memories, too. That's all. It wouldn't suddenly turn you into a mage."

Nick shoved him away. He leaned back against the wall, a lurching sensation in his stomach. "How do you know I'm not a potential mage?"

"You don't have the right signature."

"Yeah, but how do you *know* I don't have the right signature?"

"I checked for it, of course." Marlen's eyes widened. "A few hundred years ago, that is."

For some reason Nick found it harder and harder to breathe properly. "So you haven't checked *lately*."

"No." Marlen shook his head vigorously. "But it couldn't have changed."

"Why not?"

"Because. It just can't."

Nick gritted his teeth. "How do you *know* it can't change?"

Marlen took a deep breath and let it out slowly. "I don't."

It wasn't possible. Even if it were possible, Nick didn't want to believe it. *Whenever you have eliminated the probable*, he thought... muscle spasm, that's all it was. He straightened and grabbed Marlen's arm. He led him down the hall, a good fifty feet away from the ward, then turned round. "All right. There's no tingling now. I want you to keep pace beside me. Don't stop until I stop, and don't say one word. Okay?"

"Fine. Whatever you want."

"I want you to be quiet." Nick shut his eyes and slowly walked forward. He could sense Marlen walking next to him. All his concentration was focused on the chain around his neck, and when the tingling hit again, there was no doubt in his mind as to its source. Strong and sudden, it buzzed round his neck like an electric jolt. He stopped the instant he felt it. "Right here," he said, opening his eyes.

"Exactly where I feel it, too," Marlen replied. "And it's still not possible. There has to be another explanation."

"There had better be." Nick found it hard enough to handle the impossible things he'd been forced to believe in so far. There simply wasn't room for one more. "I am *not* a potential mage."

"That's what I keep telling you, mate." Marlen dug into his bag. "Can I take care of this ward now?"

"By all means, go right ahead." Nick idly waved his hand at him. *Concentrate on the mission*, he thought as he watched Marlen mess about with his powders and chants.

Ignore the memories from the past. Ignore the idea of mages in limbo, magical wards, and drones. Ignore the damn tingling. He would just focus on the ring. Brian wanted him to get that ring, and he wanted to prove himself to the PIS. Nothing else mattered. He shouldn't let himself get confused by simple little side issues, like not knowing who or what the hell he was anymore. The tingling suddenly vanished. "It's gone," he said.

"Yeah." Marlen put his things away. "Why don't you take the bedrooms on the left and I'll take the ones on the right." He strolled off down the hallway.

The ring, Nick repeated. *Find the stupid ring and get this over with.* He went to the first door on the left and opened it. The bedroom he walked into was larger than his entire flat. And it looked as if a whirlwind had recently touched down inside. All the dresser drawers were pulled out, their contents scattered. The closet had also been emptied, and even the mattresses had been slid off the bed and slit open.

Nick quickly checked the next room down and found the same chaos. As he came out of the third room, which had also seen more peaceful days, he met Marlen coming out of the third room on the right side. "Someone beat us to the search," Nick said.

Marlen nodded. "Same here. The drones?"

"Can't be Ed and Georgina, unless they can fly."

"Not without an airplane, they can't."

They checked the rest of the rooms on the floor and found them all in shambles. At the end of the hall another, narrower staircase led to the third floor. As Nick crept upward, he heard a noise. He froze; Marlen was right behind him. "Footsteps," Nick whispered. He listened as the steps drew closer to the landing above. They were heavy and methodical. He wished he had a weapon of some kind; he didn't even have his nightstick. But then the footsteps slowed, turned, and headed away from them.

"Come on." Nick slowly made his way up the steps. When he neared the top, he poked his head round the wall, just in time to see a man walking down the far end of the corridor. The fellow turned at the last room and went inside.

Marlen came up beside him. "Well?"

"The last room on the right. Big guy, maybe six three or four." He smiled. "Would you like to take the lead?"

"Very amusing. You're a cop; you know how to reconnoiter. You go first."

"Thanks." But Nick headed down the hall. He reached the edge of the doorway and peeked inside. His view was largely blocked by the tall man, whose back was to him. The man, probably a drone, faced a woman secured to a chair—a big woman with big hair. In the drone's right hand something glinted; as he waved it about, Nick made out the unmistakable outline of a gun.

He moved part way back down the hall and gestured at Marlen to join him.

"That's Isabel, all right," Marlen said when Nick described the scene. "Must be Vere's drone trying to intimidate her. What's your plan?"

Nick sighed. "My plan? Tell me, just what would you do if I hadn't come along on *your* expedition?"

"Improvise."

"So improvise."

Marlen pursed his lips. "Well, I suppose I could barge in there and distract the fellow, and then you could jump him from behind."

"What if he shoots you?"

"It'll hurt."

"Oh, for Christ's sake. You know what I mean."

"Keep your voice down," Marlen whispered. "Have you got a better plan?"

"Yeah," Nick replied. "I do. I'll stand to one side of the door, you stand on the other. Then we make some noise, and when he comes out to investigate, we both jump him."

"Might work."

"Of course it'll work." Nick spoke with more confidence than he really felt. "Come on."

They crept up to the door. Nick checked to make sure the drone still had his back to the opening then snuck across, leaving Marlen to take the near side. They both stood with their backs to the wall and listened.

"You drones are so bloody single-minded," Isabel's voice boomed out.

"Give me the ring," the drone said in a mechanical tone.

"For the hundredth time, I can't do that."

"Give me the ring, or I will shoot you."

"Go ahead." Isabel yawned. "Might make a nice change from being bored to death. Not that I can die, of course."

"Give me the ring."

"Look, this is absurd. Didn't your employer explain to you the uselessness of threatening mages with death?" There was a loud rumble. "Did you hear that? That's my stomach. Come on, have a heart. Let's call up the takeaway place."

"Give me the ring."

"I *told* you, I can't do that."

Outside the door, Nick gestured at Marlen, making bizarre hand motions at his backpack, then at the wall. He wanted the idiot to make a distracting noise, and Marlen finally figured out the meaning of his contortions. He slipped the bag off his shoulder, gave it a good swing, and let it fly. It thumped resoundingly against the far wall.

Heavy footsteps came toward the door. Nick tensed, hands out. The drone walked through the opening. Nick chopped at his gun hand, knocking the arm downward but completely failing to dislodge the weapon. As the drone turned toward Nick, bringing his arm back up, Marlen kicked the back of his knees. The drone stumbled, and Nick leaped out of his way. But the man stopped his fall, using the wall for support. Then he staggered into the center of the hall, whirling, gun hand searching for a target, while Nick and Marlen circled madly round him. Marlen got behind him again and aimed another kick at the small of his back. The drone staggered again, then fired wildly as he pivoted.

Nick dropped into a crouch and made a dash at him, tackling him at the knees and finally bringing him down. With a loud groan, the drone landed on his back. Marlen stomped on his wrist, and the gun dropped from his hand. Nick landed a vicious right hook to his jaw. The man moaned, his head lolled, and then he passed out.

Nick took a moment to catch his breath then reached down to pick up the pistol. A Browning Hi-Power. The fellow had gotten off half a dozen shots, so that left eight, assuming there was one up the spout. He put the safety catch on and pocketed the weapon.

Together they hefted the drone into the room, dropping him unceremoniously inside the door.

"You certainly know how to make a racket," Isabel said as Marlen undid the ropes binding her.

"You're welcome," he replied. He tossed the ropes to Nick, who tied the drone's hands and feet.

Isabel rubbed her arms. "It wasn't necessary, you know. I was about to use a little spell or two to take care of him myself." She paused. "Who's your friend?"

"Isabel, Nick. Nick, Isabel." Marlen gestured at the drone. "Any more of them about?"

"Haven't seen any." She bent forward to rub her ankles. "You know, something very peculiar's going on. I think Duncan has it all wrong about you."

Nick came over to join them. "Why do you say that?"

She straightened. "I asked that fellow who sent him here. I know a drone when I see one. The big disadvantage to using drones is that they'll answer any question put to them. And that one told me he'd been sent by Vere. Perhaps you can explain it to me."

"Be delighted," Marlen said.

"Over lunch," she added. She rose and stretched, and her stomach rumbled again.

"One thing," Nick asked. "Why wouldn't you give him the ring? I mean, I know you're immortal, but it's still a lot to stand up to a bullet."

Isabel chuckled—a deep, throaty sound. "I didn't say I wouldn't give it to him. I kept telling him I *didn't* have it."

Nick felt a sinking sensation. "Why not?"

"Please don't look so worried. It's perfectly safe."

"Where?" Marlen asked. "You *can* trust us, Isabel."

"Oh, I never trust anyone, dear boy. That's why I buried the ring in a quite remote spot on the other side of the island. We can go dig it up later if you must. But first, I'd like my lunch. You'll join me, won't you?"

She strode out, calling over her shoulder, "Do you two like Chinese food?"

Chapter Eleven

Nick opened one of the little white boxes. "Who got fried rice?"

"Me." Marlen looked into a box. "Steamed rice?"

"That's mine."

They exchanged containers across the dining table. The table, a twenty-five foot monstrosity, squatted in a high-ceilinged room with big beams and narrow windows which gave Nick the feeling that a Norse invasion was imminent. Isabel sat at the head, with Nick and Marlen to either side. A few dozen takeaway boxes littered the space between them.

"Sweet and sour chicken," Isabel boomed out.

Marlen raised his chopsticks. She passed it along.

"Where's my chow mein?" Nick asked.

"Beef or pork?"

Nick considered. He couldn't remember. "Whatever." He got pork. "Did we get any of those little dumpling things?"

"Potstickers." Marlen looked up guiltily. "Thought they were mine."

"Doesn't matter," Isabel said, "I just found some more." She handed them to Nick, who wolfed them down. Most of the meals on their journey had consisted of cheese and tomato sandwiches that had been sitting on roadside cafe shelves long enough to acquire a variety of mysterious gray tints, and he was famished. He found a sack filled with soy sauce packets and began squirting it over everything in sight.

"So what you're saying," Isabel said between mouthfuls, "is that you royally cocked things up."

Marlen had given her a recital of the recent events in his life during their wait for the delivery man. He swallowed a bite of sweet and sour chicken and said, "Well, you could say that."

"I did say it." She pointed her chopsticks at him. "You know, when Duncan told us you'd taken the stone, I was ready to haul your arse in front of the Council and get you sent to limbo."

"But you believe my story now, don't you? I mean, that guy upstairs did tell you Vere sent him."

"And we did save you from him," Nick added. He felt peeved that she still hadn't bothered to thank them.

"True." Isabel returned her chopsticks to their proper use. She scowled at Marlen over the lid of a fried rice box. "But you, nonetheless, are a menace to the Society."

Marlen's eyebrows knitted together; he looked genuinely hurt. "I can't help it if I don't want to be a stockbroker."

Nick didn't care for the tone of her remark, either. "Does this mean you won't give us the ring?"

"Why should I?" She grinned. "It's perfectly safe where it is."

"Possibly." Nick tried to think of a good argument. "But if you don't, and we leave, what happens if Vere sends a second drone up here? Or a third?"

"I'd find that extremely annoying," she replied. "Perhaps you'd like to leave that gun here so I can protect myself."

"Not bloody likely."

"Just asking."

"Look," Marlen said, "Nick's right. Vere can have an army of drones on their way here for all we know. And we can't count on Duncan to stop her. Either we leave the ring here and send a bunch of mages up to help guard it, or we take it back to London HQ and let 'em guard it there. Be safer to go back to Town."

Nick raised an eyebrow, mildly surprised that Marlen had managed to come up with a plausible argument."

Absolutely," he said. "We'll take good care of it. There're two of us, and I've got a gun. They won't stop us."

"You do have a point." Isabel smiled. "But at the moment, I'm afraid it's a moot one. It will take all afternoon to travel to the burial spot and dig up the ring, most likely into early evening. We won't make the last evening ferry run."

"So we go get it," Marlen said, "and leave first thing in the morning."

Nick nodded. "That's fine by me." He rummaged about for something more appetizing and found the bag of fortune cookies. He picked one then held the bag out for Marlen, who eagerly grabbed a handful. Marlen cracked a cookie open and pulled out the paper strip. "'You will go on a long journey.' Ha. Already doing that. What's yours say?"

"Nothing." Nick stared at the paper. He didn't like what it said, and he didn't feel like sharing it. He read it again to make sure his eyes weren't playing tricks on him.

"Hey, come on." Marlen snatched it from his fingers. "'The key to your soul lies in your dreams.'" He shrugged and handed it back. "Could be the gentry at work again."

"What?"

"The fairy folk. Playing tricks on you."

Nick crumpled up the fortune and tossed it aside. "I'm not amused," he replied.

Nick drew a careful line down the center of the thick cream stationery. He'd spent the afternoon exploring the castle on his own, and had found the small, quiet study— the perfect place to sort things out, a place where he wouldn't be disturbed.

The antique walnut desk contained plenty of paper and pens; writing things down always helped him make more rational decisions. He felt quite pleased with the way he'd divided the paper into two neat columns. On top of the left side he wrote "Reasons to take ring to PIS HQ." Above the right column he wrote "Reasons to take ring to ISM HQ."

Brian ordered me to he put on the left hand side. Underneath he added *Want to prove self to DI6*, followed by *It will be just as safe there anyway*, and finally *I don't owe Marlen anything*. And, he thought as he tapped the pen against the paper, he could say goodbye to Marlen's friendship. But was that a positive or a negative? The man had turned his whole life upside down, and had severely messed about with his sense of identity. The only way to maintain control of his life and his sanity was to get as far from Marlen as he possibly could, and stay there.

Nick looked at the blank right-hand column. There was only one reason to take the ring to the ISM—because it would help out Marlen. It wouldn't win him any bonus points with the Domestic Intelligence Six Service. And Marlen would remain his friend, ready and willing to find ever new ways to disturb his life for a long time to come.

It wasn't really a question of taking the ring to the DI6 or the ISM. It was a question of his old life versus a possible new one. On the left side he could just as well write *Turn my back on all this past life nonsense, ignore all evidence that it's true, and try to return to a rational existence*. And on the right he could put *Stick it out with Marlen and find out who I am. And find out what he really wants from me*.

Except he was sure he already knew the answer to that last one. And it was damn well time to confront Marlen about it. Nick drew a large X through the entire sheet of paper, crumpled it, and put it in his pocket.

Georgina sat on a bench in Hyde Park, admiring the view of the Serpentine and the willows in the distance. It was her favorite meeting place, particularly on a crisp wintry day after the tourists had diminished in number. As the early evening sunlight fell across the leaves on the path, highlighting the golds and reds, she contemplated the peacefulness of the place, and its inevitable transiency.

Oh, well, she thought. *Enjoy it while you can*. She wished she could enjoy it longer, but even as she wished it, she saw the gentleman she was meeting coming smartly along the path.

Brian Watson was a small, bald man with a neatly trimmed gray beard. He wore a light gray, three-piece suit and carried a walking stick, apparently for ornamentation rather than usefulness, as it was tucked neatly under one arm.

"Good evening, my dear," he said in a clipped, upper-class accent. "So good of you to ring."

"Of course I rang," Georgina replied. "I *am* in your employ. Please cease standing there and have a seat."

"Thank you." He joined her on the bench. "Naturally, I'm anxious to hear more. What is Duncan really up to?"

"Just as your nephew reported. He's gone to Cornwall to fight the renegade mage, Vere." Georgina paused to brush away an errant leaf which had fallen upon her sleeve. "Provided she's actually free, which I still doubt. Naturally, I've heard stories of her. Legendary, they say. Once tried to destroy all of mankind, due, I believe, to some sort of revenge plot. Silly, if you ask me. Who would the mages serve if there were no mortals?"

Brian gave a little cough in response. "Indeed. Power for the sake of power is, nonetheless, attractive to those of lesser intellect."

"I've always heard that Vere had a remarkable mind. It does make one wonder." She sighed. "It's such a lovely evening. Might we not stroll a while?"

"Certainly. It would, in fact, be advisable. In our line of work, constant movement is an asset." He rose and offered her his arm.

They walked along the Serpentine, whose calm waters glittered in the hazy light.

"The reason I asked you to return," Brian said, "is that I need someone here in London while I'm away."

"Ah. You are going to Cornwall, then." When she had phoned from Scotland, Georgina had wondered why Brian wished to call her off the pursuit of the magical ring. "And what of Nicholas?"

Brian paused to watch the ducks. "I also called you back because I need to test young Nick. Your absence, in addition to your instructions to Ed, will ensure that Nick gets a good chance at obtaining the ring. He'll have much less interference. Yet I have the feeling that he is torn in his allegiances."

"Between you and Marlen."

"Precisely."

They walked on, strolling beneath the willow trees.

"What is it you should like me to do?" Georgina asked.

"Remain at ISM headquarters, and see if Nick does as I suspect he will, which is to bring the ring there."

Georgina shook her head sadly. She couldn't understand how a solid young man such as Nick would be swayed to disobey PIS orders, especially for the sake of someone like Marlen. "And if he does, I can kindly offer to look after it. And then turn it over to the PIS." She admired Brian's prescience. He always knew how to cover all the angles.

"That is quite correct," Brian replied. "I have longed to analyze such a magical object for years and years. It will do wonders when it comes time to ask the Minister for more funding, too. He'll be terribly impressed."

"It will be a pity, though," Georgina said, "if you are right about your nephew. He has such promise as an agent. If only he weren't so influenced by that maladjusted Marlen."

"Indeed. However, even should he do as I suspect he will, it won't be the end of his career. Yes, he'd be making a major misstep, but how can he be loyal to a secret unit with which he has had no genuine contact? After all, we never had time to train Nicholas properly in PIS tactics or aims. But I never imagined he would bump into Marlen, of all people, when he did. One cannot plan for *all* contingencies."

"No." Georgina found it little short of amazing that Brian managed to plan as well as he did, given the very uncertain nature of his mission. He was a most talented man. "One can only do one's best. At least you were able to put Nick's encounter with Marlen to some good use. So we may yet salvage him as an agent. Surely his patriotism will win out over any temporary sense of friendship."

"In the end, perhaps it will. I'd be willing to give him another chance anyway, at going through the rigors of training to see what he can do. We can but hope for the best, while always planning for the worst."

Georgina turned about and headed back along the path. "What shall you do in Cornwall? I find it difficult to believe this story of Vere being on the loose. You don't really expect to find her there?"

Brian shrugged. "Something of interest appears to be occurring. Otherwise, why would Duncan have gone? It bears checking."

"Do be cautious," Georgina said.

"I always am."

She bid him farewell at the bench, and watched him admiringly until he was lost from view.

Duncan found the deserted village on St. Michael's Mount a bit eerie, especially in the dark.

He had hiked down to the Marazion beach at dusk, when the tide was out. The causeway to the island stood high and dry, blocked for ten feet on either side by the chain-link fence. Duncan used his wire cutters to make a gaping hole in it, and across he went.

On the other end of the causeway, a quarter-mile off land, stood the towering mount, a great rocky hill dotted with trees. Atop it stood the castle, once a monastery and more recently, a private home. Lying at the base of the steep hill were dozens of smaller buildings comprising the island's village, which circled its harbor. Duncan wondered how much power Vere was expending in keeping what must be hundreds of people away from their homes while she set about her tasks. Quite a lot, he imagined.

He stood in the center of the empty village. *Too quiet here.* And too dark. Black clouds obscured the moon. A storm was brewing.

Duncan gazed at the hill looming above him. A ragged, narrow footpath snaked between the rocks and trees, up towards the castle and its blockish towers.

He had no firm plan, other than to be prepared for anything magical she chose to throw at him. She couldn't have a lot of power, not in her weakened state, not with holding her drones in thrall and keeping her spells over the villagers in place. She'd have wards around the castle, probably inside as well, but those should be simple to disarm. Time-consuming, though. Then he would use his own, stronger magic to defeat her.

The sky grew darker, the wind picked up, and a little rain drizzled down. *Hell*. He studied the steep footpath. He didn't fancy hiking up it in the rain and the dark. Not if there were wards in the way, and who knew how many drones, though they were generally easy to manage. Perhaps he should put off his attack for better weather, and a bit of daylight. He looked at the empty houses of the village. He could stay out of the storm, have a nice think over his strategy, and be refreshed and ready to go at first light. Be less hazardous if he could see what he was up against.

Not far off, thunder boomed, followed swiftly by the crack of lightning. The last thing he needed was to be caught in a violent downpour. Duncan quickly trotted off towards the nearest house to wait out the storm.

Chapter Twelve

Nick found Marlen in the library, in the center of a storm.

At least, the remnants of one. The huge room certainly looked as if a hurricane had recently passed through, tossing hundreds of books with abandon, dumping them in great wild heaps about the floor.

Marlen sat hunched in a far corner, near a towering pile of oversized volumes, engrossed in a tome. Nick carefully picked his way through the mess, curious to know what new madness had struck his companion. He supposed being immortal and virtually invincible would tend to make a person careless of other people's property, but still. This chaos was a tad extreme.

He paused to glance at a large picture book, flung open to a view of Bath. His eye fell on nearby volumes, also open, each page depicting an architectural scene. After the first few, he figured out the connecting thread. They were all Regency period. As he worked through the devastation towards Marlen, Nick noted a great variety of pictures from that era—buildings, streets, gardens, people engaged in social activities, dances, sporting events. Since he sincerely doubted Marlen had suddenly developed an intense desire to research early nineteenth-century history, Nick approached him with growing interest.

"Evening." He dropped down beside Marlen, who had his nose in an art book. "Mind if I ask you something?"

Marlen looked up. "Hm?"

"What the bloody hell are you doing?"

"Oh, nothing." He shut the book with a sigh.

"Nothing?" Nick waved at the decimated bookshelves. "You must've pulled half the library down. *What* are you doing?"

In reply, Marlen shoved a book of prints towards him. "Did you look at any of the others?"

"Yeah." Nick thumbed through the pages. It brimmed with prints of corpulent men and saucy women cavorting in much revelry. "They're all early 1800s history. So?"

"Those were the best years we ever had together," Marlen replied quietly. He brushed his fingertips over a leather folio. "We did the Grand Tour of the continent, in lavish style. Wasted buckets of money gambling all across Europe, had a wonderful time. Saw all the sights. Stayed at all the finest hotels, ate in the best restaurants. Drank the most expensive wines." He paused. "Good memories, that's what I'm looking for. Something that will bring back the good times we had, trigger the things you'll *want* to remember."

"Oh." Nick solemnly gazed at the art book. A print depicted a rowdy pub scene. He imagined they must have spent a great deal of their Grand Tour exploring the pubs of Europe. But it failed to ring any of those bells Marlen so desperately wanted him to hear. "Sorry. Nothing."

"Take your time. Look at some of the others."

"No." Nick closed the volume. He struggled to push away the feeling of affection rising within. He'd come here to confront his "friend", he'd come to say things that would help sever their tie, or so he hoped. Because the last thing he needed, before betraying the man, was to experience that feeling of fondness he'd had at least once before towards the idiot. "No, it doesn't really matter." He strove to get the words out. "I know what you're after with all this, and it isn't going to happen, so you might as well leave it be."

Marlen's eyes widened. "What are you on about?"

"You. Me." Nick fingered the silver medallion around his neck. "And this. I know what you want me to remember. So go on, tell me the truth about this quote."

There was no mistaking the wariness in Marlen's face. "Can't it wait?"

"No. I'm tired of you always saying you'll tell me later. It *is* later. Tell me now. Why did you put 'remember me' on here?" He already knew the answer. Not all of it, but the important part. But he wanted Marlen to say it himself.

"Because." Marlen looked down at his hands. "Because when I gave it to you, we weren't as close anymore. Your fortieth birthday was coming up, and you'd been talking a lot about settling down at long last. No more gambling, no more drinking, no more fighting. You wanted to get married, start a family. That sort of thing. I don't know. I thought you wouldn't be seeing much of me anymore, that's all. Didn't want you to forget all the good times we had."

Nick shook his head sadly. "No, go on. There's more to it than that."

"Is there?"

So he wasn't willing to say it after all. Nick felt a knot form in his gut. Fine. Someone had to say it. "Stop edging around the truth." He took a deep breath and let it out slowly. "We were lovers, weren't we?"

"Oh, hell." Marlen looked up. "Are you getting more memories back?"

"Just say yes or no, dammit."

He looked away again. "Yes."

Nick could see him digging his nails into his palm; it seemed to be Marlen's standard reaction to stress. Nick's resolve to make this encounter painful, to sever their ties, wavered. A few years ago, he had to admit, things between them might have gone very differently. If he'd seen Marlen in one of the gay pubs he once frequented, he would have been quite interested. Right type, there was no denying it, no getting away from that basic attraction. But he had exerted an enormous amount of mental energy pushing that part of his life aside since joining the police. He knew it was still there, firmly tucked away, something he knew existed yet didn't wish to actually look at.

Remembering more of his other self, of the Nick who'd been Marlen's lover, would be fraught with danger. No doubt that was why, in part, he'd fought against the memories. What if they changed him? What if they made him want that life again, the one he thought he'd buried once and for all?

No, it couldn't be. No matter how crazy his life felt at this moment, no matter how much more turmoil he experienced, the one thing he determined to hold onto was his basic sense of who he was. Nicholas John Watson, ex-Met detective, solid citizen, a logical, practical, forthright man with a dedication to duty. He suddenly frowned. Why did it all sound so pompous?

"Hey." Marlen gently nudged his thigh. "Are you okay?"

Nick blinked. There he sat, the bane of his existence, looking helpful, concerned, and deeply worried, those nails digging veritable trenches. "Yeah, I'm okay." He hesitated. Then, because he found he couldn't handle the hurt in Marlen's eyes, said softly, "You know, there are times when I do like you. As a friend."

Marlen relaxed his hands. "Thanks. And I'm sorry about not telling you earlier. Thought it might upset you too much, what with your fiancée and all."

"My what? Oh." Nick blushed, recalling his invention of Gwen. "Actually, I made her up."

Marlen smiled. "Thought so."

Curious now more than anything else, Nick asked, "What happened back in 1500 and whatever it was? You know, when you said we drifted apart. Was it because I grew older while you stayed twenty-five? Couldn't you handle me aging?"

"Wrong," Marlen replied. "Other way round. You couldn't handle the fact that I stayed young."

"Oh." Yes, that might be rather odd, being the lover of someone who never changed, while turning gray-haired and paunch-ridden oneself. "Well, but when I came back in the next incarnation, and was young again, did we, um, you know—"

"Yeah," Marlen said. "We were lovers again. Not always, but nearly every time, when you remembered."

"And then each time, I grew old on you." Nick shivered, chilled by the thought. "You know, it might be bet-

ter for mages to stick with other mages. Can't you find
someone immortal to fall in love with? Can't you see that it's
impossible for you to keep being in love with *me*? I'll
always grow old and die on you."

"Maybe."

The word startled Nick. "Maybe? There's no 'maybe'
about it." As much as he disliked contemplating his own
mortality, it was stupid to be in denial. "I'm mortal, despite
this transmutation nonsense. Someday, I'm going to bloody
well die again. For God's sake, give it up!"

"Can't," Marlen said simply. "It's too important to me.
It's been the only important thing in my entire five-hundred-
godforsaken-years of life."

Oh, hell. Nick bent his head, studied his hands. Marlen
couldn't have picked a worse time to reveal how much
he cared. Not when the first thing Nick planned to do in
the morning was to get hold of the ring and take off for
London without him, to go straight to Brian's office. Why
did the bastard have to make things so bloody difficult?

"Look," Nick said finally, "I'm sorry, but it just isn't any
good. I'm not about to fall for you in this life, so you're
going to have to wait until next time."

"Maybe not," Marlen replied. "Don't you see? Things
are different. Something's happened to you. That tingling
you felt around the wards, I told you, that can't happen
to anyone except a mage."

Nick shook his head. "But I'm not a mage."

"So I've always believed."

The shiver returned, creeping slowly up his spine. "But...
how could it have changed?"

"I don't know. The only thing I can think of is Vere's
grimoire. It must have something to do with that.
Remember I said there was an anti-psychic block spell
that I played around with, because I thought it might help
restore your memory?"

Nick nodded. "That's why these memories keep popping
up. So?"

"So there was a lot of gibberish in the grimoire, right
before that spell, stuff I didn't completely understand.
It sounded like notes from some experiment she'd been

conducting. She'd been doing a lot of research on the nature of immortality. Remember what she'd been up to before she got so angry at the mortals?"

"She wanted to find a way to make everyone immortal." Nick had a bad feeling about where this was heading. "So she'd written down her notes from that original research?"

"I think so," Marlen said. "Didn't have time to decipher all of it." He paused. "Maybe I did something, I don't know. Maybe that anti-block spell triggered more than just memories. It would be really helpful if we could go ask her."

Nick touched the medallion, ran his fingers over the engraving. "Why did you steal it? The grimoire?"

"Told you, to find a memory-restoring spell."

"No." Nick gazed intently at him. "Tell me the truth. Why did you really take it? Because you knew she'd been researching immortality, that's why. Isn't it?" Dammit, the little bastard had been holding back on him again. He hadn't just wanted him to remember who he was, he'd damn well wanted to make him immortal as well. Nick knew it as surely as he knew day from night. "You were hoping she'd devised a spell to make mortals live forever, weren't you? *Weren't you?*"

Marlen held his gaze. "I got tired of watching you die."

"You sonofabitch." Anger flared within him, the anger he had wanted to generate earlier. "Of all the selfish—" He felt so suddenly hot that he had to move, get up, walk away. Nick paced rapidly between the book piles, slapping at them. "This isn't really for my benefit, is it? You haven't done a damn thing for *me*, or given one thought to what I might want. No, the only person you ever think about is your own lazy, greedy, good-for-nothing self!" He flailed at a stack of books, toppling them to the floor. "To hell with somebody else's memories. I don't want them, good, bad, or indifferent. Because I'm not *him*. And that's what you want. You don't want *me* to remember, you don't want *me* to wind up turning into a mage, or living forever. You want him, and he doesn't bloody well exist, not in this lifetime, anyway. But no, that's not good enough. You can't wait any longer, you're tired of the whole damn cycle. So you go and find me in spite of the fact that I'm not the Nick you're so stupidly in love with, and now you're busy trying to force me into the mold, one way or another. Not once did you think to ask if I *wanted* to remember, not once did you consider the possibility that I might not want to be immortal, that it might upset me to watch my family and friends grow old and die around me, no, you just fucking well up and did it!" He brought his fist down hard on an end table. "Christ, I'm so sick of your manipulations. You almost had me there, you know, with this 'good memories' ploy. Very clever. Well, let me explain it to you loud and clear." He thumped the table again. "I do *not* want to remember our Grand Pub Crawl of Europe." *Bang*. "I do *not* wish to remember our little lover's trysts across the ages." *Whack*. "And I do *not* want to be *your* Nick. You can take your spells and your memories and your utterly useless immortality and you can shove them up your arse!"

He turned to storm off as best he could through the mess. He'd almost been taken in, almost fallen for that sentimental streak in Marlen. Good memories. Right.

He paused at the doorway however, unable to resist looking back. Marlen sat there in his corner, unmoving, staring at the wall. Then he slowly drew his knees up, wrapped his arms around them, and bent his head.

Nick didn't know how long he stood there, watching. He never heard a sound, but he could see Marlen's shoulders shaking. Oh, hell. What was he supposed to do now? He'd got what he wanted. He wanted to not like the bastard, wanted to feel better about stealing the ring, and he'd achieved that. So why not simply walk away?

He didn't. He stayed in the doorway and waited. After what seemed a very long time indeed, Marlen stopped shaking. His head lifted, he took in a great gulp of air, and let the breath out in a great sigh. Then, as Nick kept watching, Marlen rose unsteadily, slowly picked up a stack of books, and carried them back to the shelves.

After the third dropped book, Nick couldn't take it anymore. His anger subsiding, he made his way back over.

Marlen turned at the noise of his approach. "You still here?"

Nick picked up the book he'd dropped and put it on the shelf. "Thought I'd help clean up." He attacked the nearest pile, shoving the books with no regard for order onto the shelves.

"Thanks." Marlen went to work on another huge stack.

Together they put the library into some semblance of order. Nick had no idea that moving books could be so exhausting, but he felt tired, hot, and sweaty when they finished, and his arms ached. He needed a bath. He hadn't hot a nice hot soak in a tub since... since after the trek in Wales. Nick frowned. Had it only been the night before last? Yes, just forty-eight hours ago he'd been lying in that steaming bath, where Marlen had brought him a hot cup of tea, and they'd had a laugh over the day's adventures and over Marlen's ability to get up his nose, and they had teased each other.

Marlen stretched his arms over his head, tilting his waist from side to side, then twisting. The lithe muscles of his back showed through his thin green shirt. Nick swallowed. He really didn't think that Marlen was doing it on purpose, but damn, he looked attractive. The urge to go over and wrap his arms around that body pulled at him strongly. Nick turned away.

"It's supper time."

"What? Oh." Nick looked back. It was safe now; he'd stopped stretching. "Yeah, maybe there's something in the kitchen we can cook up."

They went downstairs together, with no mention of Nick's outburst. He certainly didn't feel like bringing it up, and was glad Marlen was pretending it hadn't happened. Sooner or later, though, something would need to be said.

A note from Isabel lay on the kitchen counter, saying she had finished off the leftovers from their lunch and gone to her room, and mentioning a particularly promising-looking freezer beside the pantry. Further investigation revealed a treasure chest of prepared meals, apparently cooked up by the castle chef and frozen for future use.

A short trip to the microwave later, they were sitting at the dining table consuming a gourmet supper.

Marlen poked idly at the Chicken Kiev on his plate.

Nick had chosen trout almondine. "Um," he mumbled between bites, "forgot the wine."

The pantry had revealed a horde of wine, and Nick took his time searching out the right bottle. Two glasses later, he felt slightly more relaxed. Good food, good wine, nobody trying to kill him... that was all he really needed to feel that life was complete. Or was it?

As he and Marlen ate and he drank, there fell an uncomfortable silence between them. Nick knew he couldn't go on pretending he hadn't said what he had in the library. Some of it had been cruel. Loving someone wasn't stupid. Maybe pursuing it over a few centuries could be considered mildly daft, but it wasn't stupid. He genuinely regretted suggesting it was.

Marlen got up and disappeared into the kitchen, returning with two slices of thawed-out spice cake.

"Sorry," Nick blurted out as Marlen shoved the cake at him.

"What did you say?"

Nick coughed. His throat felt dry. "I'm sorry for what I said in the library."

Marlen raised an eyebrow. "Are you really? Are you going to try to tell me you didn't mean a word of it?"

Nick broke a piece of cake off with his fork and pushed it around on the plate. "No, I'm not going to tell you that. I did mean it. Well, most of it. I'm sorry I was so blunt."

"I see. Tell me, do you have any feelings for me at all? As a friend?"

"I said so before, didn't I?" Nick broke off more pieces of cake, but didn't eat any. "However, I happen to prefer friends who talk things over with me first before making plans that will affect my entire ruddy life!"

"You think I meant it to happen that way? I thought if I did the memory-restoring spell, then you'd be the same as you always were before, and everything would be all right. Then I was going to tackle Vere's research into immortality, and end the incarnation cycle forever." Marlen poked at his cake. "I didn't know, back when I played about with the grimoire, that you'd wind up being so damned uncooperative. I honestly didn't think you'd mind, because you'd be Nick, and *Nick* wouldn't have minded."

"Well, *I* mind. A *lot*." Nick attacked his slice of cake.

"Yeah," Marlen replied bitterly. "Something changed you."

"Maybe I decided that being a brawling, pub-crawling, general layabout didn't have a lot going for it."

"After all this time?"

Nick shrugged. "Maybe that car wreck had a sobering influence."

"Wasn't your fault," Marlen said. "Or mine."

"No, but we *were* hit by a drunkard. Even if it's buried somewhere in my subconscious, that *could* have influenced me into becoming something other than a drunken lout this lifetime."

Marlen vigorously shook his head. "But you *weren't*. All we ever did was have some fun! We never hurt anyone. Not unless they deserved it."

Nick shoved his empty plate away. "You should eat yours. It's good." He decided white wine would be the perfect chaser, and refilled his glass.

"No, listen to me." Marlen pushed aside his untouched plate. "You've been making unkind remarks about 'my friend Nick' and his general lack of character, and about the fact that neither one of us has ever done anything useful in five centuries, as if that were a major crime against humanity. I'm tired of your smugness. Who the hell cares if all we did was laze around having a good time? Who cares that we weren't exactly upstanding citizens, that we never made it into Burke's, or won any community service awards? Huh? We *lived*, that's what we did. We had adventures. We traveled, and saw things I'll bet you've only ever seen in books, and we did things you've never seen outside a movie house. Maybe you're having a wonderful time being a decent, public-minded policeman, and maybe you really enjoy nabbing all the evil-minded crooks and protecting the nice clean streets from the filth, and maybe you've got your eye on moving up the ladder by brown-nosing every politically well-aligned old fart you meet until you're so successful, admired, and virtuous that you have dreams about an O.B.E.; but in my opinion, you'll never enjoy it as much as you enjoyed the summer night we hijacked the gondola, loaded it up with champagne, and drifted out a ways into the lagoon, to lay back and watch the lights of Venice and the stars, while toasting the health of *Sparafucile*, the jet-black killer of a horse who made us half a million lira richer that day. No, do what you want, call me whatever you like, refuse to remember who and what you were, but don't ever forget those long, wondrous nights we had together. Please. It may not have changed the world, but it meant something. It really did."

Nick's hand froze on the wine glass, so stunned was he by the outburst. An eerie feeling crept through him as he recalled his own thoughts earlier in the library, about how he had always envisioned himself... solid citizen, dedicated to his public duty... and how pompous it had sounded. It was almost as if Marlen had read his mind. Venice under a starry sky, viewed from the water on a warm summer night—would he truly be happier lazing his life away like that?

He managed to raise his glass and take a sip. "When did that happen, during our Grand Tour?"

"No." Marlen took up his own glass and drank. "No, the gondola escapade happened in the life before this. 1972. Summer lasted a long time that year."

Nick idly fingered the stem of his glass. "Summer can't last forever, Marlen. Not even for you."

"Don't you think I know that?"

"Do you?"

"Oh, yeah," Marlen replied. "Trust me, I do know. But I'll tell you something. Just because I know the truth, doesn't mean I have to approve of it."

"But don't you see," Nick protested, "that denying reality won't help you any? Things can't be the way you want them to be. It doesn't matter what you try in this mad quest of yours to return to some golden image in your memories. Can't you see that it's bound to fail?"

Marlen nodded slowly. "Probably." He smiled softly. "Doesn't mean I'm going to give up trying. Maybe that's my real purpose in life. Failing. It does seem to be the one thing I'm really good at. Who knows? Maybe I've spent five centuries inadvertently teaching others what not to do in order to be successful."

"Could be." Nick wished he knew how to make things better for him. There was so much yearning in Marlen's voice that it hurt to listen to him. Yet there was nothing he could say.

"You know," Marlen went on, "sometimes it feels as if I've spent my whole life driving on the wrong side of the road, going the wrong way down one-way streets, turning left when I should have turned right. And it feels as if it doesn't matter where I wind up, because I'll always be lost."

There was nothing Nick could say to that, either.

Marlen finished off his wine and slowly rose. "I'll see you in the morning." Then he walked out of the room without looking back.

Marlen lay awake at midnight. And at one a.m. And two.

The thoughts which kept running through his mind centered on a rather serious dilemma. He had succeeded in getting Nick to start remembering his past. Unfortunately Nick was, for whatever reason, denying that that past had anything to do with him. The odds of this Nick becoming his best friend again, let alone a lover, were not looking good.

The logical thing to do was to give up this time, and wait for Nick's next incarnation, hoping everything would be back to normal then. He had gotten very good at waiting over the centuries. The problem with this plan was that Marlen had a feeling it might not come to pass. Because this time, Nick might very well not die.

Whenever the mages got together to seek out potential new members, whenever they sought the unmistakable, unique signature which marked a potential mage, they did so by performing a particular ritual. This ritual involved a specific incantation breathed over three candle flames. If a prospect existed anywhere within a hundred square miles, the flames would dance, grow, and join together to form a glowing circle. Within that circle, a picture would slowly emerge, a living portrait of their target. Never, in all the centuries of mage history, had one of these new faces turned out to belong to anyone other than a potential mage. They only needed finding, and training.

It hadn't been difficult for Marlen to find three candles in the castle. While the ritual worked best with two or more mages chanting, it could work with only one, provided the new prospect wasn't far off. He set up the spell in the library atop the massive Victorian desk in the dark with only the candles casting flickering shadows across the bookcases on all sides. Moonlight streaked through the tall leaded window as he spoke the incantation. He held his hands over the flames, then pulled them back, directing the candlelight to merge as one fiery circle. And in the circle a face had formed. Nick's face.

Somehow, Nick had changed from a transmutated soul into a mage. And Marlen had a feeling he wasn't going to be pleased by the news.

Now Marlen lay on his oversized, overstuffed bed, staring blankly at the carved ceiling, its repeating pattern long since having lulled him into a semi-trance. Immortal... it was what he'd always wanted Nick to be. He'd wanted it for five centuries. There was only one small problem. He didn't want just an immortal Nick. He wanted an immortal Nick who still loved him.

It had to have been the grimoire. Something he had inadvertently set in motion while tinkering with the spells. The fact that he'd created this state of affairs himself didn't exactly make Marlen feel any better.

What he really needed to know, before he could fall comfortably into sleep, was what the hell he should do next.

And he was at an utter loss.

Isabel finished cleaning the ring and set it on a towel on the kitchen worktop.

"There. That's got most of the grime off. I had it tucked away in a nice wooden box, but water got into the hole I'd buried it in and mucked things up."

Nick stood in the kitchen doorway, watching from a distance, since the reek of ammonia was overpowering. He waited until Isabel dumped the stuff before venturing inside.

The ring failed to impress him. Nothing more than a small silver band with strange symbols engraved on it. "So this is really a powerful magical object?"

Isabel nodded. "Rather ordinary looking, wouldn't you say?"

"Very. You'd think it would be easier for Vere to simply make another ring like this rather than go to the trouble of retrieving it."

"Possibly. But it usually takes months to infuse an object with the specific magical properties you desire. Vere must be in a hurry."

"I would be, with Duncan chasing me."

"And he has very good reason." Isabel hefted the water pot and carried it to the sink.

Nick stared at the ring. This was his chance. A clear path lay to the kitchen doorway, a scant ten feet away, and Isabel stood occupied emptying the boiling water. Marlen lay asleep upstairs. Nick had heard him snoring on the way past his room. He had already left the note, and he had armed himself with the drone's gun in case Isabel moved faster than expected. Using it didn't appeal to him, though it presented few moral qualms, since he couldn't possibly kill her, merely slow her down.

All night he had worried over the choice he had to make, but in the end, he opted for sanity. Sticking with Marlen, helping him any further, would only lead to more confusion. He'd had enough. Yes, he'd been curious earlier about who he was, but the more he found out, the less he liked it. Now he simply wanted to return to a world he understood, one that made sense. And he wanted to keep his job with Brian, wanted to make good on his first assignment. One thing he had been very well trained at during his years on the force was following orders.

No, the only course of action which would allow him to maintain his hold on reality was to get as far away from Marlen as quickly and effectively as possible, and to stay there. Besides, he had already left the note.

Feeling as if he were moving in slow motion, Nick picked up the ring, placed it in his pocket, and went for the doorway. He was running, yet it felt as if his legs were churning through molasses instead of air.

As he hit the doorway he heard the clatter behind him, as Isabel dropped the pot. He heard the shout. Ignoring her, he bolted along the corridor towards the main entrance. He didn't look back, didn't pay any attention to the pounding footsteps, which faded as he dashed outside the castle. No contest.

Nick ran to his car. He had it started and halfway down the drive before Isabel appeared; he saw her in his rear-view mirror, standing on the castle's front steps, waving and shouting for all she was worth. He pressed his foot hard on the pedal, and soon Isabel and the castle were lost from view.

CHAPTER THIRTEEN

She really shouldn't have spent so much time on research using the television and computer. Vere rubbed her eyes, tired from a poor night's rest, a night filled with images of figures on a bright screen exploding left and right. These electronics the humans had invented were amazing tools, yet also a seductive frivolity. She should not have let it draw her away from her goal.

But she had, because she had slackened her defense of the castle in her obsession with perfecting her knowledge, and she had failed to check on Duncan's whereabouts at her usual timely intervals. She would not survive to enjoy the modern age if she didn't rectify this oversight immediately.

Vere went to her workroom in the castle's armory, where she had set up her magical tools and grimoire in anticipation of completing her great spell. On a long wooden table in the center of the room she laid out a map of Cornwall, placed her seeking stone upon it, and performed the spell for locating Duncan.

The stone wobbled about, finally settling down in the island's village. So he was already here, so close. Too close, though hardly unexpected. She sighed, and took out the two amulets she used to create her wards around the castle. Time to reinforce and strengthen them, make it harder for Duncan to make his way up here. He'd break through them all eventually, yet this extra power she would put behind them would slow him down enough to give her time to strategize. She'd give him wards stronger and trickier enough to keep him occupied all day long.

An hour later, she felt satisfied with her efforts, and put her tools away. She felt calmer, more in control. Duncan had apparently come alone, as far as her magic could tell, and she could fight him one on one without fear. Not just with magic, either.

Vere left the workroom to check on the contents of the small room next to it, once used as a garrison. Inside, her drone Ron had brought a box of dynamite. He'd explained to her how the sticks inside were harmless until the detonator caps were attached and the fuses lit. She'd left the dangerous box alone until needed, and now she needed it.

She pulled a stool up to the box, retrieved the separate container of caps, and sat down to attach them to the dynamite, very carefully, one by one.

Brian Watson strolled along the empty beach below the town of Marazion. He stopped in front of a chain-link fence that blocked the head of the causeway leading to the island of St. Michael's Mount. CLOSED FOR RENOVATIONS UNTIL FURTHER NOTICE, the sign read.

"Hmpf," Brian muttered. "Renovations, my foot." He gazed across the water at the island. It jutted upwards, true to its name, mostly mountain—though a rather small one. At the top stood the castle. All he could see of it from the beach was part of a wall and one tower. Down below, in an inlet, there were more buildings, squat and gray, and a small harbor. He had already checked at the dock on the Marazion side. No one would take him over. Every single boat owner in town had been handsomely and secretly paid to refuse all such requests, and he didn't have enough money to out-bribe his competitor.

Who had to be Vere. She must have taken over the island, just as Nick had reported. She could have made the drones Nick had spoken of out of the workers there, and then booted everyone else off. And she'd paid who she needed to pay to keep quiet.

A group of boulders stood near the head of the causeway. Brian leaned against one, crossing his arms against the cold. He stared at the chain fence. Someone had cut a gaping hole in it. Handy.

After a few more minutes of consideration, he patted the Walther PPK which fitted snugly in his shoulder holster, and headed for the causeway.

His plan, such as it was, involved reconnaissance and assessment until reinforcements arrived. He didn't know how long it would take for Nick and Marlen to get from Scotland back to London, possibly most of the day. But when they did, Georgina would be poised to intercept, one way or another, and direct them both here. After that, the plan got much hazier. Even DI6 had little in its handbook on how to deal with renegade mages who might or might not be a threat to all of humanity.

He didn't mind not having a clear path to follow. He rather prided himself on playing things by ear, keeping on his toes, able to shift with the winds of chance wherever they blew. Made the game all the more exciting, made him feel young again. *Alive.*

On the other end of the causeway, the village stood empty, deadly quiet. Even the terns seemed spooked by the place. Brian ambled down the deserted main street, wondering if Vere knew he was there, if she had some magical looking glass from which to gaze at her world from on high. Georgina had told him about some of their basic spells and abilities, though he knew she kept a lot in reserve. He knew they had seeking spells for finding people and objects, spells to enslave people, or confuse them, or make them tell secrets. And they had protective spells against other mages' magic, ways to draw magical circles around themselves to keep other magic out. They had protective spells that Georgina called "wards", for blocking people's passage. Surely Vere would have a lot of those in place here on the island?

He paused, studying the landscape ahead. A few more houses, then a rocky path leading steeply up through the trees, winding and twisting its way to the castle. Georgina said you couldn't see a ward, but you'd know when you hit one. He didn't fancy running into something that might knock him out. But then how could he go on?

The answer came a moment later, when he heard a door creak open. Brian slid quietly behind a house, peering cautiously round its protective stone wall. Up ahead, a man emerged from another house, and stood gazing up at the castle path. Brian had never met Duncan Phipps, yet had no doubt as to his identity. "Starched, blond, and imperious," had been Georgina's description of the mages' leader. The man in the dark blue suit with the ramrod back and sleek blond looks fit his image of Duncan to perfection.

Brian watched as the head of all the mages produced a leather pouch, removed something from it that was too small to make out, and held it out ahead of him as he walked forward, chanting. Fascinating. From what Brian understood of mage powers, Duncan could no more hike up that path without disabling the wards any more than he could, yet there he went, slowly working his way up the hill. And very helpfully breaking all the wards as he went.

That would do nicely. Brian slid out from behind the house, crept up to the next house, and waited until Duncan hiked far enough up the hilly path to be out of sight before he moved quietly after him.

Marlen sat on Nick's empty bed, staring at the piece of notepaper in his hands.

Isabel had woken him. At first he had refused to believe what she told him, but it was hard to deny with the evidence staring him in the face. He had read Nick's note, then immediately tried to go back to sleep in an effort to wake again later to find that it had all been a dream, but had given up the plan due to the fact that Isabel kept screaming profanities at him.

Since Isabel had arrived at the castle via chartered plane and had no car, Marlen had sent her off in search of transport, a mission which left him blessedly alone to reread the note.

Marlen—No "dear", he noticed, though it hardly mattered considering the content. *Please forgive me. I can't explain why, but I have to take the ring back to London alone. Don't try to find me. I don't want to be found, and even if you do, it won't do any good, since I won't have the ring on me by the time you reach me. I didn't take it for myself, and don't worry, I'm not working for Vere. I'm truly sorry I can't explain. All I can say is that I need to do this. And I have to get away from you. I'm fond of you, and that's part of the problem. I don't know who I am anymore. I need to find out, but I need to find out by myself. Please, you have to leave me alone. Otherwise it's too hard. Things get too crazy when you're around. I'm sorry. I'm really, really sorry about this. I hope you can find him again someday. I know you need him now, but it isn't going to happen this time around. God knows the last person you need in your life is someone like me. Trust me, you can do a lot better. Nick.*

Most of it didn't make much sense to him. Why had he taken off with the ring? Why couldn't he explain anything? Didn't Nick realize that this would only make things worse for him with the Council, that the other mages would toss him into limbo without a second thought? Marlen crumpled the piece of paper, tossed it against the wall. This was the last thing in the world he had expected. Of all the people who might have turned on him when he needed help... not Nick. No, he couldn't have done this; he'd never do anything that might hurt him. But of course, that was the Nick he knew, or thought he'd known, all his life. Why had he changed? It couldn't really be that stupid theory Nick had proposed, about the "subconscious effect" of the car crash. Maybe that would explain the lack of adventurous-ness, maybe it could lie behind the refusal to budge from his current practical, no-nonsense way of life, but *nothing* could explain away this outright betrayal.

Don't try to find me. Yeah, sure, he was supposed to simply pretend it hadn't happened, pretend nothing was wrong, and do what? Calmly return to mage headquarters and tell the Council that his best friend, who was a mage himself and didn't yet know it, had stolen the ring? That would go over well. Especially as he didn't even know why, nor did he know what Nick was planning to do with it.

Marlen put his head in his hands. *Why? What the hell did you want it for?* What would a policeman want with a magical ring? The only thing he could think of was that Nick was going to hand it over to his superiors. And what the hell would *they* do with the thing? Without a knowledge of incantations and power rituals, the ring was useless. No, that made no sense. The only person who would have a use for it would be another mage. But Nick didn't know any other mages. Or did he?

He'd said he wasn't working for Vere. Maybe he was in the employ of someone else. Duncan? Marlen couldn't believe that. Spying was the only thing that made sense, though. Something suddenly flashed through Marlen's mind, a scrap of remembered dialogue from the morning after they had first met. He had come out into the living room, Nick had been on the phone. *'Who were you calling?'* he'd asked. *'My fiancée,'* Nick had answered.

Except that last night, Nick had admitted he'd invented her.

So who had he called that morning? Not his police supervisor, because he'd already called the fellow shortly before. Whoever it had been, Nick had lied about the person's identity.

It belatedly occurred to Marlen that Nick's job as a police officer might not even be real, that it could be a cover for something else. Perhaps he worked for some special branch of the police, or one of the other mysterious government organizations that liked to investigate ordinary citizens. Or not so ordinary citizens.

Marlen reached for the bedside phone. He got hold of the operator, and was put through to London, to the police station where he'd been interrogated by Nick.

"Perkins," said the voice on the other end.

"I want to speak to Detective Watson," Marlen replied.

"Watson? Nick Watson? I'm sorry, sir. Mr. Watson has left the force, and I'm not allowed to give out forwarding numbers."

"Left it when?" Marlen asked hollowly.

"Only a few days ago, sir."

"Well, can you at least tell me where he's working now, then? It's terribly important. This is his brother."

"Oh, is that David? I thought your voice sounded familiar."

"Yes, it is. Please, it's a matter of a family emergency."

"Well," said Perkins, "I can't imagine old Nick would mind. I'm surprised he hasn't bragged to you about his new employer yet. He's working for DI6. In the Paranormal Investigation Service unit. Ever heard of them? Very unusual stuff they deal with, or so I'm told."

"Really." Marlen felt his mouth drying up. He coughed. "I suppose they have an unlisted number."

"Yes, afraid so. Can't give that out. Sorry."

"That's all right," Marlen replied. "I'll find him. Ta." He hung up.

He was still staring blindly at the wall when Isabel returned twenty minutes later.

"Planes are right out," she reported. "Too much fog this morning. But I found these downstairs." She held up a large key ring. "And this one fits into a Jag in the garage. Full tank of petrol, too." She paused. "Are you still moping over that bastard 'friend' of yours?"

"He was spying on me," Marlen replied, not quite believing it yet. "All along, he's been spying on me. For some outfit called the Paranormal Investigation Service. You ever heard of them?"

"No. Private or government?"

"Government."

"I shouldn't worry, then." Isabel rattled the keys. "Can we get going? We might just catch up to him before the next ferry arrives."

Marlen nodded, though he didn't welcome the idea as much as he thought he would. While part of him wanted to confront Nick, part of him wanted very much to crawl into a deep, dark hole and stay there for a century or two.

Maybe being put into limbo wouldn't be such a bad idea after all.

An image haunted Nick's mind, an image that refused to dissolve during his long drive back to London.

He had made the seven-a.m. ferry with plenty of time to spare. Too much, in fact. He had spent some anxious minutes standing at the back railing, waiting for Isabel and Marlen to burst through the fog shrouding the dock, ready for vengeance. At last, the horn had sounded. But as the ferry began to pull away, they suddenly appeared, easily recognizable in the Jag, since they'd apparently been in such a rush they hadn't bothered to put the top up.

Isabel leapt from the car and stood at the end of the dock, shaking her fist and screaming wildly. Nick refrained from waving.

The image that haunted him wasn't hers, though. No, the sight that disturbed him most was that of Marlen, sitting motionless in the car, staring blankly at the retreating ferry, so blankly it seemed as if all the life had been drained away from him. It wasn't what he'd expected. Marlen was the most alive person he had ever known; surely he should have been shouting too, surely he should have been jumping about, angry, frustrated, and letting fly with that temper of his. Instead, he looked utterly defeated.

And he was the one who had done that. For five hundred years Marlen had eagerly taken on adventure after adventure, had thoroughly enjoyed the many and varied excitements of life, had, as he'd said himself, *lived*. Then Nick had come along to take away the one thing that kept Marlen so determined to go on. Love. It wasn't merely the fear of death that drove Marlen; he had suspected all along there was something else. And he knew what it was. Marlen was driven by something more than mere obliteration. He was driven by the fear of spending eternity alone.

That wasn't a curse Nick wished to lay on anyone, friend or foe. The only thought that helped him live with his treachery was the hope that Marlen wouldn't wind up alone forever after all. Someday, there would be a new incarnation. Maybe then things would set themselves aright.

Odd, to think that he'd be back here in the future. *But,* Nick thought, *will I really be me?* Would he remember this life, this person he was now? Would he be the same? If so, then what had happened to the other Nick, the one whose memories kept flashing through him, the one he kept striving to push away? Where was he? Would he exist again, and if he did, what would happen to *him*?

Nick shook his head. Too confusing by half. There was no need to worry over hypothetical futures when he still had a very real present to deal with.

In the early afternoon he hit the outskirts of London. There had been no sign of the Jaguar during his drive, so he had no idea how close they were in their pursuit. No doubt they would need to stop from time to time to do one of those seeking spells, to make sure of where he was heading. They would be able to track him straight to DI6 headquarters.

As Nick drove through the streets, working his way towards Whitehall, he wondered just who he should turn the ring over to when he got there. DI6 was located, ironically enough, only a block away from the spot Marlen had marked on his map for the mage's HQ. But Nick had never actually been inside the building before. Nor did he know where Brian's PIS office was located. He didn't even have any identification as an agent. For all he knew, what with Brian having gone off to Cornwall, they would refuse to believe he was a new agent, and would turn him away.

As he drew closer to Whitehall, Nick's sense of reluctance increased. He had spent a good deal of mental effort convincing himself, back at Dunvegan, that going straight to the PIS was the only thing he could do, yet now he was here, the reality of actually doing it held less appeal. He pulled off the street, parked the car, and got out to walk around a bit, needing the crisp November air to help clear his head.

Not quite knowing why, he found himself drawn to St. James's Park. He strolled along a winding path down between the bare willows. The park was quiet this afternoon. He dropped onto a stone bench, staring vacantly across the expanse of autumn-brown land to the government buildings beyond. He should just go there, explain as best he could to whoever was in the DI6 office, hand over the ring for safekeeping, and leave it at that. Then he should go out to Cornwall. Surely Brian would need some help. And perhaps somehow, some way, he could do something to help stop Vere, help Marlen after all. Not that he'd appreciate it at this point. No, there was no way Marlen would ever forgive and forget.

The image of Marlen's face came to him again. He couldn't banish it, couldn't get away from the hurt he had caused. If only there had been a way to do things differently. If only he could have saved both his career and the friendship. Nick abruptly shook himself. What was he thinking? Friendship? With that lazy, irresponsible, good-for-nothing troublemaker? No, that was precisely what he'd been running away from. Why would he want it now?

Nick sighed, more confused than ever. He had taken the ring because Brian ordered him to. But he had also taken it because he knew it would turn Marlen against him, that it would keep them apart. He had done it because he was a coward. Because he couldn't handle the emotional turmoil that being around Marlen invariably led to. He was frankly afraid of it.

But now that he was here, now that he was finally alone, Nick felt strangely at loose ends. He should have felt victorious, having gotten what he presumably wanted. He should have felt good, having returned to the sane world and logical life he'd left behind only a few days ago. So why did he feel so uncomfortable instead, so out of place?

A chill autumn breeze swirled through the park, kicking up dead leaves. Hazy afternoon sunlight skittered across the waters of the Serpentine. He should just turn the ring in.

Nick took it from his pocket, turned it round and round. So unexceptional. What did Brian want with it, anyway? To study it, of course. Supposedly to learn something about the magic powers the mages used. He ran his finger over the inscriptions, unimpressed. His own medallion looked more intriguing than this slight band.

Oh, bloody hell.

Nick cursed himself as he lifted the medallion from his neck. Larger than the ring, just as many arcane symbols on it, and while it was no doubt less powerful, it still contained some magical element. He was such a fool. All this time, when he'd been struggling to know what the right thing to do could be, and there it was, staring him in the face. The medallion. All Brian wanted was a magical object to study. He wouldn't bloody well care what it was, just something, anything. He would never have known the difference, anyway. Nick could have simply told him the ring turned out to be a red herring, he could have lied, could have told him anything. He could have handed over the medallion instead, could have told him it was the third object. How would he ever know the truth? And then he could have let Marlen keep the ring, could have let him take it to the mages' HQ, everything would have been fine. No lost points with Brian, no lost job, and no lost friend.

Some agent he had turned out to be.

Too late now. He could still hand over a magical object to the PIS, but how much more impressive would it have been to do both that *and* keep his friendship with Marlen going? For it rather belatedly occurred to Nick that Brian would want him to stay on Marlen's good side. Surely the PIS would want to continue investigating the mages. Surely they would want someone who was able to get close to them. And he'd completely blown that chance.

One of the most basic things he had learned as a police officer had been the handling of informants, or anyone else who was privy to criminal activity. You had to keep them happy. You had to keep them on your side. And you sure as hell didn't go around betraying them at the first opportunity.

Yes, Brian would have wanted him to remain friends with Marlen. But that wasn't what was bothering him most. What bothered him most was the realization that part of him still wanted Marlen in his life. Whether he was an assignment or not.

Nick turned the medallion over, stared at the *memor mihi* inscription. *Remember me.* He squeezed the silver disk tightly. "I'm sorry," he muttered aloud. "I'm sorry."

It was too late. Nothing he could do now would mend the wound. He really shouldn't care. Intelligence agents weren't supposed to care, he'd heard that somewhere. They weren't supposed to become emotionally involved, couldn't dare risk feeling anything for anyone, because it would only wind up causing pain. Nick sat there on the cold stone bench, trying very hard not to give a damn about the idiot who had turned his life inside out because he couldn't do anything about it even if he did care.

Except take the ring straight to mage headquarters.

Nick swallowed hard. He could do that. Brian would never know, probably wouldn't even care so long as he had something to study, like the medallion. It would make things better for Marlen, and he wanted to make things better. The only thing it wouldn't do was salvage their friendship.

Did that really matter so much? Was he really going to miss the bastard? Maybe he was feeling sentimental now, but wouldn't a little more time and distance put those feelings solidly to rest? He stared blankly for a while at the willow trees, whose leafless branches drifted in the wind. Out of nowhere, an image flashed through his mind, an image of those same trees, only this time with leaves, thousands of them whispering in the night. A late summer night, a warm night, with the park all to themselves.

The memory flooded through him utterly whole and real. He knew instantly which night it had been. The night of the car crash. He saw it clearly, vividly, as real as any memory of his own. He and Marlen had gone out for an unusually quiet evening for them, to a gourmet meal at a new Italian restaurant, then on to a film, and afterwards, they had come here for a peaceful stroll in the dark. As they moved between the willows, and Nick realized that no one else was near, an exciting idea struck him—to make love, right there, right then, underneath the whispering branches. And they had. He remembered the tension at first, the desperate, frantic pace they set, for fear of being discovered. And he remembered how things slowed down, how the longer they lay there, the more relaxed they became, and turned from haste to a lazy, exquisitely drawn-out love-making, full of passion and need and romance. They had held each other afterwards for a long time, two who had spent centuries being torn away from each other and had come back to each other again and again, two who belonged together always, no matter what.

Eventually they left the park, and found their car, and headed home. And they never reached it.

Nick stayed on the bench for a long time, looking at the row of willow trees. He had never been loved so strongly, or so fiercely. All of that passion had been destroyed in the twinkling of an eye. All of it had been forgotten, at least by one of them. Until now.

Oh, God. He closed his eyes. *I loved him. I really did love him.* It wasn't fair. Why the hell couldn't he have remembered earlier, why had he run away before finding out the truth?

The hurt didn't go away, not when he finally opened his eyes, nor when he rose to walk out of the park, and not when he headed for the narrow alley Marlen had marked for him not so very long ago.

He stopped at a newsagent's on the way to pick up a paper with yesterday's stock quotes. Then he found the alley and the door to mage headquarters exactly where Marlen had said it would be. Nick knocked once, and only once, and waited.

Chapter Fourteen

"You're only going ten kilometers over the speed limit," Marlen said. "I don't suppose you could drive any slower?"

"You're slipping," Isabel replied. "Last time you complained, there was at least twice as much sarcasm in your tone."

"Sorry. I'll work on it." Marlen didn't see why his bad mood should annoy her unduly anyway. What did she expect, a cheerful passenger? Hardly likely after this morning's revelation. Bad enough to find out your best friend had betrayed you, without adding on the discovery that he had never been truthful from the very beginning. And to make matters even more cheering, his perfidious, lying, treacherous best friend and former lover had also turned out to be potentially immortal. Five hundred years of friendship, and it had to end like this?

"It's not fair," he muttered.

"What," Isabel said, "life in general, or your particular part in it?"

"Everything." Might as well be angry at the whole world as well as himself. Especially since the world didn't make much sense right now. "I've been minding my own business and not bothering anyone for five centuries. So why has everything suddenly gone so sour?"

"I hate to break it to you," Isabel replied, "but trouble rarely starts all by itself."

"Thanks for the reminder." As if he needed it. One small mistake. Weren't most people allowed a few errors in judgment from time to time? It really hadn't been such a horribly wrong desire, had it? To want the one person in the world you cared anything about to stay alive? Okay, so maybe he had gone about it in a naive and foolhardy fashion, but he hadn't honestly thought of it that way at the time. The best of intentions, of course, could be punished as easily as the worst. One unhappy result would have been sufficient, though. Having accidentally sprung Vere, that would have been enough to get across the message that the status quo didn't wish to be disturbed. He could have lived with that screw-up, with just one reminder not to go messing about with things he didn't understand.

But no, he had to learn his lesson in triplicate. Not just a revenge-crazed mage on the loose, no, he had to have the rest of the mages ready to put him in limbo, and he had to go and lose Nick as well. *What next?* he wondered.

"It could be worse," Isabel said, as if reading his mind.

"How?" He didn't really want to know.

"We could have Ed and Georgina behind us."

True. He wondered where Georgina had got herself off to. Ed had been at the dock, waiting for them when they drove off the ferry. Well, more or less waiting, since he hadn't seemed terribly alert, caught in mid-yawn as they drove past his car. Despite his subsequent rapid attempt to follow, it had taken no time at all in the Jag to leave him in the dust. There had been no sign of him the rest of the day.

"I can handle Ed," Marlen replied. "If and when he ever turns up. It's Georgina I'm worried about."

"So am I," Isabel said. "She's an odd one, all right. Wonder where she's gone?"

"Wherever it is," Marlen replied, "you can bet it's right in the thick of things."

Nick was only partly surprised to find Georgina waiting for him inside mage HQ. She was, after all, the only mage he'd met so far who appeared to have any sense.

When the alley door opened, he had been greeted by a short, squat gentleman. Nick had given him the

closing quote for Arthur Lance Realities. The fellow said
nothing, but lead him down a dark, narrow set of steps
and through a winding series of corridors. The labyrin-
thine headquarters made him wish for a piece of chalk or
a very long string. They passed by dozens of closed doors,
with nothing to indicate what lay beyond them. At times
he swore they traveled the same corridor twice. A rather
dreary place, all in all, or so he thought until the fellow
showed him through an unmarked door just like all the
other unmarked doors.

Inside stood a large, high-ceilinged suite of white-walled
rooms and bright chandeliers decorated in the most lavish
style, with tapestries, statuary, and frescoed floors that
could have come from an Italian Renaissance villa. And
probably had, come to think of it. In the center of the
main room stood a marble fountain, complete with stone
dolphins spouting water. Grecian urns held bouquets of
roses, somehow fresh way down here. Velvet-cushioned
benches stood scattered about the rooms, while solid gold
trays decked with fruit and cheese perched on mahogany
side tables. Somewhere, a hidden music system piped in
Mozart.

He found Georgina sitting primly on a Louis XIV chair,
reading *Sense and Sensibility*. She set the volume aside and
waved him onto a nearby Elizabethan settee. He tried very
hard not to stare at the stuffed peacock behind her.

Georgina smiled. "A bit ostentatious, isn't it?"

"Yes," Nick replied.

"The mages have been collecting treasures from the
great houses of Europe for as long as there have been great
houses. It seems to make them happy. You see, what we
really are, is nothing more than a society of very well off,
long-lived people with a few magical abilities who don't
have much purpose. Because we are immortal, we decided
ages ago that it simply wouldn't do to spend eternity in
rags and hovels. So much nicer to spend one's time sur-
rounded by pleasant things, catered to by servants, able
to travel on a whim, and generally indulging in lavishness
whenever possible. Greedy and selfish, don't you think?"

"Oh, I don't know." Nick stopped staring at the peacock and focused on the DaVinci instead. "If I were rich, I don't suppose I'd spend my life in a hovel, either. But I thought you had a purpose. Aren't you all working as stockbrokers?"

Georgina pulled a golden rope. "Tea?"

"Thank you."

"Yes," she said. "We do dabble in portfolio investments for wealthy clients, but none of us works terribly hard at it. We don't put in ten-hour days. Heavens, we rarely put in six-hour days. The only reason we do it is to continue rationalizing our existence. The sole point to helping the rich and powerful was, from the very beginning, simply to get the rich and powerful to reward us in very rich ways. Magic itself doesn't produce a hefty bank account or a house in Belgravia. But magic worked in the proper fashion, used, for example, to confuse a king's enemies at the proper moment and thus keep the king in power, can lead to piles of gold from a grateful client. Or, say, a little spell here and a little spell there which makes the populace believe that blue velvet cloaks are *de rigueur* for the winter season, and the wealthy trader in blue velvet stays wealthy, and passes some of his gains onto his trusty mage. Thus we ensured that our years on this earth would be lived in ease. Nowadays, we are all filthy rich from centuries of amassing such payments. We don't *need* to work at all. But without something to justify ourselves, we feel a tad, well, pointless. So we continue doing what we have always done. We make rich people happy." She paused as a servant arrived with a silver tea trolley. "Two lumps for me, please. Nick?"

"Oh, um, just a drop of milk, thanks."

The servant passed him the teacup, and offered a tray of cucumber sandwiches. He took one.

"You may leave that." Georgina waved the fellow away. "Now, then, where was I?"

"Making rich people happy," Nick said, biting into his sandwich. It was delicious.

"Yes. Sad, isn't it?"

Nick had no idea how to respond to this observation. He shrugged and sipped his tea.

"I'm fairly new to this mage business myself," she went on. "I find it all a bit silly, really. There are more serious things one can find to do with one's time. All that's required is a bit of imagination, some basic intelligence, and a passion for trying new things. I suppose the older mages must have ventured into other arenas from time to time, but perhaps are jaded by now. I shouldn't blame them for being boring old sticks. Still, that's what they are. Now, I'm not saying that one shouldn't put in one's time, and I would be the last person to condone shirking one's duty. Your friend Marlen, for example, is a prize layabout. He should at least make an effort at being a stockbroker, if for no other reason than to find out what it is he's been rebelling against all these years. But that's not the worst of his crimes. Not only does he fail at being a proper mage, which in my opinion is not such a disgrace these days, but he fails at being anything else. Indolent, I believe I called him once. While I do consider the current mage philosophy of life and work to be somewhat less than inspirational, I do *not* consider general laziness to be a viable alternative. That young man really needs to find something to *do*. A sense of purpose, that's what makes life worth living. Where is he, anyway?"

Nick, still reeling from her opinionated deluge, took a moment to recover. "Oh, he's around."

"I see. And why are you here? Did you secure the ring?"

"Yes." He finished off the tiny sandwich and reached for another. "I wanted to leave it here for safekeeping. And I want the other mages to know that Marlen is perfectly harmless, and didn't mean to cause any trouble." He frowned. "Just how did you get back here from Scotland?"

"Chartered plane, of course. I highly recommend them."

"And where's Ed?"

"Still in Scotland, I suppose." She picked up the teapot. "Another cup?"

"Yes, please. But why did you come back?"

"That," she replied, "is none of your business. Let me see the ring."

He dutifully handed the small silver band over, glad to be rid of it once and for all. "You'll keep it here?"

"Naturally." She smiled. "We couldn't allow it to fall into the wrong hands now, could we?"

Somehow, she suddenly reminded Nick of Uncle Brian. He had no idea why, it was simply something about her demeanor. Maybe she and Brian were related somewhere along the line. Anything was possible. "What will you do about Vere?" he asked.

"Nothing. Duncan has gone out to deal with her. I'm sure he's capable of handling things. What, may I ask, are your future plans?"

To drown my sorrows in the nearest fifth of whiskey, he thought. Aloud, he said, "I think I'll go out there and look around."

"Ah. And have you any weapons?"

Nick fingered the Browning he'd taken from the drone in Dunvegan Castle. "I have a gun."

"I see. A pity you haven't any magical weapons."

Nick frowned. "I thought only mages could use those."

"Most of them, yes. But there might be something." Georgina took a small velvet bag from a pocket and poked about inside. "Let's see what we've got. Hm. Boundary chalk... no, that won't do. Talking amulet... not unless you're a mage, quite wrong. Aha. These should work, I've already prepared them." She pulled out two small glassy green spheres and handed them over.

"What are they?" Nick fingered them gently. They looked rather like marbles, a bit larger, though surprisingly light-weight.

"Those are confusion balls," Georgina said. "I have imbued them with the proper spell, so all you need to do is toss them to the ground when needed. They break on impact, releasing a cacophony of lights and sounds meant to disorient. Doesn't last long, though enough to distract an opponent. Try to throw them as far from yourself as possible."

Nick carefully pocketed the spheres. "Thank you."

"You're most welcome. Now then, how were you planning to get to Cornwall? It's a long drive."

"Please don't tell me you have magic carpets."

"Certainly not." Georgina raised a faintly affronted eyebrow. "But might I suggest the Chambers Chartered Flight Service? I find them most reliable."

Nick drank his tea. "Thanks." He started to rise, then paused. "Aren't you supposed to put some sort of spell on me, to make sure I don't remember how I found this place?"

For the first time he could recall, Nick heard Georgina laugh, and it was rather a pleasing sound. "No, that won't be necessary," she said. "Why, were you planning to inform the BBC? I think that would be quite delightful, actually. Might liven this place up a bit for once."

He hated to disappoint her. "Sorry, no. Just thought, well, you know, you'd want to keep it a secret."

"Oh, don't worry," she replied. "No one would believe it in a million years. I mean, would you?"

Nick shook his head sadly. "I rather wish I hadn't." Then he walked away, finding the trusty doorkeeper waiting to lead him out again.

The first thing Marlen did on arriving at mage HQ, after pausing to wave at Georgina, was to head straight to the very well stocked bar. He grabbed a fifth of whiskey and a glass of ice then laid back to relax on an eighteenth-century chaise lounge.

Georgina's presence annoyed him but didn't especially surprise him. He and Isabel had done a seeking spell on the ring when they hit London, and had traced it here. This fact confused him to no end, since it seemed like the last place Nick would have taken it. But perhaps the bastard had somehow been waylaid by Georgina. Served him right.

He poured out his drink. Isabel had gone over to have a quiet chat with Georgina, which he wasn't able to hear. No doubt discussing his many inadequacies as a mage. After a few minutes Isabel departed without so much as a parting glance.

"Hello, there," Georgina said. "Are you sure you ought to be indulging?"

Marlen downed half the drink. "Why not?"

"Because it might be wiser of you to stay sober, so that you can go out to Cornwall to help your friend Nick."

"He's not my friend," Marlen replied.

"No? Then I wonder why he brought the ring here?"

Marlen downed the other half of his drink. This made no sense at all. "Why did he do that?"

She shrugged. "He said he wanted it to be kept safe, and he also asked me to tell the mages that you had intended no harm."

More confused than ever, Marlen sat up straight. He wanted to see her eye to eye. "You're not making that up, are you?"

"Why ever should I?"

"I don't know." He poured himself another drink, but this time sipped at it slowly. "What else did he say?"

"Nothing much. Only that he was going out to Cornwall."

"When was this?"

"Oh, about half an hour ago. I believe he is taking advantage of a chartered plane service. Why, with luck, he could be there in another hour or so. We should probably all go out to have a look, don't you think?"

Marlen shook his head. Whatever that lying bastard was up to, he wanted no part of it. First he betrayed him, and then he turned around and did precisely what Marlen wanted him to do. What kind of insanity had possessed Nick?

"No," he said. "I'm staying right here. I've had enough." Getting thoroughly sloshed seemed like the only truly sensible approach to life at the moment.

"Well, I think you're being rather selfish. You started this whole debacle. Shouldn't you see it through to the finish?"

Marlen eyed the bottle of whiskey. "The only finish I'm interested in is the end of this bottle. And then I want to go into limbo for a few hundred years."

Georgina actually looked startled, a feat he had never imagined possible. "You want what? *Why?*"

"I want to give up," he replied. "Is that so hard to understand? Selfish? Yeah, it's selfish. Wanting to be happy is selfish." He drank more heavily. "I know you happen to believe that I'm a lazy, good-for-nothing fool, but what you *don't* know is that I've spent my five hundred good-for-nothing years trying to do the one thing I thought had any meaning in this world. I tried to love someone. Maybe that's not enough in your book, maybe it doesn't score any points with the Immortal ruddy Society of Mages, maybe it means I'm a complete and total failure. Fine. Think whatever the hell you like. I was happy. From time to time, whenever he remembered and whenever we were together, we were content. So I tried to make it last forever, and I failed. He doesn't want anything to do with me, and he's not going to want anything to do with me for the rest of bloody time. Did you know Nick's a mage? He has the signature. You didn't know that, did you?"

She gave a slight shake of her head. "No, I didn't."

Marlen finished off his second glass and poured another. "Well, it's true. That's what I wanted, for him to stop dying on me. I'll bet you're one of those people who appreciate irony, aren't you?"

"Marlen—"

"Oh, it's terribly ironic." He lay back on the lounge, cradling the glass to his chest. "Be careful what you wish for. Isn't that the classic warning? You'd think someone who had been around as long as I have would pay attention to things like that. Stupid. You know what I think? I think it's a crime to grant individuals immortality while leaving their mortal desires intact. It hurts, dammit. Don't any of you bloody well understand that?"

"Marlen, please—"

"Oh, go to hell." He sank further into the lounge.

A few moments later, he heard Georgina padding across the floor, and looked over to see her at the bar. "What are you doing?"

"I am fixing myself a drink," she replied calmly.

Marlen sat up. "Why?"

"Because I believe I have misjudged you slightly, and because I believe you need some company, and it is rather tedious to remain sober while one's companion is getting tipsy."

"You're going to get tipsy with me?" The notion nearly shocked him into not drinking any more at all.

"Yes." She pulled a Moroccan leather recliner towards the chaise lounge and sank into it, drink in hand. "You don't mind, do you?"

He found himself shaking his head.

"Good. Now, let's have a nice, tipsy chat. About you, and about Nick, and about a little-known organization called the PIS."

Marlen blinked. How the hell did she know about that? "Okay," he said, deciding it was time to go back to sipping slowly instead of chugging. "Let's do that."

Ed Kelly had been abandoned by Georgina in Scotland on a bitterly cold morning. Before that, he had been left alone in a freezing cold cave in Wales. Why? Because Duncan deemed it so. Why did they all jump to his commands? Because he was "Duncan the great mage who devised the Spells of Protection"? "Duncan the defender of humankind who defeated Vere"? Fine. But what had he done *lately*?

Ed had driven all the way from Scotland pondering his next move. Duty said he should report back to mage headquarters. He should tell the Inner Council that the ring had been snatched from Isabel. He should find Duncan, and let him order him off to another absurdly uncomfortable or dangerous assignment. Yes, that's what he *ought* to do.

Halfway between Scotland and London, his motor's heater broke down. An hour later the front tire blew out. Eventually, many hours later, cold, hungry, and broke from repair shop bills, Kelly arrived in London. He drove directly to his flat, packed a bag, and made a brief call to his travel agent.

Majorca sounded nice this time of year.

CHAPTER FIFTEEN

The climb to the castle had taken most of the day. Vere had set up nearly every ward and trap in the book across the path, plus a few clever variations that came close to fooling even Duncan. Detecting them and performing the necessary rituals and incantations to destroy them had been exhausting. She had obviously done a seeking on him and knew he was on his way, for the wards had progressively strengthened throughout his arduous progress.

Now, as late afternoon sun bathed the Mount in soft hazy light, Duncan had at last made it to the outskirts of the castle proper. He squatted behind a row of thick, prickly bushes near the castle wall after making a quick reconnaissance of the building. He'd found a small door near the rear marked GIFT SHOP EXIT that looked most promising as a point of entry, since its top half was glass. He rummaged through his leather bag of magical objects. Defensive magic, such as ward removal, was all well and good, but what he wanted most was a little offense to go with it.

Mages didn't have a great many weapons, having spent the centuries working together to create and then nudge along rich and powerful mortals, rather than engage in any tedious internecine warfare. Occasionally one of their own became unruly, but on the whole, they had proven to be a peaceful lot. Still, a few magical weapons never hurt, and over the years they had invented a few useful items.

He pulled out a stick of boundary chalk. If you managed to draw say, a square or a circle on the floor without your opponent noticing, and then got them to step inside of it, all of their own magic would abruptly prove useless. Of course, all they had to do was step out again, but the second it took to realize the error and rectify it might be all one needed to gain the upper hand.

Duncan had a defensive stick of protection chalk as well. This was for drawing circles to step inside of yourself, as no magic could then enter the area. The major disadvantage being that you were stuck there. This item worked best if you got into trouble but had a cohort or two somewhere nearby to come to the rescue.

If you wished to make an enemy think you were somewhere else, you used a displacement spell, which made your image appear a few feet from where you really were while momentarily hiding your real form. If you wanted to make your opponent's head feel as if it were on fire, you tried a simple enflamement spell.

One of his favorite devices was the enclosed weather spell. While no mage had the power to affect the general weather pattern, it was entirely possible to cause a very small area, particularly indoors, to suddenly experience rainfall or hail. It tended to distract people, and he had found it handy on a few past occasions.

He had his usual oeuvre of spells and powders and amulets as well, plus a few confusion balls. His plan of attack should be kept simple, forceful. Go in, find Vere, have a confusion ball and displacement spell ready to let fly, and before she managed to gather her wits, grab her and tie her up. A gag would prevent her from chanting any spells. Then he could lock her up somewhere. Surely a castle of any means would have a dungeon or cell about. It would take at least four mages working together to place Vere back in limbo, but she should keep until he could gather reinforcements from London.

Duncan put the chalk back in the small bag.

Time to get this over with, once and for all.

Brian felt grateful for the trees on St. Michael's Mount. The boulders proved useful as well, as did the twists in the path itself, all helping to hide him whenever

Duncan stopped to deal with another magical obstacle, which happened frequently. Must be an awful lot of those ward things about.

At the final turn of the path prior to reaching the castle, he settled down behind a rock for a rest. He wanted to give Duncan plenty of time to make whatever entry plans he had, and to get far ahead of him. Running into Duncan at an inopportune moment was not appealing.

From his coat, he pulled out the castle tour map he'd purchased in Marazion upon arrival. There were several entrances, though tourist entries were kept to the main entryway and a gift shop at the rear. He doubted Duncan would attack through the main door, so that might be a good candidate for his own entry. If he timed things right, Vere would be distracted by Duncan long enough for him to get inside and do a little recon.

Brian took a brief glance ahead, where the main entrance stood. No sign of Duncan. He'd give it a few more minutes just in case, then in he'd go. He spent a short time memorizing the building layout, patted his Walther PPK for good luck, and then he took off for the castle.

Duncan padded cautiously up the stairs from the gift shop towards the main floor of the castle. He tensed at each step, expecting every magical trick in the book to be thrown his way at any moment.

He had entered by the simple expedient of breaking one of the gift shop windows. He'd found souvenir maps inside and was now heading for the living chambers normally used by the family-in-residence. It seemed the most likely spot to find his quarry.

I must be vigilant, on constant guard. He held his confusion ball in one hand, ready to toss, and he had some smoking fog powder in the other. He reached the landing and took a careful look down a long corridor. According to the map, the dining hall stood off to the right about midway along. From there they could pass through another hallway to the master bedroom. He cautiously entered the corridor, waiting and watching for some form of magical attack.

What would she try? Malodorous potions? Freezing spells? Hiding spells? False images? Fake noises?

He inched his way down to the dining hall door. It was dead quiet inside. Somewhere beyond, Vere waited. Had she lined the dining room with chalk circles? He carefully scanned the floor. Nothing. Perhaps she was about to spring a small rainstorm on them. He sniffed the air, since magical storms were always preceded by an acrid smell. Nothing. He moved a bit further into the room, smiling confidently. It didn't really matter what she tried. Every possible spell and form of attack was known to him, every piece of magic she could attempt would be entirely familiar, for he had practiced them all hundreds, no, thousands of times, and there was nothing, outside of a few minor variations, which could surprise him, and even the variations were easy to deal with once he figured them out. Vere was a fool to take him on in a battle of magic. All her spells could be anticipated, and all of her attacks could be thwarted with the tools and skills he had honed over the centuries. It was simply no contest. No doubt she had hidden somewhere because she knew this, or perhaps she had already accepted her inevitable defeat and had fled the castle.

I can take her. He was ready to counter anything Vere chose to toss his way. *What am I skulking about for? She's no match for me.*

He took two more steps forward and found himself face-to-face with the muzzle of a gun.

"Looking for me?"

Vere stepped out from behind a doorway, holding the weapon steady. "Don't say one word, or make even the hint of a motion, or your face will be instantly unrecognizable."

Duncan froze. *Think.* She could shoot him, and it wouldn't kill him, but it would take days for him to recover. He'd be completely at her mercy. Of all the forms of attack he'd been expecting, the one he had failed to consider was non-magical human technology. How had she learned about modern weaponry so quickly? *Unfair.*

"It's been a long time," Vere said. "Have you missed me? Do feel free to respond, so long as you utter no chants."

"Give it up," he snarled. "The rest of the mages are on their way out here. You're outnumbered."

"I don't believe that," she replied. "Or you would have all come here at the same time." She smiled. "How do you like my little toy? Don't you think the automatic pistol is a marvelous invention?"

"Charming. And rather pathetic, that this is the only way you can try to win."

"Ah, Duncan." She shook her head. "Are you trying to appeal to my sense of fair play? I know naught of fair play. I know only how to get what I want."

"Fine. What do you want?"

"Oh, so many things. Though I must say, I am impressed at how much power human women have acquired since I left the world. Not nearly what they *ought* to have, of course. They ought to rule over the men entirely, as they are obviously more sensible."

"Funny, how that hasn't happened," Duncan sneered. "You always did claim women to be the wiser, yet they've never found a way to control men."

"Or male mages," she replied. "To my eternal regret."

"Oh, please. How I detest a whiner. Contrary to mortals, female mages have had equality with males for quite a few centuries. Much to *my* eternal regret."

"Not on the vaunted Inner Council, not where the true power lies. Not in my time."

"Well, they have it there now."

"They do not! And they *will* not until a *woman* leads them all."

"How utterly tiresome. I begin to see the form of your vengeance. You mean to talk me to death."

"Not at all," she replied calmly. "What I'm going to do now is render you unconscious, tie you up and gag you, and dump you in the cellar until I decide on the final method of your complete destruction."

"Oh, honestly. Can't we simply discuss this absurd situation like adults?"

"No, we cannot."

Duncan was afraid to ask how she planned to knock him out. She would regret it, though, whatever it was.

He viewed this little fiasco as a minor setback, albeit an embarrassing one. She was bluffing; she couldn't possibly destroy him. His anti-fire protection spell stood firmly in place, so only an explosive device could result in total obliteration. She might have learned about guns, but surely she couldn't have mastered the use of more deadly force, or gotten her hands on major weapons.

Duncan frowned. Or could she?

"Ron," Vere said to someone in the room behind her, "it's time for you to assist me."

A young man wearing a tour guide uniform came through the doorway, armed with a nightstick.

Duncan groaned.

Brian heard footsteps as he explored the ground floor's main corridor. He darted inside the nearest room, leaving the door ajar. The steps echoed closer off the stone floor. He cautiously peered through the door crack, frozen in place.

A young man wearing a tour guide uniform half-dragged, half-carried an unconscious, bound and gagged Duncan Phipps along the floor, followed by a woman in a long red dress. *Vere.* She'd captured the head of the mages. Brian stifled a sigh. This couldn't be good. The PIS brief was to observe, not to interfere. Unless the safety of a human was at stake. Was that the case now? Or did Vere merely seek revenge against Duncan, and Duncan alone?

Brian watched silently as the three moved past, until they turned a corner. He checked the castle map. The dungeon lay in that direction. Looked as if Duncan would be out of the picture for some time, but he probably wasn't in any immediate danger. So what did Vere have planned?

He scanned the corridor, then opened the door and slid along the wall in the direction from which Vere had come. He looked into each hallway and room he passed as quickly as possible, always on alert. When he found the dining hall, and took in its contents, he realized how badly everyone had underestimated Vere's ability to recover from limbo. Multiple television sets, a computer, and teetering stacks of books, magazines, newspapers. She had wasted no time in joining the contemporary world.

Brian didn't want to stay in any one room for long, anticipating Vere's return. He moved on, and not far away from the dining hall he stumbled across a more disturbing room. The castle's armory had been turned into what looked like a magical workroom, with strange symbols drawn on the walls and on top of a long narrow table, with dozens of candles, censers, stones and jewels taking up every available surface. A huge, tattered book lay open to reveal pages of ancient writing.

Perhaps the goblet was in here, and the stone. But before he could search, Brian heard a voice. He dashed to the door. He couldn't see anyone, but he could hear her coming. *Hide.* He darted into a small room next to the armory and ducked behind a large crate. Footsteps came close, but then faded off, possibly into the armory workroom. Brian let out a sigh of relief.

And then he noticed the lettering on the wooden crate. CAUTION: EXPLOSIVES.

He pried open the lid. Dynamite. A lot of dynamite. So much for observation only. Whatever Vere wanted to do with this lot, it couldn't be good, and now he'd have to find out how to stop her. Alone.

Brian patted his gun again then leaned back against the cool stonewall to have a nice long think.

The chartered plane service dropped Nick off at the town of Marazion in the early evening. He headed immediately down to the beach for a look at the island. The tide was out, so the causeway leading across stood bare. He wasn't particularly impressed by the sight across the way, a clumpy mound with a dull-looking block of stone on top which apparently qualified as a castle. What impressed him was the sky beyond, where dark, massive clouds roiled and tumbled. A storm heading in. It seemed appropriate. Cataclysmic forces might very well join in battle tonight, on land as well as in the air.

He hoped he survived the fray.

Nick walked over to the fence stretched across the start of the causeway, and slid through the gaping hole. Obviously he hadn't been the first person to try this route recently.

He hiked across to the island proper, quickly surveyed the empty village, and then headed up the path to the castle.

The narrow, rocky route took him a while to navigate. He felt out of shape. And cold. The evening air grew chillier as he climbed, and he had worn only a light jacket. The wind picked up, blowing tree branches into his face. He could smell rain coming, too. And off in the far distance, he heard a faint roll of thunder.

He came round the final turn to find a brightly lit castle, both inside and out. Vere must be running up one enormous electric bill. As he approached, Nick took out the Browning. He just hoped he didn't need to use it.

He scouted round the building, and found a broken window in the rear. The castle gift shop. He climbed through. Inside, he found a map of the place. Now, where would everyone be hanging out? Well, it was dinnertime. Might there not be someone in the dining hall?

Nick slowly made his way upstairs and down a long corridor. He peeked cautiously into each room he passed, mostly bedrooms, seeing no one. Then down the stairs at the other end, where a turn led him to a new corridor and more rooms. When he heard footsteps, he ducked inside the nearest room, but not before catching sight of a man heading his way. He'd been seen.

He shut the door, breathing hard. Now what? He glanced round the tiny room, seeing only a large wooden crate. Even if he hid behind it, the man would quickly find him. But he moved to crouch behind the crate anyway, and jumped back when he found someone else there. "Brian!"

"Nick!" He stood up.

The door swung inward. A young man wearing a uniform stood there, staring blankly at them. Brian raised his gun.

"No!" Nick gestured at him to lower it. "He's human. He's one of her drones, he's under a spell."

"You are not tour guides," the young man said.

"I think Vere's right next door," Brian whispered fiercely. "She'll hear him!"

"He won't do anything to us without being ordered to. Come on, maybe we can just slide past him." Nick moved to the doorway and gently pushed the puzzled-looking

young man aside, but as soon as he stepped into the hallway he froze. He was standing face to face with Vere, who
was speaking words he couldn't understand. Nick tried to
move, but couldn't. He looked down. A chalk circle had
been hastily drawn just outside the doorway, and he had
stepped directly into it.

"Nick, are you all right?" Brian shoved past the tour
guide, and wound up standing still beside Nick, trapped
inside the same circle.

"I'm fine," Nick said. "Now what do we do?"

Vere smiled as she finished her chanting. "Whatever I
tell you to do, of course."

Nick shrugged. A mage telling him what to do again.
"You know," he replied with resignation, "someday I'm
going to learn to stay away from you people."

Just not any time soon.

Vere instructed Ron to tie them securely to dining room
chairs while she fetched an amulet from her workroom.
Curious, to have mortals wandering about the island. Were
they working for Duncan? They couldn't have gotten all
the way to the castle unless they'd followed after him,
after he'd broken all her wards. So at least she knew they
hadn't been here very long, and hopefully, hadn't had a
chance to cause any damage.

When she returned to the dining hall, she sent Ron off
and pulled up a chair to sit across from her hostages. Ron
had already taken away their weapons and their identification, which she'd looked at without comprehension. Same
last name, but no indication of what they did or who they
worked for. She decided to question the older man first,
as he seemed to be in charge.

Vere held her talking amulet in front of his eyes, and
spun it while chanting a simple spell. The amulet was a
useful device for getting mortals to tell you whatever you
wanted to know, as they couldn't possibly lie while under
its influence. She only wished it worked on mages as well,
but alas, this was not the case.

But she didn't really want to question Duncan anyway.
Safer to keep his mouth firmly gagged. Besides, what could

he tell her, other than that he wanted to put her back into limbo? And that was not about to happen.

No, it should be much more entertaining to question this new fellow instead. What would mortals want with her? More important, how had they even found out about her existence?

Vere finished her spell and snapped her fingers. She had directed it only at the older man, and he stared at her with a glazed expression. "Good afternoon, Mr. Watson. Might I call you Brian? Yes, I think I might. First, I would like to thank you so much for not tampering with my dynamite. I have some plans for that. Now, then, what were you doing wandering about the castle?"

"Curiosity," he replied.

"I see. How did you get here?"

"Followed Duncan."

She might have guessed. It really was a pity the mages had allowed that deceitful, power-hungry fool to become head of the Society. "And why were you following Duncan? Have you been spying on him?"

"Yes."

"How long?"

"Years," Brian replied.

His companion, the young man called Nicholas, started. "*What*?"

Even more interesting. "My dear," Vere addressed him, "are you related to this gentleman?"

"He's my uncle." He glared at him.

Vere got the impression the uncle had been keeping secrets from the young man, and she had a fairly good feeling that Duncan didn't have a clue about any of this. She turned back to Brian. "Why were you spying on Duncan?"

"Been keeping an eye on the mages."

"That's all? You don't have some scheme for destroying us?"

Brian shook his head. "Studying. Observing. Not destroying."

"Well, how kind of you. Some people would take a dim view of mages running loose, mucking about with the world's finances. I'm glad your organization is sensible enough to leave us to our business. So you came out here solely from curiosity. Because you are studying us. Is that right?"

"That's true, ma'am."

She always appreciated good manners. "Well, in that case, I'm terribly sorry I had to tie you up. But these things are necessary precautions for me, I'm afraid. I have enemies, you see. Or rather, one enemy. Duncan. Did you know that he put me into limbo seven hundred years ago?"

"Yes, ma'am."

That surprised her. "Oh, and who told you that?"

"Nick did."

"And who is Nick?"

"My nephew. Nicholas John Watson."

Ah. Of course. She hadn't recognized the use of a nick-name. "I see. And who do you work for?"

"Don't tell her!" Nick cried.

"Oh, I'm sorry, my dear boy, but he can't help but respond. It's *magic*."

"We work for Domestic Intelligence Six, Paranormal Investigation Services unit."

"Both of you?"

"Yes."

"How did Nick know about me?"

"Marlen told him."

"Brian!" That was the young man again.

Vere sighed. "Really, you must cease interrupting. I could put you under the same spell, and you'd tell me exactly the same things, so it makes no nevermind if he does. Do please try to keep quiet. Now then, Brian, that would be the mage to whom I'm so indebted, yes? Marlen O'Neill?"

"Yes, that's him."

Ah. Things became clearer to her now. Her drones told her of Marlen, the one who'd freed her from limbo, the mage from whom they'd retrieved her grimoire. She owed him a great deal. "Your nephew here and Marlen are friends, then?"

He nodded.

"Not anymore," Nick muttered. "Sorry, didn't mean to interrupt."

"That's all right, dear. Do you know where Marlen is?"

"No," said Brian.

"I don't know, either," Nick said. "We had a disagreement."

"Pity. Well, never mind." She could always do a seeking spell or two. It was about time she checked up on the ring's whereabouts as well. The drone she had sent to Scotland was long overdue. "Tell me," she said to Brian, "was Nick here also spying on the mages? Was he spying on his friend Marlen?"

"Yes."

Clearer and clearer. Poor Marlen. She had a bit of a soft spot for the young mage. She hoped they had a chance to meet someday. She favored Nick with a disapproving glare.

Nick glared right back. "I'm *trying* to fix things."

"Are you? How? By coming here to interfere with my little project?"

"I don't even know what your little project is. I wanted to help Marlen somehow. The other mages, especially Duncan, aren't too happy with him for freeing you."

"Of course they're not. But that's because they don't know the real me, thanks to Duncan's lying ways. So let me guess. You thought you'd come flying in here, capture the evil mage with your gun, and all would be well again. Interesting. And only one thing wrong with it."

"Really?" Nick looked disdainful. "And what would that be?"

"Simple. You failed to chase after the right mage."

The first time Vere set eyes on Duncan, she thought, What a handsome visage. *She had traveled over a hundred miles for this meeting, a long and arduous journey in those days. Her hopes made it worth the effort.*

Yes, she found this head of all the mages to be a handsome man.

Then he opened his mouth.

"You have come here to seek admission to the Inner Council. I granted this audience knowing only your name and nothing more of you until your arrival yesterday. Is this request meant to amuse us?"

"I see no reason for amusement. The requirements have been met."

Duncan waved a dismissive hand. "Yes, yes. You are at least two hundred years of age. You have mastered the Book of Higher Spellcasting. You have authored a grimoire and created ten spells of use to the community of mages. One requirement, however, you have failed to meet."

"Of what do you speak, my lord?" She gritted her teeth, suspecting what was to come.

She was right. Duncan slowly looked her up and down, his gaze lingering far too long on her breasts. "You are clearly not male."

"I have read nothing in the Council rules stating such a requirement."

"Is that so? Your knowledge is not current. I seem to have read precisely that rule only this morning."

"You have altered them!" Why, the deceit of this man— he had seen her for the first time on her arrival yesterday, seen that "Vere" was a woman, and had the rules changed.

Duncan shrugged. "Expediency is a virtue. But you would not know of these things, as females are generally incapable of making quick and effective decisions."

Bastards, *every damnable one.* "*I have devised better spells for rapid healing. I have refined the spells of seeking, and I have greater knowledge of the Book of Higher Spellcasting than all of your precious Council members combined. More than that, I have great designs in mind for magical work which could forever change our world for the better. The sole reason you refuse me entry is that you fear my abilities!*"

"Hardly. I have a few abilities of my own, dear girl. One of my many talents is command. And as the Head of All the Mages of England, I command you to keep your place."

"I will do no such thing. I will find another way to thwart your power. I will continue my work."

Duncan merely smiled. "Do as you please. I shall be keeping watch."

To her sorrow, he did much more than that.

Vere looked sadly at her two hostages. Men. They behaved like headstrong fools, as had most of the males she had ever known.

The one called Nick stared at her, mouth agape. "What do you mean, we chased the wrong mage?"

"My words should be easy to understand. The evil mage is safely tucked away in the castle dungeon. Would you like to know why? Of course you would. All in good time, my dears. First, though, I'm curious to know where my ring has got to, and I am wondering if perhaps either of you could enlighten me."

"I'm not saying a word," Nick said.

"So unhelpful." Vere turned to Brian. "What about you, Mr. Watson? In all this spying on us, did you happen to hear anything about the three objects of power, perhaps from Marlen? Did you hear about the ring in Scotland?"

"I heard about it," Brian replied mechanically.

"And what did you do when you heard about it?"

"I asked Nicholas to retrieve it for me and bring it to London."

"Ah." She cocked her head at Nick. "And did you do that?"

The stubborn young man merely furrowed his eyebrows. Honestly. When would mortals ever learn?

Vere held up her talking amulet. "Would you like to tell me what happened under the spell, or do you prefer to keep your mind to yourself?"

Nick fidgeted, frowned, looked at his companion's glazed expression, and then let out a huge sigh. "Fine. I'll tell you of my own free will. I got the ring, and I took it to London."

"Where, exactly, in London? To this intelligence outfit?"

"No." Nick frowned, looked at Brian again, and lowered his eyes. "I took it to the mage's society."

How oddly this young man behaved. "And why ever did you do that?"

"To help Marlen."

"I thought you said you and he had a disagreement."

"We did. It's a long story. I'm sure you wouldn't be interested, and besides, you can't get the ring now anyway, so what does it matter?"

"Oh, it matters, my dear." They had no idea how much it mattered. Perhaps it was time to tell them exactly why she needed the ring, and why they needed to help her get it here. She considered herself to be a reasonable person, and these two seemed relatively reasonable as well, if a bit misguided. Once they knew the truth of the situation, they would choose to join her. Any sensible person would.

Vere snapped her fingers and spoke one word. Brian's eyes refocused as the spell dissipated.

He flushed immediately. "How dare you force me to answer like that!"

She cleared her throat. "Excuse me, but *you* are the one who broke into my home. Even if it isn't really mine."

Brian squirmed against the ropes that bound his arms. "What are you going to do to us?"

"Well," she replied, "if you promise to behave yourself and not try anything foolish, then I am going to untie you." The two fools didn't honestly seem threatening. Besides, she had taken their guns away, and she still had her drones. "Next, I am going to offer you some supper. Do you like roast beef?"

Brian raised an eyebrow. "But I thought, I mean, that is, oh bother." He looked at Nick. "Didn't Marlen tell you that Vere was a power-mad, highly dangerous mage who was out to annihilate all mankind?"

Vere's kind feelings towards Marlen altered slightly. "Oh, honestly. Well, I have news for you."

"And what news is that?" Nick asked.

"Simple." She reached round to undo the ropes. "He was wrong."

"So you're a spy, too," Marlen said. "I'll be damned."

He felt very good. He had absolutely no reason to feel good, but the whiskey had made his brain stop worrying about life, death, limbo, and treachery, and instead, he now thought mainly about truffles. Georgina had ordered the servant to bring out a box of very fine, very dark chocolate truffles, and he found them quite addictive.

"Yes," Georgina replied. "I've been working for the PIS for some years. Nick's uncle runs it, you know."

"Does he? Sly bastard." He bit into a truffle. "These are excellent."

"Aren't they?"

"Um." Marlen savored the creamy chocolate. Some pleasures in life were so simple. "So you're a spy," he repeated, wondering if had mentioned that already. His mind felt ever so slightly foggy. "And you've been spying on your own kind. Us. Your fellow mages."

"Yes. I have."

"Why?"

"Well," Georgina said with a cheerfulness he wasn't entirely used to, "because it's my duty. Brian explained to me that England needed to know about the Society. And as I am a devout patriot, it seemed the right course to take. You see, I firmly believe that England is the greatest country on the face of the earth. Nothing must ever threaten her. We must all do our duty to protect her from harm. Brian has a terribly important mission. He has been charged with making certain that no misfortune should ever befall our beloved country by the use of paranormal means. And that, of course, includes the use of magic. Now, so far, the Society has never directly posed a threat to the stability and power of England, but you never know. I am convinced that someone like Duncan needs watching, and Brian convinced me that *I* was the one to do it."

Marlen managed to process about one word in three. "So you're a spy," he said.

Georgina reached over to take his glass of whiskey away. "I think you've had enough of that for one evening."

"And Nick's a spy, and whatshisname the uncle is a spy, and how come I'm not a spy?" He licked a few dabs of chocolate off his fingertips. "Can I play, too?"

"If you want."

"Oh, good." Now, what should he do for his first mission? Who could he spy on? Georgina? Isabel? Maybe Ed. He wondered where Ed had got to.

"Now, about the ring," Georgina said. "I've been thinking about what to do with it. And I think the mages don't really need it, do you? No, of course they don't. All it does is cause endless trouble. So why don't we just hand it over to the PIS? Brian has been hounding me for a magical object for years, but they don't let you create them until you are at least a hundred years old, which I am not, and they keep the ones that have already been created carefully guarded. But now I've finally got one for him. I'll just tell Isabel and the others that it's been safely tucked away, and they need never know exactly where. And they'll all believe your story, and won't think any the worse of you for making a mess of things. Yes, I think that's a perfectly excellent plan. Right? Right." She clapped her hands. "So, the only question left now is what to do about Vere."

"And Nick," Marlen muttered. "What should we do about Nick? Can I spy on him? It's only fair."

"Yes, dear, you can spy on him as long as you like. Wonderful idea."

"Thanks." About time someone turned the tables on that sneaky bastard. Marlen reached for another truffle. Life felt pretty good. Who needed to worry when you had friends like Georgina around? Nice young woman, Georgina. And she had such good taste in food.

The servant walked in carrying a telephone.

"For me?" Georgina asked.

"Yes, ma'am."

"Who is it?"

"A party named Vere," he replied.

She had gotten the number from Brian, who, having been spying on the mages for some time, had naturally tapped their phone line ages ago.

"Good evening," she said to Georgina. "My new friends Nick and Brian tell me you have something of mine. I'd like to get it back. It's small, it's circular, and it's silver. I understand there's an excellent charter plane service with which you are acquainted."

There was a significant pause on the other end of the line. Then Georgina said, "Might I have a word with Brian?"

"Certainly." She held the receiver out to him.

"Georgina?"

"Yes. What in heaven's name is going on?"

"Just do as she says, please."

"Why? Is she holding you both hostage?"

"Of course not," Brian said. "It's really perfectly all right. We've been wrong about Vere from the start. It's *Duncan* who's the evil one."

There was another long pause. "And where is Duncan?"

"Safely locked up. Trust me, Georgina. Bring the ring here and everything will work out just fine."

Vere took the phone back. "There, you heard him. Well?"

A new voice came on the line, a male voice.

"You're holding them hostage, aren't you?" he demanded.

"Oh, hell." Her temper flared. "Yes, fine, all right, I'm holding them hostage. Bring the damn ring here immediately, or I'll toss them both off the Mount. It's a long ways down. Is this Marlen? You can come, too. I've been dying to meet you. You have precisely three hours." She rang off.

"Was that necessary?" Brian asked.

Vere shrugged. "What's necessary is whatever works. And I'm sure it worked."

"He's not my friend," Marlen said, his teeth chattering.

He and Georgina stood on a runway in the dark and the cold, waiting for the Chambers Chartered Flight Service to haul a plane from its hangar. He felt a good deal more sober than he had back at HQ, and wished he didn't.

Georgina reached into her carpetbag and produced a thermos. "Here. It's coffee."

Marlen gratefully accepted. "I don't see why I have to go out there."

"Because Nick is out there, of course."

"He's not my friend," Marlen repeated. The coffee managed to warm him up enough so that his teeth stopped chattering.

"Yes, well, I know that when he stole the ring in Scotland it must have been very shocking, but he wouldn't have brought it to the mages if he hadn't had a change of heart. And he was only trying to follow his duty to his uncle. Think how hard it must have been for Nick, a fine, upstanding young man with a devotion to public service who was given a certain task to perform, and who then became fond of the person he had to harm in order to fulfill his civic duty."

"He hates me," Marlen replied.

Georgina sighed. "I'm sure that's not true."

"Well, he can't stand to be around me," he amended.

"What you need to do," she said, "is go to him and have a nice, long, heart-to-heart. Things will work out. They always do."

Marlen laughed. "Only for people like you."

A rumbling engine sound interrupted her response. "Oh, good, the plane's ready."

He handed her the thermos, and when she reached for it, he noticed the small silver band on her hand. "Why are wearing the ring?"

She looked at her finger. "I'm not. The ring is tucked away in my bag. That's a college graduation present from my brother Ned. Nice, isn't it?"

"It looks just like Vere's ring," he said. He peered more closely. "Except for the Latin inscription. What does it say?"

"Old family motto," she shouted over noise. "'To believe in one's dreams is to spend all one's life asleep.'" She headed off towards the plane.

Marlen thought about it for a moment, and then he followed.

Duncan woke with a throbbing headache.

He was also stiff, sore, cold, and hungry. His wrists and ankles were bound with rope and a tight gag kept him from doing more than muttering.

A tiny window no more than eight inches square sat high in a wall of the brick-lined room. A thick wooden door was the only other thing to look at. Furniture wouldn't have been terribly useful in any case, since he was too neatly bound to sit or lie comfortably on anything.

As he contemplated his situation, a *boom* sounded nearby. Was Vere testing out those few dynamite sticks? A few seconds later a flash of light lit the tiny window, followed by a larger boom. Not dynamite. Thunder. They were having another storm.

The next thunderclap rattled a piece of plaster from the ceiling, which narrowly missed his head. Great. Just what he needed.

The next one, bigger and closer, loosened a brick from the ancient wall. It crashed to the floor, breaking apart near his feet.

A few clumsy maneuvers later, Duncan was busy rubbing the ropes binding his hands across the brick's jagged edge.

"You believe her story," Nick said. They sat at the dining table, a pot of tea and a plate of biscuits between them. Vere had gone off to her workshop, which she had sent up in the castle armory, to "tend to things". She obviously didn't trust them entirely, having left Mark at the door with Brian's gun in hand.

"Yes," Brian replied. "For some time now, I've had reason to suspect that Duncan was not a very forthright fellow. We will therefore do whatever we can to assist Vere in fighting him."

"You knew about them all along." Nick felt slightly ill; he felt used. "All this time, you knew about the mages. When I first told you about Marlen, and you told me to find out more about him and the others, you gave no clue that you'd ever heard about them." Anger flooded through him. "But you knew all along! You even knew the phone number of mage headquarters!"

Brian calmly poured out a cup of tea. "We've been tapping their line for some time."

"How long?" Nick couldn't believe his uncle would cover up the truth like this. "How long have you been watching them?"

Brian calmly added sugar to his tea. "Nearly thirty years."

Nick's mouth hung open. *"Thirty years?"* Bloody hell. It wasn't fair. The whole thing was entirely, utterly, and completely unfair. "Goddammit, why didn't you let me in on it?"

Brian rose to pace about the room, teacup in hand. "The PIS is a valuable organization. Lower echelon agents do a good job of investigating peculiar claims, and their work is not unappreciated. Top agents, however—those with an

"A" rating—work on a different mission. They keep tabs on members of the Immortal Society of Mages. This was the purpose for which I founded the organization all those years ago." He paused to look at Nick. "Do stop allowing your mouth to hang open."

Nick did so, only to open it again in question. "But why keep it such a secret?"

"A matter of trust. The PIS was founded with the knowledge and support of the government. The top ministers are aware of the true nature of our work. They're aware, as I have been aware, that the ISM is real, and its members' powers are genuine. Part of my agreement with Her Majesty's government is that this knowledge be restricted to as few people as possible. That's one reason we embedded the PIS within the Domestic Intelligence Six service, where we can hide within its bureaucracy. Only those PIS agents with the highest clearance can be allowed to know. Have you considered what might happen if the public were to find out there were real immortals in their midst?"

"Well, they'd be fascinated, for one thing."

"And?"

Nick thought about it. "They'd be curious—"

"And?"

"And, well, I suppose they'd be envious."

"Precisely. How long would it be before we had millions of people demanding that they be given immortality? And we wouldn't be able to."

"No? Is there research going on, though? There must be."

Brian nodded. "A select, and of course, highly secret team has been studying the medical aspects, without much progress. That's how the PIS began. That's why I was able to convince the top levels of government to fund us. I had medical records, as well as blood and tissue samples, from a mage." He paused. "From Marlen."

Nick couldn't help but let his jaw drop again. "How—or should I say, when—did you manage that?"

"Nearly thirty years ago I was in college here in London, working on a graduate degree in biology. I shared a flat with a medical student. One day he came bursting in from a long stint at the hospital casualty ward; he'd been working nearly twenty hours. He acted very odd, and didn't want to talk at first. But he couldn't hold it in, and finally told me about a strange case they had. A young man had been brought in late the night before, a car crash victim. His injuries should have been fatal. No one expected him to survive the surgery, but he did, and then, in the course of a mere twelve hours, his condition went from grave to satisfactory. Many of his more severe injuries seemed to be healing at an impossible rate. They had isolated the fellow and ordered the staff to keep quiet. Well, naturally, I was curious. I'd been working on a thesis project at the time, studying platelet action, and I couldn't resist going over there. I dressed in my lab coat and managed to sneak into his room. Got the samples and tried to ask questions, but he wasn't exactly cooperative. The next day he gave them the slip and disappeared. My flatmate told me that before he left, Marlen found the lab and destroyed the samples the hospital had taken. But he didn't know about mine. Shortly after, following my own preliminary research and a lot of talking to people in high places, the PIS was born. Marlen helped provide the proof I needed to convince the right people."

"Poor fellow." Nick smiled. "He always ends up causing trouble for the mages. The Society doesn't know about the PIS?"

"Some of them seem to know of its existence, but no more than what most people who've heard of it know. That we check out odd events and claims. They don't, as far as I'm aware, know that we've been spying on them."

"And that's all you've been doing? Keeping a watch on their activities?"

"Our missions are to watch them, to make sure they don't do any harm, and to attempt to gather information about their magic and its methods. So far, the ISM has been fairly innocuous. They don't do a whole lot, other than play with the stock market. This business though, with Vere and these objects, this is something major."

Nick wondered what else Brian would keep from him until he deemed the time right. Now that he knew he was capable of duplicity, how could he trust him? "You know," he said, having calmed down a bit from his previous anger, and more curious than anything else, "I'm surprised *more* people don't know about the mages. I mean, Marlen's not good at keeping secrets. He told me easily enough."

"The Society has a strict Code," Brian replied. "The first rule is never to reveal their nature to a mortal. But I understand Marlen's not keen on obeying rules."

"No. I think he's broken more than a few."

"He's not in a position of power, though." Brian returned to the table. "So I suppose he's less of a risk to them. The Inner Council is where the real power lies."

"How much have you found out about this Council?"

"Not a lot. I realized some time ago that while the Society may appear innocuous, that could easily be a front. Most, if not all, secret societies keep the 'real' agenda hidden, even from their own members." He smiled. "Like the PIS. So, it seemed quite possible that the Immortal Society of Mages had a more sinister purpose, known only to the Inner Council members. The only way to find out would be to plant someone on the inside."

"An infiltrator? How could you manage that?"

"I had to find a mage, someone in the lower ranks on their way up. Someone with a strong moral sense, a belief in the status quo, and a commitment to patriotism. Someone who I could entrust with the knowledge of the PIS's mission, and who would agree to act on our behalf. It wasn't easy, but I succeeded."

"Georgina Pruitt."

"Of course."

Nick nodded. Thus his recent orders to her over the phone, to bring the ring here. He wondered if Marlen would really come along with her. And he wondered what Marlen would say when he found out the truth about Vere and Duncan.

But what he most wanted to know was what to say to Marlen when they met again. Nothing he could think of seemed anywhere near to being adequate.

He reached for the teapot to pour himself a cup. He took a deep breath and let it out slowly. "I disobeyed your orders. About the ring."

"Yes." Brian refilled his own cup. "It's not a good sign, of course, but on the other hand, you haven't had the benefit of PIS training. Loyalty to an organization depends to a great extent on one's familiarity and experience within that organization, don't you think?"

Nick swallowed. "You'd let me stay on, then?"

"If you wished to. On probation, naturally."

"Naturally." He didn't know if that was what he wanted anymore, but then, he still had a lot of unanswered questions about a great many things. "If you don't mind, though, I need some time to sort my life out first. So I'd like to take a bit of a holiday after this is over." He paused. "Provided we survive." He glanced at the drone guarding the door.

"Don't worry," Brian replied. "As long as Duncan is locked away, we are perfectly safe."

He passed the biscuit tray.

It took Duncan over an hour to fray the rope enough to loosen it. Then he worked it off his wrists, which were scraped raw from encountering the brick edge. They would heal quickly, the same way his headache and other ills had vanished. He tore off the gag, undid the ropes around his ankles, and then went to work on a spell to unlock the door.

The storm still thundered overhead; rain had started pouring down. Duncan hoped this would help mask the sound of his passage through the castle. He wanted to move quickly, and act efficiently, before anyone knew he was loose.

Finishing her task in the armory had not taken long. Properly placing the fuse wire into the detonator caps really hadn't been that difficult at all, once Vere had located the proper online manual. Amazing invention, the Internet.

She cut the wire lengths fairly long, and tied the ends together for easy lighting. One good pass with that other handy invention, the cigarette lighter, should set most of them burning at once. And then it would simply be a question of time before the whole crate went up, creating a satisfying hole in the castle.

Her primary plan was to finish her spell. The ring would be arriving any minute now, according to the flight plan Georgina had relayed. Vere had placed the dynamite in a small garrison room next door to the armory. She left it and went down to the armory room itself, where she set up her work area. She found it had a certain inspiring atmosphere. Crossbows, swords, and muskets decorated the walls, and a suit of armor stood guard near the door. On the large oak table in the center of the room she had placed the stone and the goblet within a geometric diagram drawn in red chalk. Nearby lay her grimoire. The power of the unfinished spell already created a soft golden glow about the table; soon, with the addition of the ring, that power would be magnified, and hers to control.

Should her magical plan against Duncan fail, however, she had what the modern terminology called a contingency plan. She liked the phrase. Her contingency plan consisted of making certain that Duncan, should he fail to be affected by her spell, would be tied down beside the crate when she lit the fuses.

While she, of course, would quickly go elsewhere. Even if her spell did work, she wanted to set the dynamite off anyway, simply because a large hole in the castle would make her very happy. The place had been an adequate locale for her during the recovery from limbo, but she had spent seven hundred years entombed beneath it, and if she had to spend another night there, she was certain she would go quite mad.

Fierce wind shook the windows of the armory. Vere crossed to look out at the raging thunderstorm. She loved storms, the nastier, the better. She hoped it raged all night long.

Marlen slowly uncurled himself from the fetal position he had adopted when the plane hit the storm. "Are we down?" he asked, not surprised to find his voice a timid squeak.

"We've been down for five minutes," Georgina replied.

He didn't believe her. Everything felt shaky still, particularly his brain. "Are you *sure*?"

"I am more than sure, I am positive. Now please make an effort to leave the plane."

He wanted very much to leave the plane, but only if the world would stop spinning, heaving, rolling and tumbling. "Where are we?"

"Marazion, of course," Georgina replied. "Where did you think we would be?"

At the bottom of the English Channel, he thought. "You're positive we're on solid ground?"

Georgina did something he never believed she would do, though admittedly, her behavior of late had been a tad surprising. She grabbed him by both arms and hurled him towards the doorway. "Out!"

"Yes, ma'am," Marlen said meekly. He climbed unsteadily down, landing thankfully on solid, unmoving earth. Huge drops of rain immediately pummeled his head.

Georgina emerged, unfurling a large umbrella. She gave him a sour look. "Honestly, when *are* you lot going to learn to carry the proper equipment for life in Britain?"

Then she strode off towards the lights of the town.

"You're not going to just hand the ring over, are you?" Marlen asked as they approached the castle entrance. "You've got a clever plan, haven't you?" He hoped her plans involved going somewhere warm and dry very soon, as the storm had soaked him through to the skin.

Georgina, nice and dry beneath her umbrella, said, "I'm going to hand it over. That's what Brian told me to do, and I am not planning to shirk my duty."

"But he was under duress!" Marlen refused to believe she had fallen for Vere's trap. "She's holding them hostage, she threatened him into saying that. We've got to find a way to capture her."

They reached the main door. "Capture her?" Georgina cast him a disdainful look. "You're terrified of Vere. You haven't got enough courage to capture a slug."

"Watch it," he said. "You're sounding like Nick."

She tried the door. It swung open. "I'm sure Brian knows what he's doing. Come along."

"No." He followed her as far as the entry way, glad to be out of the rain. "You're only going to get caught and held hostage by her, too. We'll split up. That way, at least one of us will stay free for a while. Namely, me."

Georgina shook out her umbrella. "From where did you obtain this sense of daring?"

"Recklessness," he replied. "Not daring. I don't really care what happens to me now, you see." *Odd feeling*, he thought, *being free*. Free of his little five-hundred-year-old obsession. Being with Nick had always provided some sort of purpose in life. But now... well, now he simply no longer cared about anything much at all. Except staying warm and dry.

""Don't you want to help Nick?"

"No. I"ve moved on." He didn't need Nick anymore.

"After all this time?"

Marlen wearily nodded. "Everything changes. All relationships end some day." He seemed to remember saying that long ago. "Now, you go off wherever you want, and I'll go wherever *I* want."

"I can hardly stop you," Georgina said. "Your recklessness, however, is what landed us in this situation in the first place. Whatever you do, at least *try* not to make things worse. Please? I was beginning to like you, and I should hate to have to revise my opinion."

Marlen hadn't made up his mind yet whether Georgina's approval of him was a good thing or a bad thing. "I'll do my best."

"Perhaps this will help." She reached inside her handbag and pulled out a pistol. "You do know how to use one?"

He nodded. "It's been a while, but I know the basics." He took the gun. "There's one more thing I'd like to have. Your family ring."

Georgina smiled. "Yes, I rather thought it might come in handy." She pulled it off her finger and gave it to him. "If it should come to be lost somehow, as I expect it might, I will want you to pay for a replacement."

"Naturally."

"Good luck, then," she said.

She headed off along the corridor to the right of the entryway, while he headed off to the left.

Duncan took off in search of Vere, but when he reached the ground floor corridor, he found someone else instead.

Marlen stood in the middle of the corridor, pointing a gun at him.

Duncan smiled warmly at him. "There you are, after all this silly chasing about. Do please put that away."

His former pupil stood his ground, warily staring at him. "You're not going to put me in limbo, are you?"

"Don't be foolish. We're all here for the same purpose, I've come to realize. We want to stop Vere, isn't that right?"

Marlen slowly nodded. "I didn't mean any harm."

"Of course you didn't. But we can't stop here chatting about old times, my lad. We need to find her, and quickly."

The gun arm lowered. "Nick is here, too, with his uncle."

"Is that your old friend, then? The one who was with you in Wales?"

"Yes. Vere captured them. That's why we—" He paused. "Why I came."

"How noble of you." Thank goodness Marlen still thought Vere was evil. He could use the young fool to surprise her, and then his usefulness would be over, and he could rid the world of Marlen O'Neill once and for all.

"Come along," Duncan said. "And do give me that weapon. I'm a much better shot than you are."

Marlen frowned briefly, but then handed the gun over. "I just want this to be over."

"Of course." Duncan led the way, scouting the rooms. Marlen would make a nice distraction, exactly what he needed. She wouldn't be expecting trouble, wouldn't know he'd been freed from the dungeon cell. All he needed were a few brief seconds to get the upper hand.

Not much farther along, they found the armory workroom. Duncan peered inside. There she stood by a long table, the goblet and stone in its center, concentrating on a spell. Not so good. If she were already focused on magic, it would take her no more than a split-second to change her chant to a spell that could trap him once more. As soon as she saw him, she'd attack him. Better to have her thrown out of the magical state she was in, disrupt her concentration. Then he could take control before she regained her momentum.

Duncan waved at Marlen to go inside. "Do anything, say anything," he whispered. "Just break her out of spell-casting."

"Right." Marlen stepped into the workroom.

Duncan watched, dumbfounded, as Marlen pulled a ring from his jacket pocket. *The ring*?

"I've brought what you asked for," Marlen said.

Vere blinked, stopped chanting, and stared at him. "Oh, hello there. You must be Marlen O'Neill."

Duncan recovered, shoved past Marlen into the workroom, catching her utterly unprepared. He aimed the gun directly at her chest. "Not a sound, not a movement. You see I, too, can resort to non-magical means."

She opened her mouth, but stopped when he moved in, getting a better draw on her.

"*Not* one word," he repeated. He glanced at the table top, at the geometric pattern she had drawn around the objects. "Ah. Working on your little spell?" He shook his head. "Didn't learn your lesson last time, I see. Pity. Perhaps putting you back into limbo won't be advisable. Perhaps we can work out a more permanent solution. Marlen, find some rope, will you?"

As Marlen obediently turned to trot off, Vere did the unexpected again. She dived beneath the table.

"Come out of there!" Duncan dropped to his hands and knees. His view was partially blocked by chair legs, but he saw her scurrying towards the far end, shouting a spell as she went. He fired randomly. Bullets splintered wood. "Marlen! Do something!"

Duncan scrambled to his feet and saw Marlen working a weather spell. Useless, as usual. Duncan dashed to the other end of the table from Vere, as fat drops of rain spattered down inside the room. Vere abruptly stood up close by him. Duncan fired. Nothing happened. *Damn*. She had used a displacement spell. Where had the real Vere gone? He ducked down, searching through the chair legs.

Her laugh echoed through the room. Duncan leapt up again. Hailstones clattered on the table, wrecking the pattern she'd drawn. Blast. Marlen's storm would delay the magical working. And now Marlen himself was nowhere in sight. Had the coward fled? And for that matter, where was Vere? She had vanished completely. A hiding spell, perhaps. Time, he decided, to stop relying on non-magical means. He quickly chanted a displacement spell of his own, then reached in his bag for his boundary chalk.

He carefully drew a circle and stepped inside. None of her magic could harm him now. It would give him some time to think about his next attack. His displaced figure stood a good ten feet away.

Vere suddenly popped back into view near the doorway. She had grabbed a crossbow from the wall, and she aimed it at the figure Duncan had conjured up. He smiled. *Won't do you any good.*

Vere fired. The arrow flew harmlessly through the apparition, hitting the wall with a resounding *thunk*. "Hell." Vere turned to flee the room.

Oh, no. Loose in the castle, she could do anything.

But then she froze in place. She had stepped inside a circle drawn on the floor. Marlen walked back into the room, smiling, holding a piece of chalk.

Duncan abandoned his own circle before she could step out again. He aimed the gun directly at her face. "One more word, one move, and we'll all find out how long it takes a mage to recover from a gaping head wound."

She glowered back, but kept silent and still.

"That rope, please, Marlen."

Marlen hurried off. When he returned, he tied Vere up while Duncan kept the gun on her then placed a gag over her mouth.

"Not as hard as I thought it would be," Marlen said.

"No, it went rather well, considering." Duncan turned the gun on him. "And now it's your turn. But first, hand me that ring, won't you? There's a good lad."

He smiled at the stricken expression on Marlen's face.

Marlen wondered why things had gone so wrong.

He sat bound and gagged in a small room next to the armory, his only company being an equally bound Vere and an open crate filled with dynamite. After he had finished helping Duncan to tie Vere up, he had been completely surprised to find Duncan training the gun on him as well. He knew Duncan didn't like him, but this was a tad extreme.

A few feet away, Vere scowled ferociously at him.

Marlen sighed. He wished, not for the first time, that he knew what was happening, and whose side he was supposed to be on.

And where was Georgina, and why hadn't she come to rescue him yet?

Duncan checked the grimoire again, even though he had already checked it a dozen times. Yes, there, in Vere's neat handwriting, were the notes on the spell, with brand new additions in the margins. After cleaning up the mess from the hail and retracing the pattern, he had followed the spell all quite accurately.

He rechecked the objects. There they were on the table, set in their proper places on the pattern, from which a soft yellow glow arose. Everything was as it was supposed to be.

So why hadn't the spell worked?

According to the grimoire, as he chanted the spell, the glow should change, encompassing each object in a circle of white light. This light would enter the already magically charged stone, goblet, and ring, pick up their power, enhance and be enhanced by it, and then surge upwards, forming a ball of energy above each object which would merge into one ball, and then this new power would rush directly into him.

All he had to do then was place his hands on any mage, chant a few special words, and his victim would be thoroughly and permanently stripped of immortality and magical powers.

To think that Vere had originally intended to use it on *him*. Well, she would get her comeuppance. He wanted desperately to use it on her now, as well as that worthless Marlen. But he couldn't get it to work.

Duncan carefully studied the three objects as he tried the initial portion of the incantation again. A white light formed around the stone. A white light formed around the goblet.

Nothing at all formed around the ring.

He picked it up. If it were truly a magically empowered object, then it would have its own signature. And there were a few things he could do to test that out, provided he had the right powders to use.

Duncan set about searching Vere's work room.

"She's been gone too long," Brian observed.

"I noticed that. And Marlen and Georgina should have been here by now." Nick knew something had gone wrong. He just didn't know what. But then, if Marlen had come to rescue them, any number of things could have gone wrong. "What if Marlen thinks Vere is still the enemy? She didn't exactly tell him otherwise."

"True enough. Do you think he's gone and done something stupid?"

"I don't know what to think anymore!" Nick crossed to the window to stare out at the storm. "The plane could have had trouble landing. The causeway could have been too dangerous to cross from the waves. Duncan could have escaped, he could be hiding somewhere, waiting for his chance."

"We'll go to the armory, then." Brian stood. "That's where she said she was going."

Nick turned round. "What about that drone at the door? We haven't any weapons."

"There are two of us and only one of him."

"True, but he has a gun and a single-minded devotion to duty."

Brian sighed. "A pity we don't know how to use magic. I've been studying the mages for decades, and Georgina has given me excellent information on their abilities, yet it does no good if you're a mere mortal."

"Wait." Nick remembered what Georgina had told him back in London. "There are a few things you don't have to be a mage to use." He patted his jacket pocket. Yes, the confusion balls were still there. He pulled one out. "Georgina gave me these. She already prepared them. All I should need to do is toss one on the ground and stand back."

"And what does it do?"

"Sets off a cacophony of noise and lights."

"Good enough. You circle round to the right, I'll go left. I'll try to draw him away from the door. As soon as you have a good shot, let fly, and we'll dive through the doorway behind him."

They quickly moved into position. Brian began waving his arms and shouting madly. The drone turned towards him, taking a few steps into the room. As soon as he saw a clear path through the doorway for both of them, Nick tossed a confusion ball at the drone's feet. He dived for the threshold.

A blaze of colored lights went off, followed by a raucous bombast of random noise. Nick struggled not to look back, covered his ears, and ran.

"*Shhh!*" Nick held his fingers to his lips.

He and Brian had succeeded in escaping the drone. Nick didn't worry that the drone would come after them, as his instructions from Vere were to guard them in the dining room, and he knew that drones took their orders quite literally. If there were no longer people to guard in the dining room, the drone would wait there until new orders came.

They now stood inside the small room beside the armory, and they knew that Duncan was right next door, having caught a glimpse of his back as they snuck past. He'd got free after all.

And the sight inside the small room was even more enlightening. Vere and Marlen sat there, tied and gagged.

Marlen's first reaction on seeing them was to squirm violently and make muffled noises. Nick hushed him again and then removed the gag.

"It wasn't my fault," Marlen whispered.

Brian removed Vere's gag.

"Where is that bastard Duncan?" Vere demanded.

"Right next door," Brian whispered. "So everybody keep their voices down, okay?"

Marlen squirmed again. "Could you bother untying me, please? And would you also bother telling me what's going on?"

"Sorry." Nick set about prying loose the ropes. "You see, Vere never created a spell to destroy mortals. That was all a lie, which Duncan talked the other mages into believing."

"Why?"

"Because he's a megalomaniac," Vere put in. "Always has been. His power urge was far greater than any other mage I've ever known. He tried to stop my experiments into immortality. The ones designed to bring that gift to all humans. He saw it as a direct threat to his own power. He saw *me* as a threat to his own power because I was smarter and more talented than him. So he concocted that entire tale about the mortals trying to burn me as a witch. Never happened. He set the fire that burned my house down himself. And then used it, along with a faked grimoire purporting to contain my anti-mortal spell, to convince the Council that *I* was the real danger."

Marlen rubbed his freed wrists. "You could be lying."

"I could," she replied. "But tell me, you're the one who stole my real grimoire, aren't you? And you read through it, didn't you? Was there anything in it that looked like a spell against mortals?"

"Good point," Marlen said. "No, there wasn't."

"You might have mentioned that earlier, you know," Nick put in.

"Sorry." Marlen turned back to Vere. "There *is* a major spell in that grimoire, though, involving the three objects. If it's not an anti-mortal spell, that what is it?"

"An anti-Duncan spell," she replied. "Well, I suppose one *could* use it against any mage, but I never intended to, only against him. After he burned my house, I was furious. I'd managed to escape the fire, with my grimoire, but I knew I had very little time before he tried again to destroy me. As far as I was concerned, he didn't deserve to continue being a mage. I would have gone to the Council, but a friend warned me that he had their ear, and was spreading vicious lies about me and my work. So I empowered the three objects instead, and set about perfecting my grandest spell. What it does, when properly worked, is to strip a mage of all his powers." She paused. "Including immortality."

Nick's eyes widened. "And he's in there now, with the objects? My God, he could use it against *you*."

But he didn't look at Vere when he said this, he looked at Marlen. And Marlen pointedly turned away.

Nick swallowed. He tried to focus on the dangers at hand, not on the aching of his heart.

"I'm certain he intends to use it against me," Vere replied.

"It won't work," Marlen said. "He hasn't got the real ring."

"You gave it to him," Vere accused.

"Wrong ring. Georgina's got the real one. I left her by the castle entrance."

"It won't take him long to figure that out," Vere said. "I suggest it's time to depart. Too dangerous here. Let me do one thing first, though." She closed her eyes in concentration, spoke some names, each followed by a brief chant. "There, that should do it."

"You freed your drones," Marlen said.

"With one final command to leave the castle at once. There's no reason to endanger mortals." She favored him with a scornful look. "There never has been."

"What about immortals?" Nick asked. "Why don't we light this dynamite on our way out?"

Vere smiled. "That would definitely take care of Duncan. Shall I stay behind to light it?"

"No. I'll do it." Nick looked round for something to do the job with.

"That's dangerous," Marlen protested.

Nick didn't really care at this point. All he wanted to do was to end this business. "I'm surprised you care." He immediately wished he hadn't said it. They hadn't had a chance to talk about the betrayal, although it was a fairly good bet that Marlen would hate him for what he had done. Or at the very least, be upset enough to not want anything more to do with him.

"I hate to interrupt," Brian said, "but whatever we do, we had better do it *now*." He dug into his jacket pockets, and produced a box of matches. "Here, this should help." He handed them to Nick then tugged at Marlen's sleeve. "Come on, let's move. Quickly, and quietly."

"But—"

"Don't protest." Nick studied the crate. "I know how to handle this stuff, I've been trained in it. You haven't. Now get going."

Marlen gave Nick a long, steady look. "I want to know why you did it," he said. "And I want to know why you changed your mind after."

Nick tried his best to smile. "I'll tell you later." He gave Marlen a gentle push towards the door. "Go on, I want you all to get a nice head start before I light this."

Marlen looked briefly back at him, and then took off down the corridor with the others.

Duncan cursed.

Marlen had given him a dud ring. So much for the loyalty of his pupil. Admittedly, he'd been pointing a gun at him up at the time, but still, it hadn't been a very nice thing to do.

Had he brought the real one along at all? Time to go threaten him, he supposed. He picked up the gun and headed for the garrison room.

He didn't get far. Just outside the armory, he heard a noise from the garrison room next door. He rushed inside, in time to catch Nick lighting a match.

Duncan hurled Nick away from the fuses. "Oh, no, you don't!" He turned the gun on him. "Blow that out."

Nick blew out the match.

"Very good." Duncan moved behind Nick, shoving the gun barrel hard into the small of his back. "Where are the others?"

"They've left the castle, safely out of your reach."

"Pity. It only drags out the inevitable." He turned at the sound of footsteps. He guided Nick into the corridor. To his immense irritation, Duncan saw Georgina Pruitt prowling along.

"What are you doing here?"

She turned, took in the scene, and slowly approached. "My dear Duncan, whatever are you doing to that nice young man?"

Duncan turned enough to show her the gun. "I'm holding him hostage. You will go find Vere and the others. Tell Vere to bring the ring here—the *real* ring. Otherwise, rather unpleasant things will happen to young Nick."

"Why should Vere care what happens to me?" Nick asked.

"You have a very good point," Duncan replied, reluctantly realizing that Vere would willingly sacrifice Nick if it meant thwarting his plans. That was all right, he could deal with her later. "Marlen cares about you a great deal, though, doesn't he?" He called out to Georgina. "Tell Marlen to bring it. Alone." Once he had performed the spell and used it on Marlen as a test, then he could easily track down the others one by one. "What are you waiting for?"

Georgina crossed her arms. "You never did have good manners." Then she took off down the hallway.

Georgina found them all back in the castle entryway, where she explained Duncan's demand. "I found it a rather ironic situation that Duncan never knew I had the real ring on me the whole time. How I detest that man."

"We cannot give it to him," Vere replied.

Marlen ignored her and held out his hand to Georgina. "Give it to me. I don't care what he does to me." After all the trouble he'd put Nick through, he could at least perform this one last favor. "Please."

"But he'll use the spell against you," Georgina replied.

"Doesn't matter." Nothing really mattered except to put some kind of ending to all this madness. Marlen smiled. "I'll try to think of something to stop him, honest. Maybe I'll manage to trip over my own feet at just the right moment."

Georgina smiled back. She reached into her carpetbag and pulled out the ring. "Good luck." She handed it over.

"Fools," Vere muttered.

Marlen headed back towards the armory.

What could he do to put a stop to this madness? Nick had no idea. *There must be something, some trick, some weapon—the walls were covered with them. If only he could reach one somehow.*

"Stop looking around the room like that," Duncan said.

They had moved back into the armory. Duncan stood on one side of the table, Nick on the other, and Duncan held the gun steady, aimed at his chest. Between them, on the tabletop, sat the stone and the goblet, on a complex geometrical pattern. A soft yellow glow rose from the pattern, flickering towards the objects.

"You have great power," Nick asked in a last-ditch effort to distract him. "Why use it to destroy?"

"I use it to control."

"You don't need to strip Marlen of his powers to control him." *All you have to do is make him trust you.*

"Nonetheless, the very threat of this spell will ensure no one ever questions my rule again. It won't be a threat unless its effectiveness is proven. Now be quiet."

Nick heard someone coming down the corridor. Marlen. Of course he would come. But he shouldn't come, not when Duncan was planning to destroy him. Marlen loved life more than anything, he was terrified of oblivion. Nick couldn't let him do this.

He glanced at the wall behind him, at the antique saber hanging there. Even if he could grab it, would he be able to do any good before Duncan got off an enchantment? Nick looked wildly round the room for something, anything to stop the mage.

"I told you to stop that. Put your hands in your pockets, where they won't get up to any tricks."

Nick reluctantly obeyed. The footsteps grew louder. *No. Stay away!* he thought. Then he felt something round and hard inside his pocket.

The second confusion ball. If it had worked on the drone, would it work on Duncan? He tried very hard not to make any suspicious movement of any sort, not to make any noise of any kind. Could he simply toss the sphere to the ground now? Or was he too close, would it affect him too strongly as well?

He waited, deciding to hold off until the right moment. Maybe he could somehow slip it to Marlen. A lot depended on Duncan's plans.

Marlen walked into the armory.

"Stop there," Duncan said. "And don't make any unnecessary gestures, or try chanting any spells. I can't really miss at this range." He kept the gun aimed at Nick's chest.

"I've got the ring," Marlen replied.

No. Nick didn't want him to do it. *Not for me. I'm not worth it.* He ached to do something, anything, but was at an utter loss for ideas.

"Walk slowly to the table, and drop it there."

Marlen did so.

"Now, stand on the other side, but keep at least five feet away from your friend."

Marlen moved over to the same side as Nick, close, but not close enough to try passing him the sphere.

Duncan carefully reached over to pick up the ring then set it on the pattern. "Don't even consider trying to overpower me. You'd have to climb over or around the table to reach me, and I'm sure I can get two shots off before you do. And I don't need both hands to work the spell, either. So just stand there, and keep quiet."

Nick fingered the sphere again. Perhaps if he tossed it onto the pattern. But he would need to wait until Duncan was focused on the spell. Until precisely the right moment.

Duncan propped the grimoire up on a chair, and began chanting the spell within.

The yellow glow encompassed the ring. As Duncan chanted, the light changed to a bright white, encircling all three objects. Slowly the brilliance grew, and Nick could see the light moving into the objects and out again, growing brighter with each passage. Suddenly the circles of light joined together, then changed to a fiery orange, then red.

Duncan chanted more fiercely. The glowing red light formed three balls of flame above the three objects. And then the balls merged into one giant globe.

Nick felt mesmerized by the sight, unable to think, let alone act. The blazing red fire was unlike anything he had ever seen before, hypnotic, powerful, primal.

And then Duncan reached his free hand into the flame, and it surged towards him, into him, dying down over the pattern even as Duncan drew all that power into himself.

And then he started around the table towards Marlen.

No! Something snapped within Nick, the fascination was broken. *Not Marlen.* He took the sphere from his pocket and dashed it onto the tabletop.

The confusion ball broke apart. Duncan staggered backwards as a swirl of lights and a cacophony of sounds engulfed them all.

Nick moved towards where he thought Duncan had been. He couldn't see anything in the brightly colored fog. Nor could he hear clearly, though some of the loud bangs he heard sounded like gunfire.

He staggered round the room, banging into the table, the walls. "Marlen! Where are you?"

If Marlen replied, Nick couldn't hear him through the madness. Light and color swirled around him, bells and crashes and screeching wails pummeled his ears.

"Help me!" Was that Marlen's shout? Was it real? Nick couldn't tell where it came from. He whirled around, banged into the table, and through the confusion of colors, he saw the red raw power of the three objects enjoined as one. The source of Duncan's power.

He shoved with all his anger against the table, rocking it, breaking the objects apart.

'NO!" Suddenly Duncan stood before him with the gun.

Nick instinctively moved sideways, and tripped over a chair. As he sprawled on the floor, an arm reached out to pull him beneath the heavy table. Marlen. The confusion spell had started to clear. He saw Marlen lying on his side, clutching his shoulder. Blood seeped through his fingers.

"Bastard." Nick saw Duncan's legs through the dying colors of the spell. He lurched from under cover, tackling the man at the knees, bringing him to the floor. He still couldn't see or hear clearly in the swirling fog, he could only feel, so he felt for a gun arm, and found it. With a strength born of fear, anger, and hatred, he ripped the gun from Duncan's hand, and brought the butt down hard where he guessed his head would be.

A crack and a soft moan told him he'd succeeded. The body beneath him slumped into motionlessness.

A few moments later, the last of the noise and lights cleared away.

Marlen had crawled out to lean against the wall, one hand over the bloody wound. He smiled. "Bad aim."

Nick grabbed him and shoved him towards the door. "Wait there." He left him propped against the doorframe.

Then he dashed into the smaller room. The matches lay on the floor where he'd dropped them. The mages would have their dynamite test case after all.

Nick struck a match, and touched it to the bunched-up fuse wire. Then he ran back into the corridor. "Come on, I don't have any idea how long we've got."

"That's nice," Marlen said, and then he keeled over in a faint.

Nick dropped down to catch him before he hit the floor. *Bloody hell*. Adrenalin surging, he hefted Marlen into a fireman's hold, and hurried along the corridor as quickly as he was able, towards the main entrance.

The explosion came just as he started down the final hallway leading to the entryway room. The resounding blast threw him to the floor. He landed clumsily on top of Marlen, who stirred and moaned beneath him.

Nick waited patiently for the rumbling to stop. When it did, and he opened his eyes again, he didn't see much, as the lights had all gone out. A little cloud of dust from the damaged ceiling drifted off into the gloom, but otherwise, things were fairly normal, so far as he could see. Which wasn't far.

He sat up. His shoulders ached from carrying Marlen. "Hey." Nick poked at him as Marlen struggled to sit up as well. "Are you all right?"

"Never better." Marlen brushed the dust off his clothes. "Did you really blow Duncan up?"

"I don't know. But I certainly hope so."

They helped each other up. "Thanks," Marlen said.

"You're welcome," Nick replied. "Shall we go find the others?"

CHAPTER SIXTEEN

Nick lifted the hot, wet cloth from the wound in Marlen's shoulder. The bleeding had stopped ages ago, and it already appeared to be knitting together. There had been no sign of the bullet, as if it had disintegrated within him.

"Does it still hurt?" he asked.

"'Course not."

They had taken over one of the houses in the island village. Waiting until morning to cross back over the causeway seemed like a good idea, particularly as the tide was in, covering the route completely with water.

Brian had stayed at the castle to search the wreckage for any sign of Duncan. Vere was in the living room with the drones, to whom she was busy fabricating a highly fanciful story to explain what had happened to them. Georgina was making a pot of tea.

Marlen attempted to sit up in the bed. The resulting groan told Nick that he'd been lying about the pain. He propped all the pillows behind him and helped him lie back.

"You shouldn't have done that, you know," Nick said.

"What? Tried to sit up?"

Nick sighed. "No, I mean, you shouldn't have brought the ring to him. He was going to destroy you."

Marlen shrugged. "Worked out okay, didn't it?"

"That's not the point!" Nick wasn't entirely sure what the point was. "What I mean is," he said, struggling to figure it out as he went along, "is that you can't keep trying to save my life all the time. It's not fair."

"Don't worry," Marlen said. "Won't have to keep doing it much longer."

That sounded ominous. "Why not?"

"Because you'll be just as indestructible as I am. Well, except for random explosions."

Nick felt the color draining from his face. "I'm *not* a mage."

"Yes, you are. I performed a signature-seeking spell on you. And it worked. Sorry."

"But *how*?" He refused to believe it.

Marlen shook his head. He closed his eyes. "Don't know," he murmured. "Vere might. Go ask her."

Nick watched him drop off into sleep, and then went to confront Vere.

"During my research into immortality," she said, sipping at the tea Georgina had poured out for her, "I investigated any number of different theories. One thing that always intrigued me was the presence of transmutated souls. Not quite immortal, not quite mortal, they seemed to be some sort of intermediary being. I hoped that by studying the few I'd been able to track down, I could divine the secret which would allow mortals to achieve our own status."

Nick waved away the tea that Georgina offered him. "Is there any whiskey in this place? I'm going to need a drink."

She went off to search a nearby cabinet.

"What I discovered," Vere went on, "was that transmutated souls were really blocked mages. They *were* immortal, but had, for reasons I could never discern, become psychically blocked, and were stuck in the recurring cycle of death and rebirth. I played around with creating a spell which would break the block."

Georgina brought Nick a glass of whiskey. He took it eagerly. Maybe it would help stop his head from spinning. "Marlen said he tried out a spell like that, from your grimoire."

"Then he probably succeeded. You are a mage."

He closed his eyes. "I don't want it."

"You can't say no to something you *are*," Georgina said.

"Yes, I can." He opened his eyes to look at her. "Isn't there some kind of ritual you put new mages through? Marlen mentioned it—the immortality ritual. If I don't do that, I can go on with my life as usual, can't I?"

"Possibly," she replied. "But that would be a great shame. For I've been working on a little scheme of my own for you and Marlen."

He chugged the drink. "There may not be a 'me and Marlen.'"

"Please," she said. "Listen to me, and think about what I have to say. You and Marlen need each other, whether you want to admit it or not. And Marlen also needs something to keep him occupied. I've decided, first, that it's time the mages knew about the PIS, and that the spying stop and cooperation begin. The mages are no threat to British security, and our mutual interests will benefit by research into our powers. Naturally, we will continue to keep this all secret from the public, unless some great benefit to them develops. In the meanwhile, there are other forces abroad in the world of which we know little. The mages are not the only possessors of paranormal talents. Investigating such things is, after all, part of the PIS mission, and I think its agents would be better off looking into strange events it knows nothing about than tapping the phone lines of the ISM. You, if trained properly as a mage, would be the perfect agent, able to not only investigate such forces, but to have the means to protect yourself from them or fight them if necessary. And of course, agents always work best in pairs."

Nick stared at her for a long moment while the meaning of the words sank in. Partners? She wanted him and Marlen to work as *partners*? Would that work? A flicker of hope stirred as he wondered if Marlen would go for the idea.

"I haven't yet spoken to Brian about this," she added. "But talking him into it shouldn't pose any major problems."

The flicker of hope was merely that—a flicker. Marlen probably wanted nothing to do with him; after Nick had betrayed his trust, he could he? He should simply walk away, for Marlen's sake. "No, I don't want anything more to do with anything odd, ever again. I can't handle having my life and my world thrown into chaos. I want to go back to a sensible life."

Georgina sighed. "And what about Marlen? Don't you care for him?"

Yes, the word came unbidden. He swallowed hard. "That has nothing to do with it."

"Are you sure?"

He looked away.

"Maybe you ought to go and speak with him," Georgina said.

Nick nodded, but before going back to the bedroom, he grabbed the bottle of whiskey and another glass.

Brian returned shortly after. "No sign of Duncan in the castle," he reported. "Not even a cufflink."

"Did you get close to where the dynamite was?" Vere asked.

"As close as I could through the rubble. Took out a good quarter of the building, all in all. There was nothing."

Vere looked to Georgina. "Well, either he's been destroyed for good, or he's not and has managed to drag himself away somewhere to heal. Or—no, that doesn't bear thinking of."

"What are you thinking?" Brian asked.

"Duncan created the Spells of Protection. Who is say he didn't come up with one against explosions, and simply kept it to himself?"

"Dear God."

"He is cunning enough to do such a thing," Vere said.

"Perhaps," Georgina replied. "Though were he alive, he could have reached us here by now. I believe we are well rid of him."

"I dearly hope so," Vere said.

Marlen woke up to the sound of ice tinkling.

Nick sat on the edge of the bed, holding out a glass to him. "Whiskey."

He reached for it. "Does this mean you're confused again?"

"What?"

"You drink when you get confused. I've noticed that."

"Oh." Nick looked at his own glass. "I suppose that's true."

"I don't blame you," Marlen said. "It's not every day you find out you're going to live forever."

Nick stared solemnly at the bedspread. "That's not what I want."

"Don't be absurd. How could you not want to be immortal?"

"How could you?" Nick replied. "You were willing to risk giving it up back at the castle, when you turned the ring over to save me. Weren't you?"

Marlen drank his whiskey. "Yes."

"Why? Because of what I did? Because I betrayed you?"

"Good question. I don't know. Maybe. Why the hell did you do it?"

Nick didn't answer for a long time, looking steadily at his hands. "I had a job to do," he finally said. "I thought you'd come through all right somehow. And I couldn't handle being around you any longer. Not because I'm not fond of you, but because I couldn't handle changing into someone else."

"But you didn't," Marlen replied. "You're still *you*." He paused, uncertain where to go from here. Part of him desperately wanted Nick to stay with him, wanted to forgive him, wanted to go on loving him, for even in this strange incarnation, he still loved him. And part of him knew he had to let Nick go.

"I know," Nick said. "I'm sorry about taking the ring, I really am. When I got to London, I couldn't go through with my plans. I wound up caring too much about what happened to you."

Marlen fought back a wave of emotion. "That's okay," he replied as casually as he could manage. "I forgive you."

"Yeah?" Nick looked genuinely pleased.

"Yeah. All best mates have a few disagreements from time to time." He finished off his whiskey. "Now, tell me you're not serious about this immortality business."

Nick shook his head, a sad little motion. "Can we talk about it in the morning? I'm too tired."

Marlen needed a good night's sleep himself. "All right." In the morning, they could sort things out once and for all. If Nick truly wanted his own life, by himself, away from the mages and away from him, than he would let him go. But the fact that Nick had admitted being fond of him still... that meant something... maybe something worth fighting for.

Nick had no chance to talk to Marlen alone the next morning, not with so many people milling about, fixing breakfast, taking showers, and generally getting in each other's way. Maybe they should have taken over two houses instead of only one.

He had had a good long time, while dozing on the living room sofa, to ponder his future. There was no denying he felt a strong impulse to stay with Marlen, do what Georgina had suggested, and live forever as one of the mages, if only because it would mean being together. It would never be boring.

But impulses were not practical. His life, his family, his friends, his career—all would unalterably change; nothing about his world would ever be normal again. It would be crazy to relinquish his whole world for one person.

Or would it? Was there anyone else in his life who had cared for him as much as Marlen had? A man who would take a knife meant for him, who would always be there to carry him home after a night's revelries, a man who broke his own Society's laws to save him from dying, a man who would follow him through time itself?

After the morning preparations were out of the way, they all started off towards the causeway. The tide had gone out again; the flagstones stood high and dry.

They crossed over and climbed through the hole in the fence. Then, as they started walking along the beach towards the town of Marazlon, Nick tugged at Marlen's sleeve to hold him back. "Can we talk now? This is as good a place as any."

Marlen waited until the others were out of view. "You're selfish, you know," he said.

Nick started, unprepared for such a frontal attack. "*Me*?"

"Yes, you." Marlen prodded his chest. "You *do* care for me, but you're not willing to chance anything deeper, because it might be too upsetting. And *that* is selfish."

"All I want," Nick said uncertainly, "is to live my own life."

"Who said you couldn't? But why do you have to live it alone?"

"I don't!" Anger flashed through him, at Marlen's presumptions. "I have friends—"

"Will you ever love anyone, though?"

"Of course I will."

Marlen kicked at a pebble and sent it skittering across the sand. "I doubt it. You're too much of a coward."

"What?" He fought down an urge to take hold of Marlen and shake him. "First I'm selfish, now I'm a coward—"

"Yes," Marlen said hotly. "You're afraid of your own feelings. You don't want to ever love anyone, because then you might have to give too much of yourself, and you can't bloody well afford to do that, because you're so perfectly content in your self-contained little world." He jabbed a finger at Nick's shoulder. "Love isn't practical, is it?"

Nick batted him away. "Stop that. I just want my life to make sense, is that such a bad thing? And it never makes sense when you're in it!"

"But you love me," Marlen replied.

"No," Nick lied. He was afraid, just as Marlen claimed he was, afraid of getting too close to something so powerful, so utterly consuming. He had to keep himself strong; he couldn't let it change him. "No, I do not love you."

He regretted the pain it caused, hated seeing the hurt in Marlen's eyes. But he had to do it, had to tell a lie in order to save his sanity.

After far too long, Marlen slowly nodded. "I see. Okay." He took a deep breath. "Then I was wrong. I'm sorry."

Nick's arms were trembling uncontrollably. He wrapped them snugly around his chest. "Please," he said. "It's best we go our own ways."

Marlen looked at him steadily. "You may be right." He reached out to squeeze Nick's arm. "Believe it or not, I'll miss you." Then he turned and began to walk away.

As Nick watched him, something tugged at the back of his mind. The sight of Marlen leaving suddenly triggered a memory, a memory of another time and place, another morning when Marlen had walked away from him, a morning from five hundred years ago.

It was the day after the night when Nick had told Marlen he planned to marry. He had told him of the life he thought he wanted—a wife, a family, stability. A life that didn't include a male lover. And Marlen, for once not arguing, had walked out of his life for good. Or so he thought.

Twenty years after that day, Nick had stood outside his home beside his horse, preparing for his daily ride. His wife had long since been buried, his children were all grown and independent, and nothing gave him comfort in the night but old memories. And before he'd set out on what would be his last ride, he'd paused to look at the medallion around his neck. Memor mihi. Remember me. And he had. And he did.

He remembered all the good times—the laughter, the adventures; the hot summer days cradling mugs of beer, the noisy nights in taverns gambling their money away, the quiet autumn afternoons strolling round the farmlands, stopping to steal an overripe apple or two. And the nights of making love with a fierce joy... nights when he hadn't slept alone in a cold bed in a cold empty house.

He did remember, as he stood on the beach in the morning light, the one time before when he'd let Marlen walk out of his life, and had wished, ever after, that he hadn't.

Nick looked down the beach at the disappearing form of his friend with a lost, long ago longing that refused to die. It couldn't work. It wouldn't work. Never in a million years.

Nick ran. One hundred yards—he shouted, and Marlen stopped and turned. "You're irresponsible!" Nick yelled. Sixty yards. "Lazy!" Fifty yards. "Inconsiderate, selfish—" Thirty yards. He bore down on the startled figure, his arms flailing, sand flying. "A total slob—" Ten yards. "Impossible to live with—" He skidded to a halt, panting, and grabbed

Marlen by the shoulders. "I lied," he said. "I'm getting good at it, aren't I?" He pulled him into an embrace, arms wrapped tightly around a trembling back, warmth flowing through him. Then he stepped away a bit, cupped one hand round Marlen's neck, and kissed him.

It was full of warmth, and friendship, and a touch of passion. When they broke apart, Marlen said, "Does this mean you've changed your mind?" There was a questioning look in his eyes.

Those eyes, Nick suddenly realized, had weathered five hundred years of love, friendship, and loss. And somehow, the joy had won out over the pain. That, Nick thought, was an accomplishment worth aiming for.

He didn't want to think about how far the future spread out before them. He only knew he didn't want to spend it waking up alone in empty rooms.

Nick smiled. He wrapped his arms around Marlen again, holding him until the trembling stopped, until Marlen relaxed, and lay his head on Nick's shoulder. Nick ran his hand through the thick, wavy hair. Familiar hair. Familiar everything. He took a deep, calming breath.

"Yeah," he said. "What do you say we try this one more time?"

Our titles are available at major book stores and local independent resellers who support Science Fiction and Fantasy readers like you.

EDGE Science Fiction
and Fantasy Publishing

Tesseract Books

www.edgewebsite.com

Our titles are available at major book stores and local independent resellers who support Science Fiction and Fantasy readers like you.

Alphanauts by J. Brian Clarke (tp) - ISBN: 978-1-894063-14-2
Apparition Trail, The by Lisa Smedman (tp) - ISBN: 978-1-894063-22-7
As Fate Decrees by Denysé Bridger (tp) - ISBN: 978-1-894063-41-8
Avim's Oath (Part Six of the Okal Rel Saga) by Lynda Williams (pb)
   - ISBN: 978-1-894063-35-7

Black Chalice, The by Marie Jakober (hb) - ISBN: 978-1-894063-00-7
Blue Apes by Phyllis Gotlieb (pb) - ISBN: 978-1-895836-13-4
Blue Apes by Phyllis Gotlieb (hb) - ISBN: 978-1-895836-14-1

Children of Atwar, The by Heather Spears (pb) - ISBN: 978-0-88878-335-6
Cinco de Mayo by Michael J. Martineck (pb) - ISBN: 978-1-894063-39-5
Cinkarion - The Heart of Fire (Part Two of The Chronicles of the Karionin)
   by J. A. Cullum - (tp) - ISBN: 978-1-894063-21-0
Clan of the Dung-Sniffers by Lee Danielle Hubbard (pb)
   - ISBN: 978-1-894063-05-0
Claus Effect, The by David Nickle & Karl Schroeder (pb)
   - ISBN: 978-1-895836-34-9
Claus Effect, The by David Nickle & Karl Schroeder (hb)
   - ISBN: 978-1-895836-35-6
Courtesan Prince, The (Part One of the Okal Rel Saga) by Lynda Williams (tp)
   - ISBN: 978-1-894063-28-9

Dark Earth Dreams by Candas Dorsey & Roger Deegan (comes with a CD)
   - ISBN: 978-1-895836-05-9
Darkness of the God (Children of the Panther Part Two)
   by Amber Hayward (tp) - ISBN: 978-1-894063-44-9
Distant Signals by Andrew Weiner (tp) - ISBN: 978-0-88878-284-7
Dreams of an Unseen Planet by Teresa Plowright (tp)
   - ISBN: 978-0-88878-282-3
Dreams of the Sea (Part 1 of Tyranaël) by Élisabeth Vonarburg (tp)
   - ISBN: 978-1-895836-96-7
Dreams of the Sea (Part 1 of Tyranaël) by Élisabeth Vonarburg (hb)
   - ISBN: 978-1-895836-98-1
Druids by Barbara Galler-Smith and Josh Langston (tp)
   - ISBN: 978-1-894063-29-6

Eclipse by K. A. Bedford (tp) - ISBN: 978-1-894063-30-2
Even The Stones by Marie Jakober (tp) - ISBN: 978-1-894063-18-0
Evolve: Vampire Stories of the New Undead edited by Nancy Kilpatrick (tp)
   - ISBN: 978-1-894063-33-3

Far Arena (Part Five of the Okal Rel Saga) by Lynda Williams (tp)
   - ISBN: 978-1-894063-45-6
Fires of the Kindred by Robin Skelton (tp) - ISBN: 978-0-88878-271-7
Forbidden Cargo by Rebecca Rowe (tp) - ISBN: 978-1-894063-16-6

Game of Perfection, A (Part 2 of Tyranaël) by Élisabeth Vonarburg (tp)
- ISBN: 978-1-894063-32-6
Gaslight Grimoire: Fantastic Tales of Sherlock Holmes
edited by Jeff Campbell & Charles Prepolec (pb)
- ISBN: 978-1-8964063-17-3
Gaslight Grotesque: Nightmare Tales of Sherlock Holmes
edited by Jeff Campbell & Charles Prepolec (pb)
- ISBN: 978-1-8964063-31-9
Green Music by Ursula Pflug (tp) - ISBN: 978-1-895836-75-2
Green Music by Ursula Pflug (hb) - ISBN: 978-1-895836-77-6

Healer, The (Children of the Panther Part One) by Amber Hayward (tp)
- ISBN: 978-1-895836-89-9
Healer, The (Children of the Panther Part One) by Amber Hayward (hb)
- ISBN: 978-1-895836-91-2
Hell Can Wait by Theodore Judson (tp) - ISBN: 978-1-978-1-894063-23-4
Hounds of Ash and other tales of Fool Wolf, The by Greg Keyes (pb)
- ISBN: 978-1-894063-09-8
Hydrogen Steel by K. A. Bedford (tp) - ISBN: 978-1-894063-20-3

i-ROBOT Poetry by Jason Christie (tp) - ISBN: 978-1-894063-24-1
Immortal Quest by Alexandra MacKenzie (pb) - ISBN: 978-1-894063-46-3

Jackal Bird by Michael Barley (pb) - ISBN: 978-1-895836-07-3
Jackal Bird by Michael Barley (hb) - ISBN: 978-1-895836-11-0
JEMMA7729 by Phoebe Wray (tp) - ISBN: 978-1-894063-40-1

Keaen by Till Noever (tp) - ISBN: 978-1-894063-08-1
Keeper's Child by Leslie Davis (tp) - ISBN: 978-1-894063-01-2

Land/Space edited by Candas Jane Dorsey and Judy McCrosky (tp)
- ISBN: 978-1-895836-90-5
Land/Space edited by Candas Jane Dorsey and Judy McCrosky (hb)
- ISBN: 978-1-895836-92-9
Lyskarion: The Song of the Wind (Part One of The Chronicles of the Kario-
nin)
by J.A. Cullum (tp) - ISBN: 978-1-894063-02-9

Machine Sex and other stories by Candas Jane Dorsey (tp)
- ISBN: 978-0-88878-278-6
Maërlande Chronicles, The by Élisabeth Vonarburg (pb)
- ISBN: 978-0-88878-294-6
Moonfall by Heather Spears (pb) - ISBN: 978-0-88878-306-6

Of Wind and Sand by Sylvie Bérard (translated by Sheryl Curtis) (pb)
ISBN: 978 1 894063 19 7
On Spec: The First Five Years edited by On Spec (pb)
- ISBN: 978-1-895836-08-0
On Spec: The First Five Years edited by On Spec (hb)
- ISBN: 978-1-895836-12-7
Orbital Burn by K. A. Bedford (tp) - ISBN: 978-1-894063-10-4
Orbital Burn by K. A. Bedford (hb) - ISBN: 978-1-894063-12-8

Pallahaxi Tide by Michael Coney (pb) - ISBN: 978-0-88878-293-9
Passion Play by Sean Stewart (pb) - ISBN: 978-0-88878-314-1
Petrified World (Determine Your Destiny #1) by Piotr Brynczka (pb)
   - ISBN: 978-1-894063-11-1
Plague Saint by Rita Donovan, The (tp) - ISBN: 978-1-895836-28-8
Plague Saint by Rita Donovan, The (hb) - ISBN: 978-1-895836-29-5
Pock's World by Dave Duncan (tp) - ISBN: 978-1-894063-47-0
Pretenders (Part Three of the Okal Rel Saga) by Lynda Williams (pb)
   - ISBN: 978-1-894063-13-5

Reluctant Voyagers by Élisabeth Vonarburg (pb) - ISBN: 978-1-895836-09-7
Reluctant Voyagers by Élisabeth Vonarburg (hb) - ISBN: 978-1-895836-15-8
Resisting Adonis by Timothy J. Anderson (tp) - ISBN: 978-1-895836-84-4
Resisting Adonis by Timothy J. Anderson (hb) - ISBN: 978-1-895836-83-7
Righteous Anger (Part Two of the Okal Rel Saga) by Lynda Williams (tp)
   - ISBN: 897-1-894063-38-8

Silent City, The by Élisabeth Vonarburg (tp) - ISBN: 978-1-894063-07-4
Slow Engines of Time, The by Élisabeth Vonarburg (tp)
   - ISBN: 978-1-895836-30-1
Slow Engines of Time, The by Élisabeth Vonarburg (hb)
   - ISBN: 978-1-895836-31-8
Stealing Magic by Tanya Huff (tp) - ISBN: 978-1-894063-34-0
Strange Attractors by Tom Henighan (pb) - ISBN: 978-0-88878-312-7

Taming, The by Heather Spears (pb) - ISBN: 978-1-895836-23-3
Taming, The by Heather Spears (hb) - ISBN: 978-1-895836-24-0
Ten Monkeys, Ten Minutes by Peter Watts (tp) - ISBN: 978-1-895836-74-5
Ten Monkeys, Ten Minutes by Peter Watts (hb) - ISBN: 978-1-895836-76-9
Tesseracts 1 edited by Judith Merril (pb) - ISBN: 978-0-88878-279-3
Tesseracts 2 edited by Phyllis Gotlieb & Douglas Barbour (pb)
   - ISBN: 978-0-88878-270-0
Tesseracts 3 edited by Candas Jane Dorsey & Gerry Truscott (pb)
   - ISBN: 978-0-88878-290-8
Tesseracts 4 edited by Lorna Toolis & Michael Skeet (pb)
   - ISBN: 978-0-88878-322-6
Tesseracts 5 edited by Robert Runté & Yves Maynard (pb)
   - ISBN: 978-1-895836-25-7
Tesseracts 5 edited by Robert Runté & Yves Maynard (hb)
   - ISBN: 978-1-895836-26-4
Tesseracts 6 edited by Robert J. Sawyer & Carolyn Clink (pb)
   - ISBN: 978-1-895836-32-5
Tesseracts 6 edited by Robert J. Sawyer & Carolyn Clink (hb)
   - ISBN: 978-1-895836-33-2
Tesseracts 7 edited by Paula Johanson & Jean-Louis Trudel (tp)
   - ISBN: 978-1-895836-58-5
Tesseracts 7 edited by Paula Johanson & Jean-Louis Trudel (hb)
   - ISBN: 978-1-895836-59-2
Tesseracts 8 edited by John Clute & Candas Jane Dorsey (tp)
   - ISBN: 978-1-895836-61-5
Tesseracts 8 edited by John Clute & Candas Jane Dorsey (hb)
   - ISBN: 978-1-895836-62-2

Tesseracts Nine edited by Nalo Hopkinson and Geoff Ryman (tp)
  - ISBN: 978-1-894063-26-5
Tesseracts Ten: A Celebration of New Canadian Specuative Fiction
  edited by Robert Charles Wilson and Edo van Belkom (tp)
  - ISBN: 978-1-894063-36-4
Tesseracts Eleven: Amazing Canadian Speulative Fiction
  edited by Cory Doctorow and Holly Phillips (tp)
  - ISBN: 978-1-894063-03-6
Tesseracts Twelve: New Novellas of Canadian Fantastic Fiction
  edited by Claude Lalumière (pb)
  - ISBN: 978-1-894063-15-9
Tesseracts Thirteen: Chilling Tales from the Great White North
  edited by Nancy Kilpatrick and David Morrell (tp)
  - ISBN: 978-1-894063-25-8
Tesseracts 14: Strange Canadian Stories
  edited by John Robert Colombo and Brett Alexander Savory (tp)
  - ISBN: 978-1-894063-37-1
Tesseracts Q edited by Élisabeth Vonarburg & Jane Brierley (pb)
  - ISBN: 978-1-895836-21-9
Tesseracts Q edited by Élisabeth Vonarburg & Jane Brierley (hb)
  - ISBN: 978-1-895836-22-6
Throne Price by Lynda Williams and Alison Sinclair (tp)
  - ISBN: 978-1-894063-06-7
Time Machines Repaired While-U-Wait by K. A. Bedford (tp)
  - ISBN: 978-1-894063-42-5